Dylan de Polka, a handsome chestnut dray-horse, pulls a milk cart for his keep, but, all the while, his head is full of tap-dancing dreams. A catchy tune is all it takes to set his hooves tapping. Dylan's dancing daydreams lead to disaster and he falls into the clutches of a ruthless horse dealer, Dangerous Dennis. Red Tabby, a worldly-wise ginger cat, risks her nine lives to rescue her talented friend from a terrible fate.

With the horse dealer and his side-kick, Clumsy Golightly, hot on their trail, the two friends are forced to leave their familiar world behind. When they stumble upon the Happy Days Circus, it seems the perfect refuge. But all is far from happy with the circus animals who, that very day, have woken to find themselves abandoned. Now, to save themselves, Dylan and Red Tabby must somehow save the circus.

Dylan and Red Tabby are joined in their adventure by a colourful cast of characters: Irma the Elephant, Ranga Orang-utan, the Meerkat Clowns, Marmaduke Monkey, Ringmaster Chia, Madame Lulu Bombazine, the rock star Lord Stomper, and many more.

Born to Dance

By the same author

Safe for Life
(Dylan de Polka's and Red Tabby's Next Adventure)

For Alex and Ben

Born to Dance

Katherine Reynolds

i4w²

ideas4writers

ISBN 978-0-9550116-2-7

First published in Great Britain in 2007
by
ideas4writers
PO Box 49
Cullompton
Devon
EX15 1WX

Reprinted (with revisions) 2009

Cover design and illustrations by Charlotte Roffe-Silvester

Printed and bound in Hong Kong by
The Green Pagoda Press Limited

For

Oscar, Barnaby, Georgia

and for Annie, and all her animal friends.

Acknowledgements

My thanks are due to Dylan and Red Tabby for choosing me as their biographer. And to our publishers, ideas4writers, for their guidance and wisdom. And to Jenny Sanders, our enthusiastic, inspiring editor; Charlotte Roffe-Silvester, our illustrator who so perfectly envisioned the Happy Days Circus world; and Michael Reynolds whose contribution to the writing process ensured that Dylan and Red Tabby's story could be expressed in the best possible way.

I'd also like to thank our pioneers. Those brave adults and children who read early drafts of Born to Dance and whose insightful questions helped strengthen the finished work.

The adults: Julia Aitken, Sandi Batchelor, Trish Batten, Sue Bevan, Michelle Broughton, Faith Cochran, Helen Fletcher, Terry Fletcher, Lorna Fortune, Pat Girouard, Paula Kelso and Margaret Kennedy.

And the children: Emily Allen, Bethany Harcombe, Barnaby Fletcher-Filkins and Oscar Fletcher-Filkins.

Contents

Part III

Born to Dance

Dylan and Red Tabby's Great Adventure

Part I

In which friendship and loyalty win through
in times of hardship and danger.

1

Dylan's Big Mistake

Emlyn the Milkman flicked the reins smartly across Dylan's haunches. 'Walk on, my lad!' he called. The young chestnut dray horse put his shoulders against the harness collar and heaved. Bottles rattled and clinked and Emlyn's milk cart trundled forward. Dylan knew the milkman's delivery route by heart. Every shop, every house and cottage, every twist and turn was as familiar to him as the four walls of his stall. Eyes shut, he plodded along, the clip-clop of his hooves echoing down the empty streets.

'Tap-tap. Tippety-tap. That's it, now. Once again. Tap-tap. Tippety-tap. You're doing fine, Dylan. Keep it up!' Mr. Spatz beat out the rhythm with his stick. 'One and two and tap and two.'

'Whoa, there, Dylan, lad. You've gone and overshot again.' The milkman's voice cut like a whip across Dylan's daydream and he halted abruptly as the bit pulled hard at the corners of his mouth. Emlyn jumped down. 'What's the matter with you?' he demanded as he filled up his carrier with milk bottles. 'At this rate, you'll have me walking half my route.'

Dylan sighed. As he watched the milkman stride back along the street, he thought again of the magical world he'd known as a foal. He longed to break free from the shafts and harness that bound him to the dairyman's cart – for Dylan was born to dance.

All night the mice had led Red Tabby a merry dance. Not once, since the cheese shop had closed the evening before, had she managed even a wink of sleep. She cast a critical eye along the high shelves which held the cheeses. Nothing was amiss. She'd done her job well. A gleam of dawn light found a chink in the shutters. From outside the shop door, the clink-clink of bottles announced the daily milk delivery.

Each morning, it was Red Tabby's habit to follow Dylan on his route, for she knew that a pot of cream or a bottle of sweet milk was likely to topple from the cart as it bumped its way along the country lanes. But she daren't leave the shop before the owner opened up for the day, so she settled on the counter to wait. Paws tucked under her chest, she closed her eyes and was soon lost in her favourite dream of tall ships and billowing sails.

While still a kitten Red Tabby had run away to sea. The swashbuckling life had suited her restless nature, but it was a young cat's game and times had changed. While guarding cheeses was perfectly respectable work for any cat, she, like Dylan, yearned for livelier days gone by.

The thatched roof of Hilltop Cottage poked raggedly above the hedgerow bordering the lane. In the long grass opposite, Red Tabby waited patiently. As soon as the cheese shop had opened, the ginger cat, who knew every stop on the milkman's route, had made a bee-line for the cottage. Now a tell-tale clip-clop reached her ears and, moments later, Dylan plodded over the brow of the hill.

'Hallo Dylan! Hallo Emlyn!' Emlyn's favourite customer, Widow Medlar, stood waving from the doorstep of Hilltop Cottage. 'Kettle's on!' she called brightly.

'Be right with you, Doris,' Emlyn called back. He quickly reined Dylan to a halt and disappeared inside the cottage for his regular mid-morning cup of tea. Left to himself, Dylan moved off to enjoy some temptingly lush grass that grew at the edge of Widow Medlar's front yard. Red Tabby followed after him, a thirsty eye fixed on the equally tempting goods stacked up on Emlyn's cart.

On this particular summer's morning, Widow Medlar's windows hung wide open. As Emlyn settled to his tea, she switched on her brand new radio, sending a catchy tune dancing out onto the warm air. The lively rhythm set Dylan's fore-hooves twitching. 'Tippity-tap, tippity-tap' they went – his rear-hooves joining in, 'tappity-tip, tappity-tip.'

In his imagination, the sun became a giant spotlight beaming down on his chestnut flanks as he danced – blond mane and tail flying – before a vast audience. He lurched and lunged between the shafts, jerking and pulling on his harness, his horseshoes making satisfying clicking noises on the widow's flagstones.

That horse could be a star, mused Red Tabby as she watched Dylan's antics from a safe distance. *He could really go places – but not while he's hitched to that milk cart.*

The cart bucked and bounced as Dylan's hooves tapped faster and faster. Soon, Emlyn's milk bottles were jiggling violently up and down in time to the jaunty music. Red Tabby watched hungrily while butter pats and eggs came tumbling down. As she edged closer, eager for her long-awaited treat, Gold Top and Silver Top bottles tottered and fell, shattering on the hard ground. This was the moment she had hoped for. Milk and cream ran in little rivers along cracks and into crevices, forming deliciously inviting puddles.

But the sound of breaking glass brought Emlyn rushing from the cottage. Widow Medlar switched off her radio and came hurrying out after him. As the music stopped, Dylan's favourite daydream came to an abrupt end. Broken bottles and scattered dairy goods lay everywhere. He hung his head in shame.

'Will you never learn?' yelled the dairyman, his face turning red with anger. 'Each time this happens I lose a whole day's takings.'

Widow Medlar wrung her hands in dismay. 'Poor Dylan. He couldn't help it,' she pleaded. 'It was a catchy tune, after all.'

But Emlyn wasn't having it. 'No, Doris, I'm only a small dairyman and I can't afford it. For that matter,' he went on, turning to Dylan, 'I'm beginning to think I can't afford you.' Dylan had never seen his owner so worked up before and he began to feel frightened as well as ashamed. Emlyn's outburst had alarmed Red Tabby too. She hastily licked the last delicious drops from a puddle of cream and stole away through the hedge.

The angry dairyman began cleaning up Widow Medlar's front yard and tidying the cart. When he'd done the best he could, he took Dylan by the bridle and led him out into the lane. 'Goodbye, Doris,' he called over his shoulder. 'Sorry about the mess Dylan made. Hope I've left things tidy enough.'

'You've left everything lovely, Emlyn,' Widow Medlar called back. 'And try not to be too hard on that poor horse. See you both tomorrow!' Then she hurried inside to telephone her friends and neighbours with news of the morning's excitement.

To Dylan's credit, he felt truly sorry about what had happened. All day long, as he plodded through the rest of his rounds, he wished with all his heart that he could undo the damage he'd done. It was true that Dylan didn't much like being hitched to Emlyn's cart, but he did always try his best because the dairyman cared for him well. There were oats aplenty and crunchy apples for treats. His name was neatly lettered above the door of his stall for all to see. And better still, above his manger, the kindly Emlyn had pinned the only reminder Dylan had of his long-lost family – a small, treasured photograph of his mother – Desiree de Polka. *Yes!* he decided, as Emlyn made his last call and turned the cart around, *I am a lot luckier than most.* But, somehow, as he began the long trudge home, the notion failed to lift his spirits.

Wherever you find a framed space like this in 'Born to Dance', why not draw a picture of Dylan and Red Tabby's adventures?

2

Emlyn's Bad News

Back at the dairy, Emlyn led Dylan to his stall, inspected his hooves for stones, then fetched him his evening nosebag of fresh, crisp oats. While Dylan munched, the dairyman ran a hand down the horse's silken mane, tweaked his ear, and patted his neck. Dylan found Emlyn's gentle touch reassuring and hoped that his terrible mistake, if not forgotten, was at least forgiven. Then the blow fell.

'Well, my lad,' began Emlyn, looking steadily into Dylan's soft, brown eyes, 'it seems we've come to a parting of the ways. I've thought long and hard on our way home and I've decided to replace you with one of those electric trucks. Tomorrow you'll be moving on.'

Dylan let out a frightened whinny.

'Come on, Dylan, lad. Haven't I always seen you right?' the dairyman protested. 'You'll go to a good home, I promise you.' And with that, he strode off across the yard to get his dinner. But, as Emlyn made his way towards the dairy, two ominous figures slipped from the shadows of the stable and hurried after him.

'Not so fast!' came a harsh voice. The dairyman stopped and peered warily at the tall, gangly man approaching him.

'We 'ear you're a mite unhappy with that nag – er – with that 'orse of yours over there,' the man said. Dylan, watching from his stall, felt his ears tingle.

'And who might you two be?' asked Emlyn, as the second man, puffing heavily, joined his companion.

'Dennis is me name and 'orseflesh – I mean 'orses – are me game,' came the answer.

'And you?' asked Emlyn, turning to the second man and eyeing the whip he held coiled in his hand.

'Golightly's my name,' the dumpy one wheezed.

'Otherwise known as *Clumsy*,' sneered the one who had called himself Dennis.

'And my boss, here,' the little man added, 'is otherwise known as *Dangerous*.' An elbow shot out, catching Clumsy sharply on the ear and sending him sprawling.

'Watch yer mouth!' Dennis hissed as he pretended to help his victim to his feet.

'Did you say *dangerous*?' asked Emlyn warily.

'Oh, no,' replied Dennis in a soothing tone. ''E said *Generous*. And it's true! I'm known far and wide as Generous Dennis, though I say so meself as shouldn't!' Clumsy rubbed his sore ear ruefully and stayed silent.

'Well then, Mr Generous Dennis and Mr Clumsy Golightly,' said Emlyn uncertainly, 'what's all this about my horse?'

'Well, you see, everyone in town is talkin' of today's unfortunate little accident,' Dennis explained, 'so we've come a'callin' to see if we can be of 'elp.'

'And just what sort of help might you have in mind?' the dairyman inquired.

Dennis smiled an oily smile. 'Sell us your fine animal and he

10

will enjoy rich, green pastures and soft country breezes, in return for some light and pleasant work.'

'Pleasant, certainly,' smirked Clumsy Golightly. 'Well, for me at least!' he added, fingering his whip. Dennis frowned and cocked a warning elbow at his tubby assistant, who hastily stepped beyond reach.

'Light and pleasant work you say?' Emlyn repeated, still hesitating.

'Indeed! Very light and very pleasant,' the wily horse dealer assured him – and added cunningly, 'then you might afford that electric truck we 'ear you want.'

Emlyn shot the man a sharp glance. 'How did you come to learn about that?'

'Why, just now, sir, while you were biddin' your fine steed goodnight,' came the swift reply. 'And, anyway,' Dennis went on, his voice dripping flattery, 'it only stands to reason that a smart businessman like yourself, sir, would want to move with the times.'

For a long moment, the dairyman peered intently at the two men standing before him in the half-shadows. 'Makes sense to me,' he agreed finally. 'So long as you promise that Dylan will go to a good home.'

Dennis put on his sincerest expression. 'Rest assured, Squire. No 'appier steed will exist in the whole of the land. You 'ave me word on it as a gentleman.' Clumsy rolled his eyes and suppressed a snicker.

Dylan peered anxiously over the stable door. He saw bank notes change hands, then heard the dreaded words, 'We'll come for 'im at first light tomorrow.'

3

A Big Shock for Red Tabby

Next morning, after another busy night at the cheese shop, Red Tabby set off later than usual to follow Dylan. With the sun riding high in the sky, she judged it was nearing midday, so she took a shortcut to Widow Medlar's hilltop cottage. Just as she arrived, a shiny new milk truck hummed past her, coming to a smooth stop in the front yard. And who should be sitting at the wheel wearing a stylish new cap but Emlyn the dairyman. Dylan was nowhere to be seen.

Emlyn stepped down from the truck, whistling jauntily. Widow Medlar's front door stood open and he vanished inside. Red Tabby heard the radio burst into life and, as before, a lively tune floated out of the window. The electric truck sat silent and unmoving on the flagstones.

Nobody's dancing today, thought Tabby. *I wonder what's happened?*

She crept up to the open window and jumped onto the sill to see what she could find out. 'Well, I've done it, Doris,' she heard Emlyn say. 'I've sold that darned Dylan. No more spilt milk to cry over.'

Dylan sold? Tabby could hardly believe her ears. *Well, there's an end to my fine morning feasts. Rats! I'm really going to miss that horse!*

'You were pretty quick!' Widow Medlar exclaimed. 'Who took him?'

'An odd sort of chap with fancy stables in the country, or so it seems,' Emlyn replied. 'Calls himself Generous Dennis.'

That's funny, Tabby mused. *I've never heard tell of a Generous Dennis.* Then a dreadful thought struck her. What if Emlyn's Generous Dennis was actually the villainous horse dealer, Dangerous Dennis? *Shiver my whiskers,* she thought. *I've got to warn that horse before it's too late!*

Creamy treats forgotten, Red Tabby raced off to the dairy, only to find Dylan's stall empty and his name already gone from above the door. All that remained was a small photograph of a mare pinned up over the manger. Something about the photograph seemed familiar and Tabby climbed up onto a rail to get a better look. Seen close to, the mare looked a lot like Dylan. 'Of course!' Tabby exclaimed aloud. 'That's the famous Desiree de Polka. She must be Dylan's mother. No wonder he can dance the way he does.'

She was just wondering where to look next for the missing horse when her sharp ears picked up the distant whistle of a train. *That's it,* she decided. *They must have taken him to the railway yards.* She snatched the photograph from its place, jumped to the ground, and ran.

Down at the railway yards, Dylan found himself herded into the livestock pens along with a number of other horses, all waiting to be transported. He was quite enjoying the experience, despite all the noise and commotion. At heart, he trusted Emlyn's promise of a good home and managed to stay cheerful – even when Clumsy gave a nearby mare a stinging flick on her flank with his whip.

The whistle shrieked again as an old engine, pulling a dozen or more wagons behind it, chuffed towards the milling animals and halted with a noisy burst of steam. Wasting no time, Dennis and Clumsy drove the horses out of the pens, up the ramps, and into the waiting wagons. Then, with loading complete and the bolts slammed shut on the wagon doors, the two men clambered into the guard's van. The yardmaster blew his whistle, waved his green flag, and the train, with Dylan and all the other horses crammed aboard, pulled slowly away from the loading ramps – just as Red Tabby came panting into the yards.

'Rats!' she cried in dismay. 'I'm too late.'

As the guard's van at the rear of the train trundled past, she caught a fleeting glimpse through its window of Dangerous Dennis, his face set in a cruel, self-satisfied smile. 'It *is* him,' she groaned. 'I knew it all along.'

For a moment, Red Tabby considered chasing after the train in the hope of getting on board, but it was clearly much too late. 'Who's going to help poor Dylan now?' she sighed.

Just then the yardmaster, off to his lunch, came wheeling his bicycle around the corner of the switching shed. The exertions of the morning had left Tabby feeling weary and she knew that the man's lodgings stood close to the cheese shop where she worked. *A ride home is better than a long walk,* she thought eyeing the wicker basket strapped behind the bicycle's saddle. While the yardmaster bent to tuck his baggy trousers into the tops of his socks, Red Tabby crept close, awaiting the right moment to slip into the basket. The yardmaster glanced skyward as he swung himself onto the saddle.

'Rain coming on,' he muttered. Over the tree tops beyond the yards, Red Tabby could see black clouds piling up and threatening to block out the sun. *I'm not getting caught in that,* she vowed and leapt into the basket just as the yardmaster's foot came down on the pedal. Head down, the man raced off along the road in a valiant bid to outrun the fast-approaching storm.

The basket was roomy and deep and the yardmaster's uniform jacket lay folded neatly at the bottom. Red Tabby settled down on it with a grateful sigh. But, no sooner had she closed her eyes than she felt a deep pang of guilt at the thought of Dylan, boxed up in a dark wagon, bound for a fate unknown. *Poor horse,* she thought. *If only I could have warned him!*

A sharp whistle sounded unexpectedly close by. Red Tabby sat up with a start and, digging her claws into the wicker-work, she hauled herself up to peer over the basket's rim.

There, in the railway cutting below and a good way behind her, she could see the train. The driver had stopped to take on water from the great, high tank at the edge of the shunting yards. The whistle blew again and the puffing engine with its rattling wagons began to gather speed once more.

Red Tabby's memory of Dennis's cruel face squinting out of the window of the guard's van flashed through her mind. *What more can I do?* she asked herself helplessly. *What more can I possibly do?*

A warning rumble of thunder sounded from the darkened sky. Ahead, Red Tabby could see a little humpbacked bridge where the lane turned abruptly to cross over the railway line. The yard-master, still pedalling furiously, swerved sharply, and reached the crest of the bridge just as Red Tabby felt the first drops of rain splash around her. The bicycle came to a skidding stop and the yardmaster, anxious to keep dry, reached hurriedly into the basket behind him for his jacket. Red Tabby, dodging the groping fingers, scrambled out onto the stone parapet of the bridge.

Now the black heavens opened and the rain came bucketing down. Sharp hailstones rattled all around as the yardmaster pulled on his jacket and pedalled off again through the driving rain. Red Tabby could see Dylan's train puffing its way towards the little bridge, blowing its whistle and sending out clouds of steam. On and on it came, faster and faster.

How Red Tabby came to do what she did next, she never really knew. One moment she stood atop the stone parapet in a fever of indecision; the next, heart in mouth, just as the train came rumbling through beneath her, she jumped.

4

A Bid to Save Dylan

Soundlessly, seemingly without weight or speed, Red Tabby soared through the enveloping smoke and steam, landing with a hard bump on top of the guard's van. The roof was slippery and wet and only her strong claws saved her from sliding off onto the steel rails and wooden sleepers flashing past beneath.

Not far from where she'd landed, a dull glow emerged feebly from a vent in the van's roof. She steadied herself and made her way towards it. Looking down through the slats, she could see the guard – and near him, already dozing, Dangerous Dennis and Clumsy Golightly, their faces mean even as they slept. With scarcely a pause to catch her breath, she set off along the tops of the bouncing wagons in search of Dylan.

Like the guard's van, each wagon had a vent in its roof. Through the first of these she saw only boxes and crates; through the next a dozen or more horses, but no Dylan; the next revealed a group of small ponies, but still no Dylan.

As the train screamed along the track, the wind blew Tabby's whiskers painfully flat against her face but still she searched on, crawling determinedly from one wagon to the next. Then a perilously low tunnel loomed ahead. To save herself from being swept away, Tabby hurriedly squeezed through a hatch in the nearest wagon and dropped into the dimness beneath.

For a while she lay unmoving in a damp and shivering ball, not knowing or caring what might happen next. By the time the train pulled out of the tunnel, the sudden storm had passed and the returning sun flooded down through the hatch, warming her fur. Recovering a little, Tabby lifted her head, only to find herself looking straight up into Dylan's gentle face.

'Red Tabby! It's you!' exclaimed Dylan, staring wide-eyed at the rain-soaked cat.

'Yes, it's me all right,' Tabby assured him, wearily.

Dylan's eyes lit up with excitement. 'What luck – you being here too. What a great adventure we can have together.'

'Believe me, there'd be nothing great about it,' Tabby said, scrambling to her feet. 'That's why I'm here. I've come to warn you.'

Dylan peered down at her. 'Warn me? What about? I don't understand.'

'It's simple, Dylan. You're in terrible danger. In fact you're *all* in danger,' she went on, turning urgently to the other horses. 'You *must* escape at once.'

The horses neighed with nervous laughter. Tabby struggled to stay upright against the jolting of the wagon. 'Dylan,' she cried. 'You have to listen to me. Please!'

Dylan felt bewildered. He knew Red Tabby to be a sensible cat, yet he still trusted his Emlyn's promise of a good home. It was all turning into such a muddle.

The train rattled noisily over a set of points and lurched into a long, wide curve in the track. The horses shifted unsteadily in the leaning wagons. 'We're turning north,' cried Tabby with mounting alarm. 'Can't you see? Dangerous Dennis must have sold you all to the stone quarries.'

'Dangerous Dennis? Stone quarries?' blurted Dylan, growing more confused than ever.

The train was now well into the long curve. Great hooves lifted and fell uncomfortably close to Red Tabby as the crowded horses tried to keep their balance.

'It's too hard to explain,' replied Tabby, nervously eyeing the forest of legs that towered above her. 'But trust me, Dylan, and promise to do exactly as I say when the moment comes.'

'I promise,' Dylan agreed.

Reassured, Tabby jumped to safety on a ledge by a small, square window, high above the stamping hooves. There she lay for a long time, her clever mind racing. *I must find a way to get us all out of this,* she told herself. *I must!*

The train, with its load of innocent captives, sped through towns and villages, fields and forests. From her window ledge, Red Tabby gazed out at the changing countryside as it flashed past. Eventually, the landscape became wilder and less inhabited, finally giving way to rough, gorse-covered moorland, shrouded in mist.

After a while the engine driver, no longer able to see along the track ahead, throttled back his speed. *This is my chance,* Tabby thought as the train slowed. She scrambled up through the hatch in Dylan's wagon and made her way back along the wagon tops to the guard's van. Through the vent, she could see the two horse dealers still fast asleep. By now, the guard had joined the snoozing pair and the three heads lolled back and forth with the gentle motion of the train.

Tabby's keen eyes swept round the van, looking for the emergency brake. Sure enough, there it was – a red-painted lever high on the wall. She wriggled through the vent, reached for the lever and, bracing herself, pulled on it with all her might. Then, before the sleep-befuddled trio could gather their wits, she hurriedly squeezed back through the vent and was safely away.

Moments later, the engine's massive drive-wheels began to respond, screeching and sparking against the iron rails, and the train juddered to a halt. The wagons banged against each other so hard that their door bolts flew open. The frightened, tightly-packed horses and ponies, sensing freedom, leapt down from the halted train and galloped off across the moors. The thickening mist swiftly swallowed their legs and bodies and then, finally, their manes and heads, until all were lost from sight, away and safe. All, that is, but one who remained behind, trustingly waiting for Red Tabby, exactly as he had promised he would.

By now, the engine driver had climbed down from the foot-plate and was standing by the mist-shrouded track, scratching his head in confusion while the guard waved a torch around uselessly in the fog. A furious Dangerous Dennis held Clumsy Golightly by the collar, lifting him so high that the tubby little man's feet dangled in mid-air.

'Oo pulled the emergency brake?' roared Dennis, shaking Clumsy until his teeth rattled.

'I already told you, Boss,' Clumsy gasped, 'It was a cat.'

'A cat? You're tellin' me it was a cat? You expect me to swallow that?' Dennis shouted, giving Clumsy another teeth-rattling shake.

'But I saw it, Boss. I really did!' Clumsy pleaded.

'He's right!' protested the guard. 'I saw it, too. A big, ginger cat. Made off just now on the back of a chestnut dray horse.'

Dennis let go of Clumsy's collar and the hapless little man landed in an untidy heap on the ground.

'I'll get 'em for this!' Dennis cried, vainly shaking his fist at the enveloping fog. 'No one crosses Dangerous Dennis and gets to tell the tale!'

Red Tabby urged Dylan away from the angry, shouting men and into the all-concealing mist. From her place, high on his broad back, she set him off at a gentle pace. A welcome silence soon replaced the noise and confusion of their great escape and the world became peaceful once more.

Before long, the fog began to clear and a setting sun emerged, bathing a large farm and fields of quietly grazing horses in its warm glow. 'We'll stop here for the night,' Tabby announced, and she jumped from Dylan's back onto a low wall to look about. 'No safer place to hide, Dylan, than among your own kind.'

'But why must I hide?' asked Dylan. 'Perhaps this is the fine home Dangerous Dennis meant to bring me to!' Tabby's warning glance silenced him. *Oh dear*, he thought, *I must have got it wrong again.*

At that moment, a strong smell of 'mouse' tickled Tabby's nose and she shot down from the wall to investigate. Sure enough, there was a mouse hole in the hedge but, since there was no one at home, she gave up and rejoined the trusting but bemused horse. 'Oh, Dylan,' she sighed. 'Use your head! How do you imagine Dangerous Dennis got that name?'

Dylan looked blank, so Red Tabby drew a deep breath and patiently spelt it out.

'Listen,' she began. 'He's called *Dangerous* because he *is*. Dangerous, I mean. Everyone knows about him. Everyone, it seems, except you and Emlyn.'

Dylan stared intently at Tabby's face, trying hard to understand. 'Dennis is no friend of working animals,' Tabby persisted. 'He travels all over the countryside buying horses and selling them on. He doesn't care what happens to them as long as he makes a profit. Can't you see the trouble you'd be in if I hadn't come to your rescue?'

Dylan gave a bleak whinny and nodded. 'Can we go back now, Red Tabby?' he asked. 'To be honest, I've had enough for one day.'

Tabby shook her head ruefully. 'We can never go back,' she warned. 'Dangerous Dennis would only track us down and capture you again – and take his revenge on me. No! We have to start afresh – somewhere far, far away.'

Dylan gulped as the truth of their situation finally sank in. 'So you've given up your job and your home just to save me?'

Red Tabby shrugged. 'We animals have to stick together. You'd do the same for me, I expect.'

With nightfall came a sharp drop in the temperature. Dylan, unused to being out so late, shivered in the damp cold. 'You're not really cut out for this life, are you?' remarked Tabby as she hollowed out a spot under a hedge and curled up for the night.

'Perhaps I can learn,' the horse pleaded bleakly.

'Not without me to teach you,' Tabby replied drowsily. Dylan dropped down beside the cat, relieved to hear that she meant to stay by him. And despite the damp and lumpy ground he was soon lost in a deep and trusting sleep.

5

The Open Road

It was the dawn of a new day. Not far from where Dylan and Red Tabby lay asleep, a plump cockerel strutted along the top of a farm gate, waiting to greet the sunrise. As he puffed up his chest for his first crow of the morning, he spotted two shadowy figures clambering over the fence at the far end of the meadow. The cockerel held his breath.

'This must be the nearest farm to where the train stopped,' the larger of the two shadows hissed at the smaller, rounder one. 'We'll find that rotten moggie sneakin' around 'ere somewhere, I'll be bound. *And* that dratted 'orse.'

'Here's hoping,' the second shadow grumbled. 'I ain't got the right shoes for all this mud.'

The cockerel, becoming more and more alarmed by the approach of the ghostly trespassers, broke his silence with an ear splitting 'Cock-a-doodle-doo!'

Red Tabby woke with a start. There, not a hundred yards from where she lay, stood the tubby figure of Clumsy Glightly. The sinister silhouette of his boss loomed up beside him.

'Dylan! Dylan!' she hissed.

At first Dylan couldn't think where he was, and began to get up. 'Don't!' Tabby warned. 'Stay down and do what I do.' Dylan obeyed and flattened his great body awkwardly beneath the hedge, trying his best to imitate his companion's actions.

By now, the cockerel's frantic crowing had roused the farmer from his bed, and he came running down the path towards the gate, nightshirt flapping. Dennis walked boldly towards the groggy landowner, a greasy smile warping his face. 'Good mornin', kind sir,' he began. 'Sorry to disturb you so early in the day. We're on the look out for our dray 'orse what strayed.'

'And a ginger cat,' added Clumsy.

'Dylan!' whispered Tabby urgently. 'While they're talking, get up and edge down the field away from the gate.'

Dylan struggled up and crept as cautiously as he could along the hedgerow behind Red Tabby. *But how can we get out of the field?* he wondered as he worked his way towards the fence. As if in answer to Dylan's thoughts, Red Tabby leapt onto his back.

'Jump!' she told him and, much to his surprise, Dylan did.

Red Tabby led Dylan along narrow, twisting lanes with hedgerows high enough to shield them from their pursuers. At last, she chanced upon a bridle path that led into a deep forest. The two fugitives plunged into the shelter of the dense foliage.

As they journeyed deeper into the woods, Dylan stole a glance over his shoulder at the cat who had rescued him from a dreadful fate. She was stretched out comfortably on his broad back, washing her face with her paws. She seemed so sure of herself, so at ease. Red Tabby caught Dylan's look and suddenly felt glad to be adventuring with this large, graceful creature.

Time we got to know each other better, she decided. So she began by telling Dylan how, as a kitten, she'd found herself alone and how she had knocked around the world for much of her life, doing whatever came to hand, even being a ship's cat for a time.

'I have no fear of heights, you know,' she boasted. 'I often climbed to the crow's nest when we were at sea.'

'Do crows really nest at sea?' Dylan asked, and then felt flustered when Tabby let out an amused meow.

'A crow's nest is a lookout place, high on a ship's mast,' she explained. 'Sailors climb up to the crow's nest so they can spot other ships or see land from a long way off.'

Dylan looked round at Red Tabby when her tale was done. 'You're lucky, you know,' he told her shyly. 'Being so used to moving about, I mean. I don't suppose you miss having a home.'

'Oh, believe me, I do, Dylan,' Tabby replied. 'But hey! Summer's only just started. Suppose we stick together? For a while anyway. I'll hunt, while you graze. We'll make a lazy time of it.'

'It sounds like fun, Tabby, but I don't know,' Dylan replied wistfully. 'How will we keep ourselves when winter comes?'

Tabby paused to consider. 'You're right,' she admitted finally. 'I suppose we'll both have to find work.'

'I could pull another milk cart,' offered Dylan. 'That might keep us going for a bit.'

'Not a good plan, Dylan,' Tabby joked, 'You'd only break more bottles.'

Dylan found himself feeling awkward again. 'How about a bread wagon then? Loaves don't break – at least, I don't think they do.'

'What we need most is a caring owner,' observed Tabby, and Dylan heartily agreed. But neither cat nor horse had the least idea where to find one. All they could do for now was to keep moving and hope for the best.

Further into the forest, they came upon a clear, sparkling pool and paused to quench their thirst. Side-by-side they stood, lapping the cool, clean water. In that quiet moment, Dylan realised that he would never be able to manage in the big wide world without Red Tabby's courage and guidance. 'You know, it's really kind of you to bother about me at all,' he blurted out to the ginger cat beside him. 'I don't know how to thank you for all you've done for me. Really, I don't.'

Tabby gazed thoughtfully at their reflections shimmering in the pool. 'Dylan,' she asked after a bit, 'where did you learn to dance?'

And so Dylan began to tell how he had been born into a travelling theatre troupe. And how, one terrible day, all the animal performers were sold off and he never saw his mother again. Then Emlyn had come along and offered him a home. Since when he'd spent his waking hours strapped between the shafts of the dairyman's cart – his freedom gone.

Red Tabby shook the last drops of the refreshing water from her whiskers and settled back on her haunches. 'There's an important detail you've left out, I think,' she teased. 'Who's this?' And she held out a small picture for him to see.

Dylan stared in astonishment. There before him was the precious photograph that was once pinned above his manger at the dairy. 'That's my mother!' he exclaimed.

'I knew it,' said Tabby. 'She's the famous dancer, Desiree de Polka, isn't she?'

'Well, yes,' Dylan admitted. 'Only our real name is Jones.'

'Well, "suffering succotash!" as a movie star relative of mine always says,' exclaimed Tabby.

Dylan's eyes widened. 'You have a relative in the movies?' he asked.

'Well, a distant sort of relative,' she admitted, looking up into Dylan's big, glowing brown eyes. Dylan gazed back at the brave ginger cat and, in that special moment, the pair became firm friends.

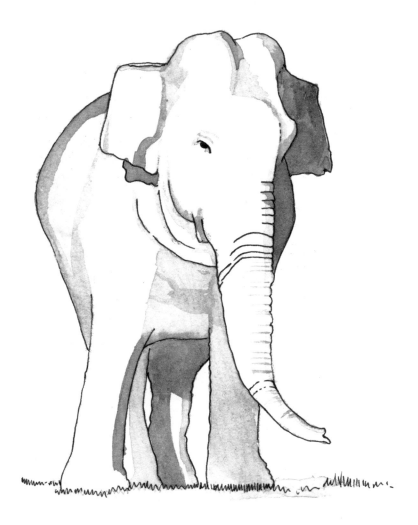

6

Red Tabby's Big Idea

Next morning, Dylan and Red Tabby rose with the sun and continued their journey to they knew not where. Their desperate bid to escape from Dennis and Clumsy had left them both feeling tired and in urgent need of proper rest. As they travelled on with no safe haven in sight, it was hard for them not to lose heart.

Around midday, as the quiet, sheltering forest began to thin, a distant sound of hammering reached their ears. Curious, as cats are, Tabby asked Dylan to wait while she shinned up a nearby tree to find out where it could be coming from.

From her perch amongst the tree's highest branches, Red Tabby could see a long field and in it a tall, brightly striped tent decked out with colourful flags. She knew at once what she was looking at, but all the same she rubbed her eyes just to make certain she wasn't mistaken. *That's it!* she thought. *The absolute perfect place for Dylan and me!* In her enthusiasm, she dropped straight down from the tree, landing with a wallop on her friend's patiently waiting back. Dylan skittered sideways in surprise.

'Dylan!' Red Tabby began eagerly when the horse had regained his composure. 'Where's the one sure spot to find food, shelter, friends and work, all under one roof? Come on! You should know!'

Dylan simply couldn't imagine.

'A spot where we could stay together and work together maybe for a long, long time,' Tabby persisted. 'If you'd like to, that is.'

Dylan's ears pricked up. 'I think I would like that more than anything in the whole world,' he said. 'But, Tabby, I'm no good at puzzles. Just tell me the answer, please!'

'Right then,' she cried triumphantly. 'We're off to join the circus!'

'The circus?' Dylan repeated. 'Wherever can we find a circus?'

'Turn left up this lane and follow the sound of that hammering,' Tabby directed. Dylan did as she asked and they soon found themselves on the edge of the circus field.

Seen close to, the striped tent, so imposing from a distance, proved to be torn and tattered; its canvas and bleakly fluttering flags in urgent need of repair. Beside it stood a huddle of dilapidated trailers – homes, perhaps, to the circus performers. But, apart from an elephant awkwardly hammering at one of the tent pegs with a mallet, there seemed to be no one about.

Red Tabby and Dylan crossed the field and were soon threading their way amongst the trailers. A large red and white poster pinned to the side of one of the caravans read: 'Happy Days Circus. Tickets Half-Price. Last Performance Tonight!' *Good,* thought Tabby. *They're moving on, and with any luck we can move with them – far away from Dangerous Dennis.* And she urged Dylan onward, towards the Big Top.

*

But the Happy Days Circus was far from happy. That very morning the animals had woken to find their owner, and all the other circus folk, gone – vanished without a trace. There was no one to help get breakfast and the animals had milled about in confusion, hardly knowing what to do next. At last, the tiger had called for a council of war.

As Dylan and Red Tabby came round the side of the Big Top, a murmur of urgent voices reached their ears. 'I wonder what's going on,' Dylan whispered.

'Push that canvas flap aside and let's find out,' Tabby suggested.

'Dare we? Do you think they'd mind?' asked Dylan.

'We'll blame it on my curiosity!' Tabby teased as she jumped down from his back and disappeared under the flap.

Eager not to be left out, Dylan nosed aside the canvas and followed after her. In the patches of sunlight that filtered through the rips and rents in the old canvas, the two friends could just make out a forlorn group of animals gathered together in the centre of the ring.

The urgent murmur Dylan and Tabby had heard outside now rose to an anxious hubbub. Then, from the dimness, came an awesome roar. Dylan's ears went back flat against his head in alarm. 'Don't worry, Dylan,' Tabby reassured him. 'If I'm not mistaken, that's a relation of mine.'

'You mean the movie star?' asked Dylan.

'No. Not him. Another one,' replied Tabby. 'Let's listen, shall we?' The huge roar came again, and now Dylan could just begin to make out the meaning.

'Everyone quiet!' The commanding voice belonged to the tiger.

'There's news,' the tiger said. 'And someone tell Irma to stop that hammering. It's giving me a headache.' A small meerkat scuttled out under the canvas and returned with the elephant that Dylan and Red Tabby had spotted earlier. The assembled animals gradually fell silent and, at the tiger's bidding, a long-limbed monkey stepped forward into the centre of the group.

'We've searched everywhere,' the monkey reported. 'They're nowhere to be found. Even our ringmaster's gone.' A groan went up, so loud that it set the highwire rigging vibrating mournfully.

'They can't all have left,' barked a sea lion. 'They can't have gone off without giving us breakfast.'

'I fear they have,' the monkey replied.

'But the show! What about tonight's show?' asked an orang-utan.

'It must go on of course, Ranga!' the tiger declared.

'But who'll be Clown?' a chimpanzee protested. 'Who'll play the music? Who'll work the lights?'

'And who'll go up on the trapeze?' chirruped a small voice. 'We meerkats can't. We're much too small. We'd never manage.'

'And my family can't,' protested the sea lion. 'Not with our flippers.'

'Getting some food inside us,' piped up a small terrier dog. 'That's the main thing.'

'We'll manage somehow,' said the elephant.

'No, Irma! *No. No.* We *won't* be able to,' a deep voice rumbled from the back of the group. 'The Happy Days Circus is done for. This is the end!'

It was a magnificent lion who had voiced the fear that, so far, no one had dared to face. And now pandemonium broke out with the whole troupe chattering and babbling at once.

Dylan looked at Tabby anxiously. 'Things don't look too good, do they?' he muttered. But, before Tabby could reply, the tiger's roar cut through the din again.

'Listen, Lion! Listen, all of you! Listen to me!' Again, the others quietened down. 'What do you think will become of us if the Happy Days Circus folds its tent?' he demanded, eyes flashing. 'If we don't keep it going we'll be caged and sold on – or worse!' A solemn hush fell at these dreadful words.

'Look, everyone,' Ranga Orang-utan ventured at last. 'Perhaps we're fussing over nothing. Perhaps our people will come back. But in case they don't, I vote we take Tiger and Irma's advice and put on tonight's show. After all, we *are* professionals.'

7

Bumps and Bruises

And so, after a little jostling and confusion, there began to unfold under that ragged Big Top a scene so unusual that it filled Dylan with delight. And Red Tabby, who had seen a thing or two in her day, found herself with her mouth hanging open in amazement. For the abandoned performers began to rehearse – not only their own acts, which they already knew by heart, but also the tricks their runaway humans would have performed.

The two chimpanzees gamely scrambled up the rope ladders to the high trapezes and started somersaulting through the air, catching the wildly swinging bars with abandon. In the ring below, the meerkats clowned around, throwing pails of sawdust 'water' over each other. One of them dashed out of the ring and came chugging back steering a small car. The others all piled in on top of him until, as the last meerkat squeezed inside, the trick car promptly fell apart, tumbling everyone out in a heap.

Up on the band podium the sea lion tapped the music stand with his flipper to call his musicians to order. The small terrier, who everyone called Dancing Dog, settled down on the drums. The monkey, whose name was Marmaduke, stretched his long fingers over the keyboard and tried out a chord or two. Ranga Orang-utan vigorously pumped the valves of a silver trumpet, while Irma Elephant tucked a huge tuba under her forefoot and blew a thunderous note through the mouthpiece with her trunk. 'All right!' called Bandmaster Sea Lion. 'Here we go. And-a-one-and-a-two-and-a-one, two, three, four.'

The makeshift band's playing was a bit uncertain at first, but soon they were tootling away for all they were worth, encouraged by delighted shouts from the other performers and the exertions of the bandmaster as he attempted to conduct them. 'Faster, Marmaduke,' he called. 'Keep the tempo, Dancing Dog. More puff on that tuba, Irma.' The musicians did their best to follow their new bandmaster's flying flippers as he raced them into a fast-paced number.

All the while, the lion sat majestically on his stand, while the tiger practised mighty leaps through a series of hoops. Then it was Lion's turn, but he hesitated, turning to the tiger with an upturned paw. 'Hang on a minute, Tiger,' he said with a worried frown. 'How will we light the fiery hoops tonight? Jumping through unlit hoops isn't much of a trick.'

'I'm sure Ranga will help us light the matches, Lion,' said Tiger. Tiger's reassuring words were hardly out of his mouth when, high up on the trapeze, something went badly wrong. Prudence Chimpanzee, soaring through the air, missed her brother Charlie's outstretched hands and plummeted, squealing, into the safety net far below. The rehearsal stopped abruptly as everyone rushed to see if she was injured.

'Prudence? Charlie? Are you hurt?' the others cried anxiously. Luckily, Prudence was only shaken by her fall, but the near accident rattled everyone's confidence. Doubts held at bay in the rush to rehearse now crowded back.

'Oh, dear,' sighed Irma, sitting down with a heavy thump. 'What Lion said is true. It's no good. It won't work.'

'Of course it will,' called a rich, warm voice from the stands. 'After all, you are the bravest, most magnificent circus troupe ever to exist in the whole wide world.'

Everyone stopped abruptly and, for a moment, just stared unbelievingly at the impressive figure in top hat and scarlet tailcoat gazing down at them. Then Irma raised her trunk and trumpeted. 'We're saved! Now everything will be all right.'

'Ringmaster Chee-ah! It's Chee-ah! Chee-ah!' The excited babble of voices washed over Dylan and Red as they watched the ringmaster stride confidently into the arena. 'It's Chee-ah! He's back! He's come back! It's Ringmaster Chee-ah!'

'Who's Chee-ah?' asked Dylan, almost shouting to be heard.

'It must their ringmaster, Chia,' Red Tabby answered over the din. 'I saw his name on their poster.'

The troupe crowded around the new arrival, everyone asking questions all at once.

'Where have they all gone?'

'Will they be back for tonight's show?'

'Can we eat now?' And so on and so on until the ringmaster had to raise his hands for silence.

'They won't be back,' Chia stated with a sad shake of his head. 'They left on the early train this morning, each and every one of them. The stationmaster himself saw them go.'

'Even our owner?' asked Tiger, incredulous.

'Even our owner,' Chia confirmed. 'And there's worse,' he continued. 'The Happy Days Circus bank account has been cleaned out. We're penniless.'

'Then it's just as we feared,' observed Tiger grimly. 'We really have been abandoned.' The harsh word 'abandoned' set the babbling, hooting and trumpeting off yet again.

'But what can I do? Where shall I go?' cried Lion, his deep voice rising above the babble.

'Where we'll all go, I expect,' Ranga muttered gloomily, 'to a zoo.'

'Come on, Ranga, old thing,' Ringmaster Chia comforted. 'It may not come to that.'

'But I am a performer!' Lion burst out in distress. 'I am an artiste. I cannot be shut up in a cage.'

'Dignity, Lion! Remember your dignity,' urged Tiger.

Again, Chia held up his hands for silence. 'Please, please! We *can't* let this be the end for the Happy Days Circus. For our days together have been truly happy, have they not?'

'Yes! *Yes!*' the others cried.

'Then why don't we give it a try?' Chia urged. 'Tonight's show could at least bring us money for food, and we could see where we go from there.'

'But are we up to it, Ringmaster?' asked Charlie.

'I watched you rehearse,' Chia assured him. 'You weren't that bad.'

'We weren't that good either,' mumbled Dancing Dog bleakly, remembering his drumming.

'Boooom!' A huge puff of smoke billowed across the ring and Marmaduke came hurtling through the air, landing neatly at Chia's feet with a cheerful 'Ta daaa!'

'Well, bless me!' grinned Chia, 'Someone must have worked out how to fire the cannon. That's a start anyway.'

'I seem a lot better at blowing the cannon than the trumpet,' admitted Ranga, who had magically emerged from the cloud of smoke.

'Wonderful! Wonderful! Well done both of you!' enthused Chia amid loud whoops from the rest of the troupe.

'I vote we give it all we've got!' cried Tiger. With a mighty cheer, the troupe eagerly resumed their rehearsals, their spirits lifted by Chia's return and encouragement.

Red Tabby caught Dylan's eye and the two adventurers, still unnoticed, slipped quietly out of the big tent. 'Aren't we going to join the circus after all?' Dylan asked as he and Tabby made their way back across the field the way they had come.

'We'll have to wait and see,' she answered.

Dylan looked back doubtfully at the ragged and battered Big Top. 'With all their troubles, they won't want to take us on as well,' he said, his voice full of disappointment.

They reached a clump of willows by the stream that bounded the circus field. Red Tabby made a quick inspection of the little copse then turned to Dylan. 'I want you to stay here, out of sight, until I get back,' she said.

'Back?' Dylan blurted. 'Back from where?'

'There's something I need to do,' she told him, 'and it's best I do it alone.'

'You will come and fetch me, won't you?' Dylan asked with a nervous gulp.

'Dylan, do you really think I'd let you down, even for a minute?' Tabby protested. Dylan shook his head. 'Well, then,' she continued, 'I'll be off, and I'll try not to be too long.'

Dylan watched his friend bound across the open field towards the Big Top. 'Sometimes she's just too mysterious,' he sighed, and he took himself down to the stream for a drink.

8

Red Tabby Makes Her Move

Tiger was concentrating hard. Jumping through one hoop was difficult enough, but his new trick – jumping through three hoops at once – took extra care. If you got it wrong, you risked scraping your shins quite badly. Nearby, Lion sat peering intently into a long piece of broken mirror, carefully rearranging the curly locks of his magnificent mane.

'Who's that?' he roared suddenly. Lion's unexpected exclamation caught Tiger in mid-jump, and he came down with a bump and a clatter of dislodged hoops.

Tiger rubbed a scraped shin with a big paw. 'Who's what?' he demanded.

'Who's *that?*' Lion repeated and peered closely into his shard of mirror. Reflected in the silvered glass, Red Tabby sat waiting patiently at the ringside, her tail curled neatly around her haunches.

'What do you want with us?' Tiger called across to her. His shin still smarted and his voice betrayed more than a touch of crossness.

'A moment of your time, wise Tiger,' the smaller cat replied politely, 'if you can possibly spare it from your rehearsals.'

'You may approach,' interrupted Lion in his most regal tones. Tiger shot him a look of exasperation.

'What can we do for you, small ginger one?' Tiger asked gently, his sore shin now almost forgotten.

Red Tabby padded across the sawdust-covered ring and, keeping a respectful distance from her large and powerful cousins, sat once more. 'My name is Red Tabby,' she began – and proceeded to tell the two great cats of the predicament she and Dylan found themselves in.

When she had finished, Tiger remained thoughtful for some moments. 'Rehearsals will have to wait,' he declared at last. 'I sense that this may be a matter of great importance to the Happy Days Circus. May we use your trailer, Lion – for privacy?'

Lion nodded grandly. 'As the star of the Happy Days Circus, my quarters are naturally the largest,' he boasted to Red Tabby as the three cats made their way to the huddle of caravans behind the Big Top.

'The Happy Days Circus is well named,' Tiger began once they were settled comfortably and introductions were complete. 'We all pull together as a team.'

'Some team when all the humans run away,' grumbled Lion.

'Not quite all,' corrected Tiger as he offered Tabby a welcome bowl of fresh milk. 'Our ringmaster is still with us.'

'Thank goodness for small mercies!' Lion remarked wanly.

Tabby eagerly lapped up the delicious milk to the last drop then asked, 'Why do you think the others left?'

'Got cowardly when the money ran short,' snorted Lion.

'It's not quite as simple as that, Lion,' said Tiger. 'If I may be permitted to explain?'

Lion shrugged, and Tiger continued. 'As you know, performing animals are often badly treated. They can be over-worked and underfed.'

Tabby nodded. She'd heard as much.

'There are laws that are meant to protect us,' Tiger went on, 'but owners don't always obey them. As a result, many animal-loving families refuse to go to circuses altogether – even to ours which is the finest.'

'We *are* the finest! We *are!*' Lion echoed.

'And so, the long and the short of it is, the Happy Days Circus has found it harder and harder to pay its way,' Tiger went on. 'And now we've been abandoned into the bargain.'

'And we'll all be split up,' Lion moaned. 'And the circus is all I know and I've absolutely nowhere else to go.'

'Oh, do try to cheer up,' urged Tiger. 'All's not yet lost.'

The King of the Beasts gave a great sniff. 'I'm ready for a lie-down,' he said with a weary sigh. 'All this stress is bad for my digestion. Pleased to meet you, Red Tabby. Call me when you need me to rehearse, Tiger.'

'A little temperamental?' suggested Red Tabby as she and Tiger climbed down from Lion's trailer.

'More than a little,' Tiger admitted, 'but a fine artiste for all that. And who knows?' he continued solemnly. 'He could be right. Perhaps there *is* nowhere for us to go – except, as Ranga says, to a zoo.'

'Can you and Mr Chia really run the Happy Days Circus without the other humans?' Red Tabby asked hesitantly – for, as she well knew, *that* was the big question.

'That's anybody's guess, Red Tabby,' Tiger told her frankly. 'I only know we can't go down without a fight.'

'That's all I need to hear,' Tabby replied.

Tiger gave the smaller cat a shrewd glance. 'Perhaps you might care to meet Ringmaster Chia,' he suggested. Red Tabby looked up hopefully at her large relative, but Tiger gave no hint of what he had in mind.

'He'll be hard at it, trying to sort everything out, as you can imagine,' Tiger went on, 'but let me at least introduce you.'

To Dylan, it seemed ages since Red Tabby had gone on her mysterious errand. The clump of willow, though a perfect hiding place, was small, and he had first grown bored and then restless. He shut his eyes and lifted his nose to the warm summer breeze. Delicious scents teased his quivering nostrils. He sniffed again and again.

What does that remind me of? he mused. *Sweet hay with just a hint of fresh sawdust. Why, it smells almost like our dear old travelling theatre.* Memories of his days as a foal, dancing at his mother's side, again flooded back to him. 'Dear Mr. Spatz,' he sighed. 'I wonder where he is now?' At the thought of his old dancing master, Dylan's hooves began to twitch. 'Toe-tippity. Tap-tippity. Tap-tippity toe.'

'You'll want to save that for later, Dylan.' The sound of Red Tabby's voice startled Dylan from his daydream and he looked round to see her standing before him holding up two tickets in her paw.

'Hurry up,' she cried. 'It's Showtime! Ringmaster Chia has given us special places.'

'Are they going to let us join the circus?' Dylan asked fretfully.

Tabby chose not to reply, but led the trusting Dylan back across the field towards the Big Top where the last of a sparse audience could be seen going in.

A sea lion pup in an outsized uniform took their tickets, and the two friends made their way down the aisle just as the lights began to dim. 'Come on. We're down front,' urged Tabby as Dylan hesitated in the sudden gloom.

An uncertain roll of drums announced that the show was about to begin. High up in the rigging, Ranga Orang-utan stood by the great spotlight. With an unsure wobble, the spotlight's dazzling beam picked up Ringmaster Chia as he came striding into the ring, looking splendid in his gold and scarlet tailcoat, gleaming top hat, and high leather boots. In one hand, he carried a short riding crop, in the other, a large megaphone. Dancing Dog's drum roll rattled to a close.

The ringmaster took a deep breath and raised the megaphone to his lips. 'Greetings, ladies, gentlemen and little people!' he boomed. 'Welcome to the Happy Days Circus!' The half-price crowd clapped politely. Chia hurriedly slapped the riding crop against his boot to signal the start of the performance and the little band struck up the Grand Parade March.

In the lead came Charlie and Prudence Chimpanzee, decked out in makeshift high-wire costumes. In the centre of the ring they bowed graciously to the sparse crowd and shinned swiftly up the rope ladder and onto the high trapeze. Dancing Dog, whose turn came next, jumped nimbly from his place on the bandstand and pranced around yapping, somersaulting and turning cartwheels. As the small terrier scampered back to his drums, the small red clown car roared into the Big Top and tumbled a crowd of chattering Meerkat Clowns onto the sawdust-strewn ground. Bandmaster Sea Lion's wife, Celia, followed close behind with her five pups, whose lively juggling set the scattered groups of children in the stands squealing with laughter. Tiger and Irma marching side by side around the ring, brought an extra air of dignity to the spectacle as the Grand Parade moved towards its climax – the entrance of Lion, mighty King of the Beasts.

From his ringside vantage point, Dylan looked on entranced, while beside him, Red Tabby, with a cool head and a watchful eye, awaited the moment she knew must surely come. The little band tooted and honked for all they were worth, and, as the music rose to a crescendo, Lion strode proudly into the ring.

9

Lion on the Spot

Dylan's eyes widened in disbelief as the great cat struck a regal pose in the centre of the dazzling spotlight. Shocked gasps came from the scattered spectators.

There stood the King of the Beasts, his handsome features rimmed not by the magnificence of a majestic golden mane, but by a halo of giant pink hair rollers.

A nervous giggle followed him as he strutted grandly around the ring. Then somebody laughed out loud, and soon the great tent echoed with cheery shouts and whistles. Lion, blissfully unaware of his comical appearance, looked about him for the cause of the merriment.

Bother those Meerkat Clowns, he fumed. *This is my moment, not theirs,* and he shook his great head in irritation. With a pop, a gaudy pink roller sprang loose and bounced cheekily across the ring.

At once, poor Lion realised it was *he* who was the butt of the joke. With a roar of despair, he fled from the Big Top to the refuge of his trailer, all dignity lost. 'Oh, dear!' he wailed as he peered into the mirror at the rollers dangling from his mane. 'How is one to manage without one's own dresser?'

With Lion's hasty exit, everything began to go wrong. The makeshift band, thoroughly rattled, lost the tempo of the Grand

Parade March and the bright music died away. With no tune to march to, the rest of the troupe milled around in confusion. The crowd, already fretful, began to heckle. Sea Lion tried desperately to get the band playing again, but all they managed were a few uncertain notes.

As the jeers from the stands grew louder, pop bottles and cans began sailing into the ring, and soon the performers had to duck and dive to avoid being hit by the rain of rubbish. High overhead, Prudence and Charlie danced and cavorted on the trapezes trying in vain to recapture the crowd's attention.

Dylan looked around the Big Top in dismay. Never, even in his worst dreams, had he imagined a scene such as this. 'Oh, Tabby!' he cried. 'This is terrible. Isn't there anything we can do?' But Red Tabby, her eyes fixed resolutely on the ringmaster, gave no reply. All about them, the jeers were growing louder and people were getting up to leave.

Across the ring, a despairing Chia caught Red Tabby's urgent look. *Well, why not?* he thought. *After all, we've nothing left to lose.* Dylan saw the ringmaster give Tabby a vigorous nod and, in a flash, she was gone from her place. Up the long rope ladder she climbed. Swiftly, up towards the trapeze.

What on earth is she doing now? Dylan worried.

'And now, my friends, allow me to present our next, amazing act.' Chia had to shout the words into his uplifted megaphone as he struggled to be heard over the babble of the unruly crowd.

Dylan anxiously followed Tabby's progress as she reached the trapeze platform and scrambled through the high rigging to where the spotlights hung.

Again Chia's voice came booming out through his megaphone. 'Dear patrons, pray silence as I introduce to you a talent unique to the Happy Days Circus. The only act of its kind in the entire world!' A ripple of curiosity ran through the crowd, replacing the raucous chatter of a moment before. Families stopped in the aisles or sat back down in their seats. 'Prepare to be astounded!' announced Chia as the people settled.

Dylan craned his neck to look for Red Tabby. What sort of daring and dangerous stunt could she be planning? For a moment, he glimpsed her high up near the very peak of the Big Top. Then the spotlight seemed to focus directly on him, and he heard Chia's voice solemnly intone: 'I give you the Fred Astaire of the equine world. The incredible tap-dancing horse. The one, the only, Dylan de Polka!'

Just as the sun had done on that fateful day outside Widow Medlar's cottage, the great spotlight blazed down, beckoning him forward. As he stepped into the ring Dylan felt the dazzling beam warm his flanks and his eyes shone with anticipation.

With an encouraging nod from Chia, Sea Lion's little band pulled itself together and launched into a lively number. Dylan's hooves began to twitch as he picked up the beat. The tap steps Mr. Spatz had taught him as a foal came back to him now as if it were yesterday: the Hop Shuffle, the Scuff and Scuffle, the Riff and Riffle, the Irish, the Buffalo, the Cincinnati, the Pirouette.

With no shafts or yoke to hold him down, Dylan danced as he'd never danced before. Right, left. Right, right, left, went his fore hooves. Left, right. Left, left, right, his rear hooves replied. Soon he was moving so fast on his great long legs that Red Tabby, even with Charlie Chimpanzee's help, found it hard to follow him with the spotlight's beam.

The spectators sat wide-eyed as round and round the ring Dylan pranced and capered in time to the upbeat music. Breathless, Dylan signalled to Bandmaster Sea Lion to slow the tempo, and he slipped deftly into the Waltz Clog and a gentle

Soft Shoe Shuffle. The music rose to a gentle climax, and, remembering how his mother used to end each performance, Dylan glided smoothly to a stop, stood very still, and modestly bowed his head.

Cheers filled the Big Top that night – its tattered canvas shaking with the applause that came from audience and performers alike.

'Saved!' Chia shouted unheard in the general din. 'All of us saved by this incredible, brilliant, wonderful, splendid dancing horse!'

Lion, in his trailer, heard the jeers turn to cheers and ventured back, his rollers now removed, to see what was going on. With the tiny crowd now firmly on their side, the troupe carried on with the show. Tiger even managed to persuade Lion to put aside his wounded pride and join in.

Wild with delight, the audience wouldn't leave the Big Top until Dylan had danced encore after encore. When, finally, they filed out into the night, their talk was of nothing but the wonderful Happy Days Circus and how they couldn't wait to tell their friends about its remarkable tap-dancing horse.

With the last of the crowd gone home, the tired but elated troupe lingered on in the Big Top, unwilling to let the magical evening end. Dylan found himself at the centre of a circle of star-struck admirers, and facing a barrage of eager questions.

'Where did you learn to dance like that?'

'Did you grow up in a circus?'

'How did you meet Red Tabby?'

The questions tumbled out, one after another in an endless stream.

At last, Red Tabby reappeared from wherever she had been, with Ringmaster Chia following close behind. Chia spoke above the excited chatter. 'Tiger,' he asked, 'might I ask you to gather everyone together? We've a big decision to make.' Then he turned to Dylan and Red Tabby and bowed solemnly. 'Will you please excuse us while I have a short consultation with the others?'

As the troupe huddled together on the far side of the ring, Dylan threw Tabby a worried glance. 'Are they talking about us?' he whispered. But the ginger cat merely fixed a knowing eye on an imaginary spot high in the Big Top rigging and said nothing.

After what seemed to Dylan to be the longest moment of his life, the huddle of performers disentangled itself and came towards them, with Tiger in the lead, Chia grinning from ear to ear.

'Dylan and Red Tabby,' Tiger began, 'with your kind permission, we have something of great importance to ask of you.'

'I'm sure I speak for us both when I say "ask away",' Red Tabby replied. Dylan nodded eagerly.

'Well, it comes down to this,' Tiger went on. 'We've talked it over and, well, we're all hoping you'll both join our company and help us start a new Happy Days Circus.'

Red Tabby and Dylan looked at each other and then at the troupe, which gazed back at them, hope alight in every eye. 'We would be greatly honoured,' replied Red Tabby. 'Wouldn't we, Dylan?' Dylan, too overcome to reply, could only nod his head and stamp a fore hoof.

'They've said "Yes!" my friends,' Chia shouted. Overjoyed, the troupe hooted, honked, roared, and trumpeted their welcome.

When the hubbub had finally died down, Red Tabby went off with Ringmaster Chia to settle the details. Dylan felt quite overwhelmed, but trotted away with Dancing Dog to see the trailer which was to be his and Red Tabby's new home. So much was happening, and so quickly, that he could scarcely make sense of it all.

10

The Troupe Gets to Work

Next morning, while Chia was off fetching food for everyone, Tiger gathered the troupe together in the Big Top. They were all bubbling with excitement about the previous night's show and the fact that Dylan and Red Tabby had agreed to stay on to help make the circus a success.

'Last night was truly remarkable,' began Tiger. A loud cheer went up. 'Hurray for Dylan! Hurray!' Dylan, brimming inwardly with delight, glanced gratefully at Red Tabby.

'And Hurray for Red Tabby, too,' Tiger added firmly. 'But we're not out of the woods yet, if you'll pardon the phrase.' The big striped cat paced up and down, warming to his theme. 'It will take more than one performance to put the Happy Days Circus back on its feet,' he warned. 'As more families hear that we're running our own show, they may choose to support us, but there's no guarantee.'

'Nothing is guaranteed in this world,' intoned Lion mournfully. He'd heard someone say that once and had rather liked the sound of it. 'Not even stardom,' he added bleakly. Red Tabby and Dylan exchanged worried glances.

'Thank you for that, Lion,' Tiger said dryly. 'What I mean is, we can't leave it at that. When Ringmaster Chia returns, he should find every last one of us rehearsing as if our very freedom depends on it – which, in fact, it does.'

Tiger's pep talk did its work, and when Chia returned with the day's rations, he found everyone hard at work perfecting their routines.

'Now, we need to spread the word,' Tiger advised the ringmaster. 'With Dylan's act in the line-up, we might even manage a full house!'

'Leave all that to me, Tiger,' Chia offered. 'I'll get onto it right away.' And he hurried back to his trailer, his head spinning with ideas.

Red Tabby caught up with Tiger as the big cat was on his way to join Lion for rehearsals. 'How is Lion taking all this?' she asked in a concerned tone.

'As well as may be expected, I suppose,' Tiger told her. 'He doesn't much like being bumped from top spot.'

'Who can blame him?' agreed Tabby. 'It's not what we intended. How can we cheer him up?'

'Time is the greatest healer,' Tiger answered. 'Give him a day or two to sulk and he'll be his own pompous self again. For all his fancy airs, he's a good sort at heart.'

Ringmaster Chia was as true as his word. Before long, colourful posters appeared – stuck up in windows, plastered on walls, and pinned to noticeboards in the town and nearby villages. 'Roll Up! Roll Up!' the posters boldly proclaimed. 'Don't miss Dylan de Polka! The Horse with the Magical Hooves. Brought to you by the Happy Days Circus.' And, emblazoned across the bottom, the magic words, 'Under Entirely New Management.'

While Chia dashed about putting up his posters and promoting the next performance, Dylan and Red Tabby settled into their new routine – rehearsing with the troupe under Tiger's inspired direction and getting to know all their new friends.

A few days after their arrival, the Animal Rescue vet came by at Chia's request. Both Red Tabby and Dylan got a thorough check-up, and the vet showed Ranga and Charlie how to groom Dylan's coat until it shone. That done, Dylan was whisked off to the nearest blacksmith to have his hooves trimmed and horseshoes fitted.

With flanks gleaming, his mane and tail freshly combed and new shoes on his hooves, Dylan felt better than he had done since his days as a foal. As time slipped by, the harrowing escape from a fate unknown, and the dark menace of the cruel horse dealer faded further and further from his mind. But the ever-wise Red Tabby knew that the very success that had brought them a fresh start could bring danger into their lives once more.

In a sleepy country town, not many miles from where the Big Top's flags fluttered gently in the summer breeze, Dangerous Dennis stood before the noticeboard of the local livestock market, writing down the times of the upcoming horse sales.

'Hey, Boss! Look!'

Dennis turned abruptly at the sudden shout. Further down the street, his tubby assistant beckoned to him excitedly.

'Look, Boss! Look at this!' Clumsy shouted again, jabbing a stubby finger at a poster plastered on the wall before him.

'What are you natterin' on about now?' glowered Dennis as he strode over.

'He's joined the circus, he has, Boss, and he's their star turn!' Clumsy managed to blurt out before being roughly elbowed aside.

Dennis planted himself squarely in front of the Happy Days Circus poster, propped his reading glasses on the end of his nose, and inspected it closely. 'A dancer is 'e now?' he mused. 'Well fancy that!'

'He'll be worth a pretty penny now, he will,' said Clumsy, eager to please. 'Pity we let him get away.'

But Dennis was too absorbed in the poster to take notice of Clumsy's unguarded remark. 'Oo knows,' the horse dealer muttered to himself, ''e might just make me fortune yet – if 'e really is the dairyman's nag.'

'It's him all right, Boss,' Clumsy insisted, eagerly pushing in again. 'That's his whole name, down there, at the bottom. See? Dylan de Polka.'

In a flash, Dennis had Clumsy by the throat. 'What name did I hear you say?' he hissed full in Clumsy's face. 'What name?'

'de Polka!' Clumsy blurted. 'Dylan de Polka!'

'de Polka, eh?' Dennis roared, and shoved Clumsy so hard that the little man staggered backward and landed on his bottom with a wallop. 'Never!' Dennis rasped, shaking a clenched fist at his cowering assistant, 'Never dare speak the name "de Polka" again!'

For a long moment, Dennis stood glaring at the fallen figure. Then Clumsy saw the fierce eyes take on a pained look. Like a stricken man, Dennis dropped his gaze and turned back to his battered truck. Clumsy picked himself up awkwardly and hurried after him, baffled by his boss's sudden, savage mood.

As Clumsy clambered into the cab, Dennis thrust a map at him. 'That's where we're bound,' he snapped, poking at the map with his forefinger. 'Now navigate.' And before long, they were clear of the town, barrelling down the country roads on the trail of the Happy Days Circus.

*

The afternoon had grown hot. With Dylan safely dozing in their trailer, Red Tabby decided to wander off on her own for a while. After a short stroll amongst the circus wagons, she came upon Ringmaster Chia's caravan. The grass beneath its wheels looked cool and sweet and she settled herself there contentedly. It wasn't long before the heat and the lazy hum of insects made her sleepy – very sleepy indeed. But, just as she'd laid her head on her paws and let her eyes droop shut, an impatient knocking on Chia's door startled her awake. She found herself gazing out upon two pairs of rather muddy boots.

'Chia! We want to see Chia!' one of the visitors demanded in a harsh tone. Tabby's fur bristled and she edged further back into the shadows under the caravan. Surely she knew that voice. The visitors knocked loudly again. Footfalls sounded above Tabby's head and she heard Chia's caravan door creak open.

'Are you Chia?' the familiar voice rasped.

'That's me,' Tabby heard Chia reply. 'How may I help you?'

'Give us our horse back,' piped up a second voice, squeakier than the first.

'Do I know you?' asked Chia. 'You are …?'

'I'm Dennis,' came the brusque answer.

'And this gentleman?' enquired the ringmaster.

'Never you mind,' Dennis snorted impatiently. 'You're wastin' me time. That 'orse is mine and I can prove it.'

Ah ha! thought Chia. *These must the men Red Tabby warned me about.* He rubbed his chin with his hand and smiled politely.

'I see,' he said, and eyed his visitors steadily. 'It would seem you're in search of a horse, sir. Now, tell me, won't you, which horse might that be?'

'Dylan the dancer of course,' Dennis snapped back. 'Like I said, that nag is mine.'

'Yours, you say?' Chia said, keeping a warm tone in his voice. His visitors nodded emphatically. Dennis eyed the ringmaster disdainfully. *This,* he chuckled to himself, *is going to be a doddle!*

'All very well and good,' Chia continued, pleasantly. 'Then, may I see your proof of ownership?'

Dennis gave an oily smirk. He was ready for this. When Emlyn the Dairyman had received payment for Dylan, he'd given Dennis a receipt, fair and square. Dennis prodded his assistant. Clumsy rummaged in his many pockets, producing, at last, a scruffy envelope. 'Well, pass it to the nice man,' snapped Dennis.

Chia's heart sank as he took the envelope from Clumsy's grubby fingers. Slowly, he opened it and drew out a soiled sheet of paper which he unfolded carefully. 'Mrs Goodbottom,' he read aloud. 'Week Ending the Ninth of June. Six pints of best, fresh cow's milk. £1.80, received with thanks. Signed, Emlyn the Dairyman.' Chia looked up at the two expectant faces. 'This appears to be a milk receipt,' he observed, and just managed to refrain from smiling. 'There's something here to do with cows, but no mention of any horse.'

Dennis snatched the paper back and stared at it in disbelief while Clumsy delved frantically about in his other pockets. His search proved fruitless and he shot Dennis a frightened glance. With an ominous growl, the bested horse dealer turned and stomped off, with Clumsy trailing a safe distance behind. Chia stepped back into his caravan, and, once inside, and with the door firmly shut, let out a bellow of unrestrained glee. 'Yippee, yippee, yippee!'

'Yippee, indeed!' echoed a much relieved Tabby, as she emerged from her grassy hiding place beneath the caravan. And she raced across the circus grounds to tell Dylan the news.

11

Stumbles in the Dark

It was midnight, and a full moon bathed the Big Top in its pale light. Dylan and the Happy Days troupe slept soundly in their beds. Perched high in a tall tree, a handsome tawny owl scanned the field below, searching for his next juicy morsel. He was not alone in his vigil. Red Tabby, too, kept watch over the silvery night, guessing that Dennis and Clumsy, foiled in their earlier attempt, would surely decide to return under cover of darkness.

Something moved in the blackness below the owl and his big, round eyes widened expectantly. But rather than a plump, tasty field mouse rustling in the long grass, he spotted two shadowy human figures creeping stealthily across the field. Disappointed, he blinked and gave two loud hoots of complaint.

Red Tabby, on the prowl nearby, heard the owl's cries and her sharp eyes soon picked out Dennis and Clumsy edging their way nearer and nearer to the Big Top. For a moment she crouched, watching the two intruders intently, then swiftly and silently made her way to Tiger's trailer. Inside, she prodded the great cat awake. 'Psst, psst! Tiger, it's me, Tabby,' she whispered.

'Hi, Tabby,' the drowsy animal growled. 'What's happening?'

'Quiet!' she warned. 'Horse thieves are sneaking up on the Big Top. They're out to steal Dylan. I need you to keep an eye on them while I fetch Lion and the others – but don't let them know you're there.' Tiger shook himself awake and padded off towards the great tent.

In the next trailer along, Tabby found Lion slumbering soundly on his big straw bed. Startled by Tabby's sudden appearance at his side, Lion lifted his great head and shook his mane vigorously, setting his big, pink rollers rattling.

'Ssshhh, good friend,' whispered Tabby.

'What is it?' mumbled Lion sleepily.

'Wake up! Horse thieves have come to steal Dylan. Tiger's already in the Big Top keeping watch. He needs your help. But don't let the thieves know you're there.'

Lion raised an anxious paw to his mane. 'I'm in my rollers!' he objected.

'There's no time to waste,' Red Tabby urged.

'But I can't be seen in public in my rollers – not again!' wailed Lion.

'Don't worry, Lion,' she assured him, 'Humans can't see in the dark. But remember, they *can* hear!'

'All right, Tabby. If you say so,' Lion snuffled.

While Red Tabby raced off to get the others, Lion heaved himself down from his trailer and set off towards the Big Top. Nosing back its entrance flap, he soon picked out Tiger waiting silently in the centre of the ring and ambled over to join him. 'I can't bear missing my sleep,' he whispered grumpily, remembering just in time not to shake his great head and set his rollers rattling.

'Nor can I,' muttered Tiger with a half-stifled yawn.

Shoulder to shoulder, the two big cats stood under the darkened canvas awaiting the horse thieves. They were beginning to wonder whether Tabby could have imagined the whole business when a rustling sound reached their ears. Under the edge of the tent crawled Dennis, with Clumsy following closely behind. Sleep forgotten, Lion and Tiger crouched on full alert.

Unable to see even their hands in front of their faces, Dennis and Clumsy groped their way forward into the Big Top's black interior. Lion and Tiger watched in amusement as the two scoundrels staggered about, stumbling first this way, then that. And Tiger had to smother a chuckle as Dennis collided abruptly with his tubby assistant, sending him sprawling onto something sharp.

'Oooww!' squealed the little man, 'That hurt!'

'Quiet, darn you!' rasped Dennis in a harsh whisper. 'Where's that torch of yours, anyway?'

Clumsy tugged a torch from his pocket. Click! The faint beam glowed dully, then faded to nothing. 'Battery must be dead, Boss,' Clumsy gulped.

'You'll be dead next if you don't look out!' hissed Dennis, and now it was Lion's turn to suppress a chuckle as Clumsy ducked an imagined jab from Dennis's sharp elbow.

'That 'orse is in 'ere somewhere,' declared Dennis.

'You must be right, Boss,' Clumsy agreed. 'You always are.'

''E'll be stabled somewhere out back, I'll wager,' Dennis added, and he blundered out of the ring, bangs and muffled curses marking his progress through the inky dark.

'Stick to the short one like glue,' Tiger whispered in Lion's ear. 'I'll keep with the tall one.' And he padded silently after Dennis.

'Hey, Boss,' Lion heard Clumsy call bleakly. 'It's dark in here. Don't leave me all alone.'

'Fear not, little man,' Lion muttered under his breath. 'You won't *be* alone. You'll have the King of the Beasts for company.'

Clumsy stood for a while in the blackness, wondering what to do next. *I suppose I'd best help look for that wretched nag,* he grumbled, *or I'll be in more trouble.* Cautiously, he felt his way forward until his boots clonked noisily against the low, ringside barrier. With a half-hearted effort to keep a quaver from his voice, he called into the pitch-black spaces under the stands.

'Horsey,' he croaked. 'Good horsey! Nice horsey. Come to Uncle Clumsy.' Nothing stirred. Clumsy shuddered. 'This place gives me the creeps,' he muttered.

Outside the Big Top, the moon emerged from behind a cloud and a bright beam of light streamed through a hole in the top of the great tent, illuminating a sign over the main entrance that read, 'Exit.'

'Exit!' cried Clumsy. 'That's for me. I'm getting out of here.'

He had hardly taken a step before a sudden, sharp yank on his collar brought him up short. *Blast! I've snagged meself,* he thought and, with rising panic, he reached back over his shoulder to unhook his clothing. But twist and turn as he might, he simply could not break free. Whatever it was that was holding him fast lay well beyond the reach of his short arms. The moonbeam marking the exit vanished as quickly as it had come, and, once more, Clumsy found himself plunged in darkness.

Matches. That's what I need. He foraged in his trouser pockets for the battered box he always carried in case of emergency and, with trembling fingers, felt for a match and struck it.

The match head flared briefly then went out in a sudden rush of what seemed to the scared little man like rather smelly breath. He struck another with the same disquieting result. He was almost sure he could feel a hot, moist breeze playing about the back of his neck. Frantically, he began striking one match after another, only to have each small flame wink out in another gust of that horrible, humid air.

The sulphurous smoke from the blown-out matches had set Clumsy's eyes watering and his nose running. He had just fished his hanky from a pocket when … 'Aaaah! Aaaaah! Aaaah! Choooo!' … close to his ear came a loud, wet sneeze followed by a peculiar clicking noise.

'Whaaaa!'

Clumsy's terrified screech brought Dennis stumbling back from his fruitless search.

'Wherever you are, Clumsy,' Dennis hissed into the darkness, 'shut up, or you'll 'ave 'em all awake!'

'Well, someone in here just sneezed,' wailed Clumsy. 'And it wasn't me! Anyway, my collar's hooked on something so's I can't move, and the matches won't stay lit, and something's going clickety-clack close behind me.'

'I'll give you clickety-clack,' growled Dennis.

'Clickety-click!' The rattling noise came again.

'There! I told you!' squealed Clumsy.

'Scratch,' came the sound of Clumsy's last match against the box. The flame flared, flickered, and steadied, revealing a full set of bright-pink, rattling rollers in the mane of a huge lion, standing right beside them. The lion had one long, strong, curvy claw firmly anchored in Clumsy's coat collar. Beside the lion loomed the ferocious face of a tiger, big jaws open wide and long, sharp teeth glittering like ivory in the warm pool of light.

The flame sputtered and went out.

'They can keep the 'orse,' Dennis yowled. 'I'm away.'

'Don't leave me, Boss. Please!' Clumsy pleaded as he struggled in vain against Lion's grip.

But the terrified Dennis was off. 'Good luck, matey,' he called back, his voice fading rapidly into the black void.

'Aaaah! Aaaah! Aaaah! Chooooo!' This time Lion's huge sneeze shook his great claw loose from Clumsy's collar. Clumsy, finding himself unexpectedly released, lurched blindly after his fleeing boss.

'They're making a break for it,' warned Tiger, and with Lion at his side, he bounded off in pursuit.

'Stop right there!'

The commanding voice seemed to come from everywhere at once. Lights flooded the Big Top, banishing the shadows and revealing Chia, megaphone at his lips. Like two scruffy statues, the two horse thieves stood frozen at the foot of the great King Pole with Lion and Tiger, fangs bared, crouching one on each side. Encircling them, barring their way, stood a determined ring of circus animals.

Dennis swivelled slowly around, glaring in renewed fury at his opponents. There in the middle of the circle stood Dylan, unwavering, Red Tabby perched on his back.

'You'll suffer for this, the pair of you!' Dennis yelled as he caught sight of the two friends. 'No rotten slab of 'orseflesh or meddlin' moggie ever got the better of Dangerous Dennis. Just you wait and see!'

'My friends,' growled Tiger, his whiskers bristling, 'perhaps this might be a good moment to teach these two bullies some manners. Are you all with me?' A rumble of agreement met the big, striped cat's suggestion. Dennis and Clumsy's eyes widened in panic.

As the Happy Days Circus troupe slowly closed in on them, the two villains looked round wildly for some avenue of escape. Through the Big Top entrance, they could glimpse the moonlit fields outside, open and inviting. 'They're only a bunch of stupid animals,' Dennis hissed through clenched teeth. 'Come on, Clumsy, when I give the say-so, bolt for it.' But even as Dennis spoke, a blast of icy cold water caught him and Clumsy full in the chest, knocking them both off balance.

The little meerkats, manning their clown-act water hose, chirruped and cheered loudly. The two scoundrels ducked behind the King Pole, frantic to avoid the freezing stream, but Charlie and Prudence stood ready with a well-aimed volley of custard pies.

'Get away, you big, hairy brutes,' spluttered Clumsy, trying desperately to wipe the creamy mess from his face.

'Hairy brutes are we? Who's for seconds?' yelled Charlie, and he launched another volley. Dennis lunged blindly at the two chimpanzees, fists flying and spitting custard in every direction. Charlie and Prudence skipped nimbly out of harm's way as Dennis careered across the ring and skidded to a stop in front of Irma's ample body. She seized a large bucket of sawdust with her trunk and dumped it all over him.

Through streaks of gooey custard, Clumsy spied the meerkats' trick car parked at the ringside. He jammed himself in behind the wheel and stamped hard on the accelerator. The car careered round and round in circles until, with a sudden bang, it fell apart, throwing the plump little villain out on his bottom, with the steering wheel still firmly clamped in his sticky fingers.

Covered in sawdust and custard, Dennis staggered back across the ring, only to stumble over Clumsy. Before the two dazed men could get up, Sea Lion and his family flopped into the ring with a huge basket of juggling balls that they tipped over the hapless pair. Dennis and Clumsy scrambled to their feet, but whichever way they ran in the sea of coloured balls, their legs flew out from under them. Arms flailing like windmills, they thrashed about, sliding and rolling across the ring, ending up all of a tangle on the end of the meerkats' seesaw.

'Stand by, Dylan,' cried Red Tabby from her place on his back. 'Here comes our turn!'

'Now?' asked Dylan.

'Now!' cried Tabby, her tail puffed out with excitement. Down came Dylan's great fore hoof on the high end of the seesaw. Up, up, up in a slow, graceful arc went the two horse thieves. Ranga and Marmaduke swung the trampoline around, expertly manoeuvring it into position as down, down, down plummeted Dennis and Clumsy, turning head over heels as they came.

'A bit to your left, Ranga,' called Marmaduke, his eye on the flying figures. 'Perfect!'

Dennis and Clumsy landed slap, bang into the centre of the trampoline. In a flash, Ranga and Marmaduke were jumping vigorously up and down beside them. 'Boing!' Up Dennis and Clumsy bounced. 'Boing!' Up they bounced again, and again and again.

Ranga and Marmaduke went on leaping and jumping, until the two bewildered intruders were tumbling and bouncing about uncontrollably.

'Aahh!' wailed Clumsy.

'Noooo!' howled Dennis.

The Happy Days troupe hooted and hollered with delight at the sight of Dylan and Red Tabby's foes in such a pickle.

'Keep it going!' called Chia over the din 'We're on our way.' Into the ring he strode, towing the great cannon with Irma pushing from behind.

'Over here, everyone,' called Red Tabby as the huge gun settled into its place. 'This should be fun!'

'Boing!' went Dennis once more, and this time Irma deftly caught the bewildered villain around the waist with her trunk, carried him over to the cannon, and popped him into its gaping mouth. Then it was Clumsy's turn, and with Irma's help, he rapidly followed his boss down the cannon's long, dark barrel.

'Here goes!' shouted Ranga, as he and Marmaduke jumped down from the trampoline and raced to the back of the cannon. Dancing Dog began a long roll on his snare drum.

Chia raised his riding crop high into the air. 'Safe journey to you, gentlemen,' he called down the barrel, 'and try not disturb the Happy Days Circus again.' From the depths of the barrel came the muffled sound of cursing.

Dancing Dog's drumming rose to a climax. Together, Ranga and Marmaduke pulled the cannon's great spring as far back as it could possibly go. Chia's riding crop came swishing down against his boot. Ranga and Marmaduke let go of the coiled spring; 'Boom!' went the cannon; and 'Whoosh!' went Dennis and Clumsy as they shot out of the gun's gaping mouth.

'Goodbye!' the Happy Days Circus troupe shouted together. 'Goodbye!' Up, up soared the troublesome pair, right through a raggedy hole near the very top of the great tent.

High on his moonlit perch, the tawny owl blinked with surprise to see two human figures sail soundlessly across the midnight sky, tumbling and twisting as they went. For the briefest moment, they hung motionless against the glowing disc of the full moon. Then, as he watched, they began to fall – down, down, towards the darkened earth where, far below, the village pond winked back the moon's reflection.

'Well, I never,' hooted the owl. 'Will wonders never cease? Who? Who? Who would have thought it?'

With a mighty splash, Dennis and Clumsy plunged into the middle of the pond, shattering the moon's reflection into a thousand glittering ripples. Down, down the scoundrels sank, deep into the pond's murky depths. 'Quack, quack!' cried Alice, the village duck, roused from her pond-side sleep.

The ripples died away and, piece by piece, the moon's reflection stitched itself back together. Silence returned. Then the silvery mirror shattered once more as Dylan's tormentors broke the surface of the pond – dripping mud, festooned in weed, and gasping desperately for air. The bedraggled men struggled, spluttering and cursing, to the bank, while Alice, upset at being woken at such an untimely hour and unhappy with the bad language she had heard, nipped angrily at their heels.

'Hello! Hello! Hello! What have we here?' A large policeman in an even larger pair of boots stood at the water's edge, gazing sternly down at the two villains.

12

Back on the Road

Seated side by side in the police station, Dennis and Clumsy shook and shivered despite the piping hot tea and warm blankets the policeman had given them. 'Names, please,' the duty sergeant began.

'D-D-Dangerous D-D-D-Dennis,' Dennis chattered.

'C-C-C-Clumsy G-G-G-Golightly,' Clumsy stuttered.

The man wrote the two names neatly in his shiny notebook then leant forward, pen at the ready. 'Now,' he began in a severe voice, 'may I ask you two – ahem – oddly-named gentlemen – exactly how you came to be splashing about in our pond in the dead of night?'

Dennis gave a loud sniff. 'It's all down to that meddlin' cat,' he complained.

'He's right!' Clumsy sniffled and noisily wiped his nose on his sleeve. 'If that moggie hadn't got into the guard's van and pulled the emergency brake –'

'Which stopped the train,' Dennis broke in, 'lettin' all me 'orses get away …'

The sergeant held up a restraining hand. 'Are you two telling me that a cat got into a guard's van, pulled the emergency brake, stopped a train, and set loose a number of horses?'

'Not any old cat!' exclaimed Dennis heatedly. 'That rotten ginger cat.'

'Long-haired,' added Clumsy.

The duty sergeant snapped his notebook shut and put the cap back on his pen. 'Well! Well! Well!' he said, staring guardedly at the two shivering men. 'We can't be having that, can we? More tea for these two, Nellie,' he told his assistant. 'Crackers!' he muttered as Nellie refilled the mugs. 'Both of them. Absolutely crackers!' And he slipped off to make a telephone call.

'I've been ordered to keep you in for the night,' he announced on his return. Dennis and Clumsy looked at each other glumly. 'Tomorrow morning, my superintendent wants a word with the pair of you,' he continued. 'Not a happy man, my super. What with you taking a midnight dip in our pond, frightening our poor duck, Alice, to say nothing of spouting tall tales concerning escaped horses and ginger cats.'

Dennis silently ground his teeth, and Clumsy, feeling very miserable indeed, looked down at his boots. The sergeant tapped the side of his nose with his pen.

'A word of advice,' he said. 'Best not to rant on that way when you see my super. He doesn't take kindly to tall tales, he doesn't.' He led the two miserable horse dealers back to the cells.

Next morning, the superintendent ordered his overnight guests on their way with a stern warning never to return again. And, with the trials of the previous night still vivid in their minds, the two villains were only too happy to comply.

When Dylan woke that day, he could scarcely believe his luck. He was free from the shafts of Emlyn's cart; free from Dangerous Dennis and Clumsy Golightly; and free, at last, to dance to his heart's content. The Happy Days Circus was packing up and moving on, and he and Red Tabby were moving on with them. He had never felt happier.

The pair watched with admiration as Irma and Ranga skilfully lowered the tattered old Big Top down the King Pole. Charlie, Prudence and Marmaduke coiled the long ropes, and in what seemed like no time, the weighty tent was securely stowed in its place on the transporter. With a final flurry of packing and stowing, the Happy Days Circus rolled out of the field, onto the road, and away towards its next destination.

Chia's posters had done their work well and word-of-mouth had travelled quickly to the next town. As the transporter turned onto the high street, passers-by waved an enthusiastic welcome, with everyone keen to catch a glimpse of the remarkable tap-dancing horse.

By Showtime, the stands of the freshly erected Big Top were packed to bursting. As he took his place in the wings for the start of the Grand Parade, Dylan could just make out Red Tabby sitting front row centre, her face alight with anticipation. *I owe everything to her,* he thought and he felt his heart swell with gratitude.

At last, the show neared its climax and Dylan's big moment came. Charlie trained his spotlight down on the ring, Dancing Dog 'rat-tatted' a long roll on his snare drum and the band struck up a fast-paced tune. Dylan stepped smartly into the dazzling circle of light and began his act. 'Tippity-tip tap. Tippity-tap tip. Tippy-tap toe.' This was no milk-cart daydream. Wide awake and loving every moment, he danced with sheer exhilaration.

The jam-packed crowd roared their delight, and, watching from her ringside seat, Red Tabby glowed with pride. *I knew he was good,* she thought to herself, *but never this good!*

On and on Dylan danced until the catchy melody swept to a rousing crescendo. Up, up he leapt, high in the air, all four hooves clicking together at once with a resounding crack. Then down he came again. For a moment he held his balance, forelegs churning the air. Then, slowly, he sank to his knees in a graceful bow.

The cheering audience, unable to contain themselves any longer, rose to their feet in a standing ovation. Chia stepped into the ring and, eyes sparkling, stretched out a triumphant hand towards Dylan.

'Ladies, gentlemen and little folk,' he bellowed over the uproar, 'I give you the incredible, the spectacular, the one and only Dylan de Polka! Truly, my friends, tonight, a star is born!'

Wave after wave of applause filled the Big Top, yet the new star paid no heed to the delighted, cheering crowd. He crossed the ring and stood humbly before the ginger cat who had guessed his dreams, and risked her nine lives to make those dreams come true. Dylan bowed his deepest, finest bow to his true heroine, the wise and wonderful Red Tabby.

By the time the last of the excited audience had melted away, the long summer twilight had faded into night. The Big Top stood dark and empty once more, silent but for the occasional flap of ragged canvas in the light breeze. One by one, the Happy Days troupe went off for a well-deserved rest.

When Dylan and Red Tabby returned to their trailer they saw, pinned to their door, a shiny gold-spangled star.

'That's meant for you, Dylan,' said Tabby proudly. 'Ringmaster Chia was right. You're a true star now.'

'Really, it's for us both,' Dylan answered. 'After all, we're a team!'

'And always will be,' agreed Tabby.

Inside their cosy home, they found a bed of fresh, sweet straw laid out for Dylan, and, hanging above it, the photograph of Desiree de Polka – his long-lost mother. Nor had Red Tabby been forgotten. There, in a corner, a deep wicker cat basket awaited her, complete with puffy, velvet-covered cushion.

'Purrrfect,' purred Red Tabby contentedly. 'Just purrrfect.' She jumped into her soft bed and turned around twice before settling down. 'We have work, food, a home, and a real family of our very own. Everything we need – well, for now, at least.'

Dylan's ears pricked up. 'For now?' he asked, a hint of concern in his voice. 'Red Tabby whatever do you mean, "for now"?'

'Well, who knows?' came the drowsy reply. 'We might not want to stay with a circus all our lives.'

'Oh dear!' Dylan mumbled. 'Oh dear, Oh dear. Here we go again!' But before he could manage further protest, his eyelids shut and he dropped off into a blissful sleep.

Born to Dance

Dylan and Red Tabby's Great Adventure

Part II

In which desperate situations
give way to courage and determination.

13

Winter Fun

Winter had come, and with the final performance of the year behind them, the Happy Days Circus found time at last to rest and prepare for next spring's tour. Each morning, the Big Top echoed to the sounds of rehearsals as the troupe polished up old tricks and tried out new ones.

'Stand back everyone,' warned Ranga Orang-utan as Marmaduke Monkey climbed inside the great long-barrelled cannon.

'Ready?' Ranga asked.

At Marmaduke's muffled 'yes', he released the cannon's firing spring and 'Boom!' Marmaduke shot right out of the barrel and up into the air. Head over heels he turned – once – twice – three times, before landing safely in the thick sawdust of the ring. 'I did it, Ranga, I did it!' he shouted exuberantly. 'Three mid-air somersaults in a row!'

Near the top of the great tent Charlie Chimpanzee's sister, Prudence, teetered precariously on the high wire as she practised the ballet steps for her new act. 'Well done, my dear,' Irma Elephant called up to her. 'You'll make a fabulous funambulist yet.'

For a moment, Prudence wobbled unsteadily on her highwire. 'Funfab …? Fabfumb …?' she asked, peering down anxiously at her friend.

'From the Latin for acrobat, you know,' Irma explained, trying to sound helpful. But Irma's long word had flustered Prudence and she had to flap her gangly arms wildly to regain her balance.

Dylan had found a private corner of the Big Top behind some bales of hay and spent his waking hours happily trying out steps and routines for the coming season. Dancing Dog, who loved a snappy beat as much as Dylan, often settled himself on a nearby bale to watch the big horse work and, much to the small terrier's delight, it wasn't long before Dylan offered to teach him a step or two.

Red Tabby, under the watchful eyes of Charlie and Prudence, had a try at the flying trapeze. Her days as a ship's cat had given her a natural head for heights and soon, much to Dylan's alarm, she was performing daredevil aerial stunts with the greatest of ease. 'Don't worry,' she told him when he protested. 'Cats always land on their paws!'

Ringmaster Chia looked in on rehearsals whenever he could, with a word of praise for each of the troupe in turn. Often he would call Red Tabby down from the high trapeze and the two of them would go off together for hours at a time. Dylan found it all very mysterious.

One never-to-be-forgotten day, the mystery was solved when, bubbling over with excitement, Chia and Red Tabby burst into the Big Top. Chia was waving what looked like a large, important document, all rolled up, and tied with scarlet ribbon.

'Friends! Friends!' he cried in his finest ringmaster's voice. 'Gather round if you please. We have the most incredible, the most remarkable, the most glorious news.' Everyone stopped what they were doing and hurried over to him, the Meerkat Clowns chattering with excitement. Chia raised his hands for silence and nodded to Red Tabby to make the announcement.

'It amounts to this,' she began. 'Now that the Happy Days Circus is up on its feet, our future might appear safe. But what if the old owners were to return and spoil everything for us? It seemed to Chia and me that we could never be truly protected until we made ourselves official.'

'And we have! We really have!' Chia couldn't help interrupting. 'We've pleaded Animal Rights and we've won! Better yet,' he raced on, raising the rolled and beribboned document in the air, 'we've set a legal precedent.'

Chia and Red Tabby seemed enormously pleased with themselves, but the troupe, feeling a bit left behind, could only look at each other in bewilderment. 'Animal Rights?' 'Regal President?' What could all this mean?

'This Regal President you mention,' Dancing Dog ventured. 'Is he going to rule over us?'

'That's not it, Dancing Dog,' Irma corrected him. 'Ringmaster Chia didn't say "regal", he said "legal", meaning it's the proper thing to do, and "a precedent" just means it's the first time that a particular "something" has ever been done.'

'But the first time that *what* particular "something" has ever been done?' protested Sea Lion, feeling all at sea.

Tiger gave a low growl. 'I've got it,' he declared with a frown. 'We've got new owners, haven't we?'

'Well, yes,' Chia admitted, the corners of his mouth twitching strangely as he spoke.

'And just who might these new owners be?' Lion asked doubtfully as the others began to look at Chia and Red Tabby with suspicion.

'Well, *you* for a start,' replied Tabby merrily. As she spoke, Chia slipped off the scarlet ribbon, unrolled the document, and pointed to the name 'Lion' neatly written on the parchment. Lion's mouth gaped open in surprise.

'And you, Tiger,' went on Chia, grinning broadly now as he ran his finger down the list. 'And Dylan, naturally, and Red Tabby, of course. After all, this was her idea. Then, there's myself, Dancing Dog, Marmaduke, Irma, Charlie, Prudence, Ranga, Bandmaster Sea Lion and his family, and our Meerkat Clowns.'

'In fact, all of us,' Tabby finished.

'Do you mean to say that the Happy Days Circus has actually become ours?' asked Irma cautiously as she struggled to take it all in. 'It really *is* our very own?'

'For ever and ever,' Tabby replied.

'To do whatever we like with?' asked Sea Lion.

'Exactly so,' beamed Chia.

'Then we're free!' cried Marmaduke. 'For the first time in our whole lives, we're truly, wonderfully free!' And he flung his long arms high above his head in sheer delight. A joyful chorus of hoots, roars and trumpetings echoed through the Big Top as the Happy Days troupe realised their good fortune.

14

Lovely Sizzling Sausages

With spring just around the corner, the Happy Days Circus prepared to leave their winter quarters and take what was now their very own show out on the road.

Chia wasted no time in spreading the word about the animal-owned circus and its unique tap-dancing horse. Then he sat back and waited for offers to flood in. But, to the troupe's disappointment, by the time they were ready to leave they had only received three bookings.

'This is a sorry business!' Chia admitted to Red Tabby. 'The truth is I'm only a ringmaster really, not a promoter.'

'It's a start,' Tabby replied, trying hard to look cheerful. 'Once word gets around about Dylan, things are sure to get better.'

Dylan was forbidden from helping to load the transporter for fear of injury. So, while the others packed up, he and Red Tabby tucked themselves out of the way in their trailer 'for a cat nap', as Red Tabby put it. Seconds later, or so it felt, Tiger was prodding them awake with a gentle paw. 'Come on, you two,' he whispered, 'Time to go.'

Dylan and Red Tabby stumbled sleepily into the chill night air. They shivered as Irma pushed their trailer up the ramp and Ranga roped it onto the transporter. Eager to return to the warmth of their snug home, the two friends hurriedly climbed back inside again and settled down for the coming journey.

Chia had the transporter out on the highway long before midnight. While Red Tabby dozed contentedly in her basket, Dylan stood at the window, staring out at the dark landscape and at car lights flashing past. The transporter juddered as Chia shifted gears, making Dylan's treasured picture of his mother swing to and fro on its peg. Dylan glanced fondly at the comforting image, then down at his very best friend, curled up in her cosy bed.

Here we go again, he mused drowsily. *Off together to exciting new places.* Moments later, his head nodded forward and he fell asleep while still standing, a trick he'd learnt as a foal while travelling with his show-business family.

Dawn was breaking as they arrived at their first town. Ringmaster Chia pulled the transporter into the wide, green field where the Big Top was to go up. After a leg stretch and a good meal, the troupe began unloading the equipment while Chia started to compose his usual huge shopping list.

'Let me see,' he muttered, chewing on the end of his pencil. 'Lots more steak for Tiger and Lion, more carrots for Dylan, fresh fish for Sea Lion's family, post the letters, go to the local newspaper, be sure to call on the Animal Rescue vet, order the posters. Oh, dear! Oh, dear! Such a lot to be done and all before lunch!'

As Chia set off on his errands, the others prepared to erect the Big Top. Irma heaved its huge canvas from the transporter, while the Chimpanzee family sorted out the ropes and poles. Dylan knew he wasn't really allowed to pitch in, but he felt he had to. He was busy dragging the King Pole into position when Red Tabby appeared from nowhere.

'What do you think you're up to?' she demanded in an alarmed tone. 'Come away at once.'

'But I must pull my weight!' Dylan protested. 'Please, let me! It's only right.'

'It's only wrong,' Red Tabby told him firmly, then added gently. 'I know you mean well, Dylan, but where would we all be if you got hurt?'

Dylan was crestfallen. 'Just standing watching makes me feel so useless,' he said. 'Besides, what else is there to do?'

Red Tabby pointed beyond the circus field. 'Just look at those rolling hills!' she exclaimed. 'I wonder what we might find on the other side.' And before Dylan could protest, she scrambled up to her favourite spot close behind his ears. 'What do you say we go exploring?' she asked.

'Are you sure?' Dylan asked.

'It's what we two do best,' Red Tabby purred.

'All right, then,' Dylan agreed. Tabby dug her claws into her friend's thick mane and held on tight as Dylan, perked up at the prospect of an adventure, broke into a cheerful canter.

The day was soft and breezy and, as the two friends made their way across the fields and up into the hills, pungent, spring-like smells reached their nostrils. When Dylan reached the top of the first rise, Red Tabby jumped down from her place and began to roll over and over on the sun-warmed ground.

Dylan caught her gleeful mood at once. 'Catch me!' he challenged – and galloped off, his long, blond mane streaming out behind him. Red Tabby gave chase and the pair raced each other across the carpet of meadow grass. Dylan slowed to a walk at last and Tabby, drawing level, took a long, running jump that landed her squarely in the middle of his waiting back.

'Oh, Dylan!' she puffed. 'This is just like the old days. Just you and me and secret places full of mice and sweet grass.'

'They really were great days,' Dylan agreed. 'Except for those cruel horse thieves.' A tremble ran from the points of Dylan's ears to the tip of his tail at the memory of their lucky escape from the scrawny horse dealer, Dangerous Dennis, and his dumpy assistant, Clumsy Golightly. 'If you hadn't come to my rescue,' he blurted out, 'I'd be chained to a cart deep down in some awful mine – or worse.'

'But I did, and you're not,' Red Tabby chided him. 'And look what fun we're having now!'

'But, who knows?' Dylan pressed on. 'They could still come back for me.'

'They wouldn't get you. Not with me on the case,' Red Tabby said firmly. 'And anyway,' she added, 'I suppose we should thank them, really.'

'What for?' exclaimed Dylan, astonished.

'Well, it's only because of those two baddies that we're together now, isn't it?'

Dylan considered for a moment. 'You're always so wise,' he answered. 'But all the same …'

'Oh, come on Dylan,' Tabby urged, 'it's too fine a day for fretting. Let's go up that next hill. I want to get a really good look around.'

Back in the circus field, the rest of the troupe was getting ready to haul the Big Top into place. Ranga had made sure that the King Pole was standing straight and true. Next, he checked the quarter and side poles and, when he felt certain these were firm and solid, gave the all clear.

Irma, with a harness hitched around her broad shoulders, moved slowly forward, leaning her weight on the main hauling rope as she came. Charlie, and his sister, Prudence, grabbed the stout guy ropes and pulled with all their might. Everyone helped, and with a mighty heave the huge canvas began its slow, creaky rise up the King Pole and into the air.

As Dylan and Red Tabby reached the brow of the next hill, Dylan glanced back the way they had come. 'Red Tabby! Look there!' he cried. 'Look what's happening!'

Far behind them, the tip of the great tent rose over the treetops and then settled into position, its many-coloured flags fluttering from the crown of the King Pole. 'The Big Top's up,' said Dylan. 'Let's go back.'

'Not yet,' pleaded Tabby, 'We've hardly begun to explore.'

From where they stood, the land fell away before them and they could see straight down into the next valley. A flock of rooks, cawing raucously, swooped and circled over an ancient oak that towered majestically against the blue sky. Tabby slipped to the ground and ran down the hill towards the noisy, wheeling birds. Dylan followed willingly after her.

The ancient tree stood behind a high, pink stone wall in a handsome but overgrown park. The park's untended lawns, all spattered with wild spring flowers, stretched away towards thick woodland. A silvery stream wound its way through the magical scene – and further off sprawled a crumbling old stately home, half-hidden amongst the thick growth of trees and shrubs. There seemed to be outbuildings and stables too.

'It would be fun to nose about in there,' murmured Red Tabby.

'Oh, dear me,' sighed Dylan. 'You cats! You always need to know what's round the next corner.'

'It's our curiosity, remember?' Tabby teased as she scrambled back up onto Dylan's broad shoulders.

The two friends ambled along, half-seeking a way in, but the park's wall seemed to run on forever with no sign of any gate.

They'd gone about a mile when the tantalising smell of frying sausages wafted up to them from beyond the wall. Red Tabby felt a sudden twinge of hunger. From her place high on Dylan's back, she saw an unusual-looking man tending a pan balanced precariously over a small fire. He wore trousers of red-and-orange check and a long overcoat of shiny purple cloth trimmed with gold braiding. Long, fair hair tumbled wildly over his shoulders. The smell of the sizzling sausages tickled Tabby's nose again. She licked her lips greedily.

As he straightened up from his cooking, the tall, oddly-dressed figure caught sight of the two friends and waved a cheery greeting. Red Tabby returned the wave hopefully, but Dylan, who was not partial to sausages, turned and trotted back the way they had come. Tabby gazed longingly over to where the stranger stood, still waving. 'But it's sausages!' she protested. 'Lovely, sizzling sausages!'

'I know, I know,' said Dylan, 'but the others are bound to be ready for us by now, and we can't miss rehearsals.'

'You're right,' Tabby reluctantly agreed after a last, long sniff at the savoury smells. 'Let's go, then.'

With that, Dylan quickened his pace to a steady canter which brought them swiftly home to the Big Top.

15

The Newcomer

Ringmaster Chia shook the Animal Rescue vet warmly by the hand and stepped out of her office into the High Street. He was just turning towards the shops when a cheery, sunshine-yellow car came barrelling down the road, pulling behind it a trailer piled high with filing cabinets, chairs, a sofa, and an ornate iron bed. With a loud blast of its horn, the car lurched to an abrupt halt beside the startled ringmaster, its trailer-load wobbling alarmingly.

'What on earth?' Chia gasped and ducked hurriedly back into the safety of the vet's doorway. The driver, who wore an exotic golden turban and outsized sunglasses, leant out of the window and beckoned to him. Chia stepped forward cautiously.

'You must be Ringmaster Chia!' said a deep and melodious voice.

'That is me, most certainly,' Chia replied, 'but should I know you, sir?'

With a flourish the dark glasses were swept off and Chia found himself gazing into the largest, most splendidly luminous green eyes he had ever seen in his life. 'Please, forgive my error, madam,' he cried, his cheeks turning red with embarrassment.

The woman nodded graciously. 'I am Madame Lulu Bombazine,' she announced.

Chia threw his hands up in amazement. 'Not the renowned circus impresario?' he breathed.

'The very same,' she assured him.

'But what could possibly bring a celebrity such as yourself to this small town?' Chia asked.

'Why, you of course!' Madame Bombazine laughed.

'Me?' spluttered Chia.

'You and the Happy Days Circus. I come to bring you the fame and fortune you so richly deserve.' Overcome, Chia stood speechless. 'I'm off to find somewhere to stay for the meantime,' said Madame Bombazine. 'I'll be over to see you all tomorrow.' And before Chia could recover his wits, she was gone.

'Excuse me, Ringmaster Chia,' Marmaduke said later, 'but what does "impresario" mean?' It was teatime and the troupe had gathered around Chia to hear his astonishing news.

Chia smiled. 'An "impresario"?' he repeated, savouring the word for a moment. 'Well, this particular impresario is able to make us the most famous circus in the whole country and, maybe, even in the whole world.'

'The whole country?' gasped Dancing Dog.

'The whole world?' echoed the meerkats doubtfully.

'But are we quite ready for all that?' Lion asked. 'I singed my mane last time I jumped through the fiery hoops and it's not quite grown back yet.'

'Of course we're ready,' insisted Prudence. 'You know we always feel nervous before a new season.'

'And let's remember, Lion,' observed Tiger, 'the more famous we are, the bigger and juicier the steaks!'

'Sounds good to me,' Lion responded, cheering up at once.

'Then may Madame Bombazine come to our dress rehearsal?' Chia asked. A rousing chorus of roars, barks and squeaks answered his question. Chia clapped his hands over his ears. 'A simple "yes" or "no" was all I needed!' he laughed.

The renowned impresario was due any minute, and Tiger intended everything to be perfect before she arrived. He hurried around checking the props for the ninetieth time – the Meerkat Clowns' custard pies, the sea lion pups' juggling balls, and Prudence and Charlie's trampoline. Then he carefully examined the big cannon that was to send Marmaduke somersaulting through the air.

Bandmaster Sea Lion flopped up to the podium, a bundle of music sheets tucked under one flipper. He had just got them sorted out when Irma arrived with her tuba. Dancing Dog followed with his drums.

'Where's Marmaduke?' asked the bandmaster.

'Having a little snack, the last I saw of him,' replied Dancing Dog. 'Shall I fetch him?'

'If you would,' said Sea Lion. 'I want to run through these numbers with him again.' Dancing Dog scampered off.

In the privacy of his trailer, Lion peered anxiously into his mirror at the circle of pink rollers surrounding his handsome features. 'Carefully now, carefully,' he warned himself as he removed one roller, then another. 'Ouch! Drat!' he yelped, as a tuft of singed fur came away with the last of them. He examined the damage and sighed. 'It'll have to do, I suppose,' he groaned and hid the singed spot with a curl.

'Remember,' said Tiger as he came past the trailer door, 'Head up, chest out, show off that magnificent mane.' Lion glanced again in the mirror and beamed.

High up in the rigging, Charlie was fussing with the spotlight when he noticed Dylan trotting into the ring. 'Hold still for a bit will you?' he shouted down, and the great circle of light swept across the golden sawdust, coming to rest on the motionless horse. Dylan's hooves tapped out a short, staccato rhythm and he made a graceful bow. Overhead, Charlie slapped his haunches gleefully.

On the far side of the ring, oblivious to the noise and bustle of the preparations swirling around him, Chia sat carefully brushing out his gold and scarlet tailcoat. He was eager to look his best when Madame Bombazine arrived.

'Costume parade's starting,' Tiger called up to Charlie.

'I'll be down in two ticks,' Charlie answered and he switched off the great lamp, slid down the King Pole and rushed off to his trailer to get dressed.

Bandmaster Sea Lion's pups were already lined up with their mother, Celia, in red-striped waistcoats. Dancing Dog wore his black-and-white chequered ruff and stylish top hat, while Irma used her trunk to make last minute adjustments to her glittering, jewel-encrusted headdress. Dylan and Red Tabby took their places with the others.

Tiger padded along the line of costumed performers. 'You're a credit to the Happy Days Circus, all of you!' he enthused. Then, looking around, 'All of you who are here, that is.' Just at that moment the missing Marmaduke came bouncing into the ring.

Tiger's brow puckered into a frown. 'And what might this be?' he enquired, pointing to the front of Marmaduke's costume. 'The last of your lunch perhaps?'

'Oh, dear!' cried Marmaduke, brushing away the offending crumbs with a hasty paw.

'And where, might I ask, is Ranga?' demanded Tiger.

'I saw him in the dressing trailer just now, trying on a new clown costume,' offered Charlie.

'Here he is!' cried the Meerkat Clowns in unison, pointing towards the entrance. All eyes turned to look as Ranga appeared in blue dungarees and yellow shirt. A giant orange-and-white spotted bow-tie was clipped jauntily beneath his chin. Everyone burst into applause, and with a boisterous 'whoop' Ranga began turning energetic cartwheels around the ring.

Perfect! Ringmaster Chia decided as he held his scarlet tailcoat up to the light and examined it minutely. He gave one sleeve a last careful flick of his brush and slipped the coat on. But, just as he had fastened the last of his bright gold buttons, Ranga came cartwheeling along and landed in a sprawl before him, throwing up a billowing cloud of sawdust.

'Oh, I'm really sorry,' blurted Ranga. 'It's my first go as a clown and I must have got carried away.'

Before Chia could respond, the sharp 'beep' of a car horn sounded outside the Big Top.

'It's Madame Bombazine,' cried Chia. 'She's here!'

He glanced ruefully at his now dusty costume and sighed. Giving himself a vigorous shake, he smoothed down his thick black hair, and rushed out to greet the new arrival.

A hush fell over the Big Top. All eyes were riveted on the entrance as Chia reappeared, the impresario on his arm. Proudly, he led her forward into the ring. She, too, had dressed carefully for the occasion, her flowing, tiger-striped dress set off by a swirl of sparkling necklaces.

'Just look at that hair,' Red Tabby whispered in Dylan's ear. Madame Bombazine's auburn tresses lay piled in luxuriant sweeps above her head, secured with a myriad of bejewelled pins. 'And such tiny feet in such stylish boots,' added Tabby, spellbound. The high-heeled boots, along with the hairstyle, contrived to make the newcomer appear a good deal taller than she actually was.

'Allow me to present the world-renowned circus impresario, the one and only, Madame Lulu Bombazine!' cried Chia, and waited for the expected greeting. But to his dismay, apart from a welcoming 'Meow' from Red Tabby and an enthusiastic whinny from Dylan, the troupe stood still and silent. Chia swallowed nervously, and tried again a little louder. 'I said "ALLOW ME TO PRESENT THE RENOWNED CIRCUS IMPRESARIO, THE ONE AND ONLY, MADAME LULU BOMBAZINE!"'

Still no one moved. Now, even Red Tabby remained silent. Chia peered intently at the circle of animals. 'But my dear friends, whatever can be the matter?' he asked. 'Why will you not welcome our honoured guest?' Anxious eyes turned towards Chia, then to the newcomer, and then back to Chia again.

'It's her dress,' wailed Prudence. Chia looked baffled. 'It's Madame Bombazine's dress.' Prudence repeated. 'Oh, dear! It isn't – surely, it *can't* be made of tiger skin!'

Madame Bombazine left Chia's side to step into the circle of worried animals. 'Oh, never!' she exclaimed. 'Never tiger skin.' And she lifted a fold of the filmy material in her delicate hands and held it out for all to see. 'It's simply my favourite pattern,' she explained. 'Tiger stripes – hand painted on silk.'

Lion, who had been holding his breath, let out a huge sigh. 'That comes as a big relief!' he said, just a little too loudly.

'Manners, Lion,' Irma whispered. 'For Heaven's sake, Lion! Manners!'

With the misunderstanding settled, everyone brightened up. Chia took Madame Bombazine around the troupe, introducing her to each of the performers in turn. When they came to Dylan, Madame Bombazine beamed up at him. 'You must be our star,' she remarked, her green eyes sparkling.

'Well, sort of, I suppose,' Dylan replied shyly.

The renowned impresario reached up and gently stroked his mane, then glanced up at Red Tabby stretched out on Dylan's broad back.

'So elegant!' she remarked.

'But hardly as elegant as you, Madame,' Tabby replied.

Tiger gave an amused grunt. The meerkats tittered and even Dylan gave a cheerful snort. Red Tabby found herself blushing under her fur. The troupe gathered eagerly around their visitor, the ice well and truly broken. 'This is wonderful!' declared the great woman, clapping her hands with delight. 'But shall we be getting on?'

16

Star Quality

Chia settled Madame Bombazine at the ringside, and the performers hastened to take their places. The band struck up a catchy tune, and the all-important rehearsal began.

Into the ring tumbled the Meerkat Clowns, with Ranga hot on their heels. Then the meerkats jumped into their trick car and began chasing *him* around the ring. He somersaulted and cartwheeled ahead of his pursuers, tootling away all the while on his silver trumpet.

The wilder the antics became, the more Bandmaster Sea Lion quickened the tempo. Marmaduke's fingers flew faster and faster across his keyboard, and Dancing Dog could scarcely keep pace on his drums. As a finale, Ranga lassoed all the meerkats together and bundled them out of the ring in a bright orange wheelbarrow, making Madame Bombazine laugh until tears ran down her cheeks.

As the renowned impresario wiped her eyes with a delicate hanky, Lion made his grand entry into the ring. 'Oh! What a magnificent mane!' she gasped.

Tiger, his stripes combed to perfection, strutted in to join him, and the two mighty cats padded round each other, growling ferociously. Chia smiled proudly. 'It's all part of their act,' he confided to his guest. 'They're great friends really.'

Bandmaster Sea Lion's throbbing jungle music soared to a climax with a crash of cymbals. This was Lion's cue. To a long drum roll from Dancing Dog, he strolled into the centre of the ring and settled himself on his great haunches. Then, with a fearsome roar, he opened his jaws wide and held absolutely still. The drum roll ended and Tiger, snarling impressively, walked boldly up to the King of the Beasts. Ever so carefully, the great striped feline lowered his head into Lion's gaping mouth, skilfully avoiding the sharp and rather yellow teeth.

Dancing Dog 'rat-tat-tatted' again and Lion's jaws slowly but surely began to close around Tiger's head. No one dared breathe. At the last possible moment, the jaws snapped wide open again and Tiger bounded free. Stirring jungle music brought the act to a triumphant close. Tiger carefully dabbed at his damp whiskers and the two great cats turned and bowed respectfully to Madame Bombazine.

The renowned impresario clapped furiously. 'Absolutely brilliant,' she told Chia. 'A top class act! Who's on next?' As if in answer to her question, Sea Lion's little band struck up a lively seafaring hornpipe and Red Tabby stepped into the spotlight. For her costume Tabby had chosen a deep-blue velvet waistcoat studded with small pieces of multi-coloured mirror that flashed and glittered under the dazzling lights. Perched on her head she wore a jaunty sailor's cap. Tabby bowed and stepped nimbly onto the rope ladder, which rose to the aerial platform high above the ring. Madame Bombazine's eyebrows shot up in surprise.

'An aerial cat?' she exclaimed. 'This I have to see!' Backstage, Dylan gulped anxiously as he watched his dear friend climb paw over paw up the long, long ladder. Once aloft, Red Tabby stepped boldly onto her trapeze and began to swing back and forth, back and forth, going faster and faster with each swing.

From the platform facing Tabby, Prudence Chimpanzee stepped onto her trapeze and began to swing to and fro. Tabby, eyes fixed firmly on Prudence, swung higher and higher. When the two were swinging in ever-widening arcs so high that they almost met, Prudence let herself fall backwards so she hung from the crossbar by her knees.

Red Tabby dropped from her perch, caught her own crossbar with her paws, then swung outwards towards Prudence. Suddenly, she let go her hold and flew free – blazing a trail of twinkling blue velvet and bright ginger fur.

Far below the flying cat, Dylan shut his eyes and turned away from the awful sight of Red Tabby's dangerous feat. He didn't know how many of her nine lives she'd already used up, but he feared there couldn't be that many left. A rousing cheer rang out and he opened his eyes again to see Tabby and Prudence slithering down a long rope to the ground and safety. Prudence – dear Prudence – must have played her part and caught his friend in mid-air exactly as she was meant to do.

'You were breathtaking,' Dylan told Tabby when the applause had died away and she came backstage. 'But, all the same, I do wish you wouldn't.'

'Really, Dylan! I *was* a ship's cat, remember?' Tabby chided him. 'It's not much different from climbing up to the crow's nest.'

Madame Bombazine's excitement grew by the minute as the troupe performed their carefully-rehearsed routines. 'When am I to see the star of the show?' she asked Chia at last.

Chia smiled and put a finger to his lips. 'We have saved him for the grand finale,' he whispered and nodded towards the ring. Bandmaster Sea Lion tapped his podium, signalled to his players, and with a 'one-and-a-two' and a 'one-two-three' they struck up their latest composition, 'Dylan's Tune'.

Into Charlie's great spotlight trotted the star of the Happy Days Circus. To everyone's surprise, he was not alone. There, jogging along beside the tall, long-legged dray horse was Dancing Dog, his black-and-white ruff and top hat echoing the little terrier's markings perfectly.

'What on earth is that meant for?' asked Madame Bombazine, pointing to a tiny platform strapped to Dylan's back.

'We shall soon see,' teased Chia, his eyes alight with pride.

Dylan felt the great spotlight's comforting warmth as he and Dancing Dog took their places in the ring. He caught the little terrier's eye. 'Ready?' he whispered. Dancing Dog swallowed hard and nodded back.

As Bandmaster Sea Lion brought the entrance music to a close, Dylan dropped to his knees so that Dancing Dog could reach the tiny platform. Once he was in place, Dylan got up and the band struck up again.

'Tip-tippity tap' Dylan's great feathered hooves began. 'Click-clickety-click clack' Dancing Dog's sharp little claws replied.

In the stands, Madame Bombazine forgot for a moment that she was a world-renowned impresario and squealed with delight.

The band kept a steady tempo, not daring to play too fast, for fear that Dancing Dog couldn't keep up. But he easily followed the big horse, matching his every move step for step.

As the duet ended, Madame Bombazine, Chia and the entire Happy Days troupe shouted and stamped their approval. Breathless with excitement, Dancing Dog jumped to the ground, only to be mobbed by the admiring meerkats.

'Dylan taught me. Really, it was Dylan. I could only twirl and cartwheel before,' he burbled happily.

Ranga swiftly unstrapped the platform from Dylan's back, and Dancing Dog cartwheeled all the way over to the bandstand and his place on the drums. Now came a flurry of chords from Marmaduke's keyboard. This was Dylan's special moment. Alone in the centre of the ring, he swung into his solo routine.

It was a dazzling performance. The Riff and Riffle, the Hop Shuffle, the Buffalo, the Cincinnati. All those steps his old tap-dancing master, Mr. Spatz, had taught him long ago, and clever routines he'd invented on his own. With hooves flashing and tail swishing, he beat out a lively syncopated rhythm that soon had everyone's toes tapping. Faster and faster he went until he seemed just a whirling blur. To end his act he leapt high above the sawdust-covered ring, clicking all four hooves together with a mighty crack. For a moment, he seemed to hang in mid-air. Then, landing gracefully, he bowed a deep bow.

'Bravo! Bravo!' shouted Madame Bombazine. Beside her, a beaming Chia 'hurrahed' with abandon, while the Big Top echoed with whoops and hollers from the rest of the troupe. When the hubbub had finally died down, Chia escorted the impresario back to her car.

'Dear Madame Bombazine,' he asked hesitantly, 'how did you like our little show?'

'You may call me Madame Lulu from now on,' the great lady told him, eyes twinkling. 'And now, Ringmaster, you and I need to talk.' It was quite some time before Chia returned to the Big Top.

'What did she think of us?' Tiger asked as everyone gathered round to hear his news. 'Were we all right?'

'Were you all right?' Chia looked strangely gloomy as he echoed Tiger's question. 'Oh, I wouldn't put it quite like that.' The troupe stared at each other in dismay.

'But we have to be all right,' protested Irma. 'We open three days from now.'

To everyone's surprise, Chia began to laugh. 'My dear, dear friends,' he chuckled, 'Madame Bomba ... I should say Madame Lulu ... thinks you're a very great deal more than all right! She thinks – and, believe me, she should know – that you are remarkable! Marvellous! Splendiferous! Stupendous! Unbeatable! Nothing less, in fact, than the greatest show on Earth!'

'The greatest show on Earth!' mused Dylan, as he and Red Tabby returned to their trailer. 'That would be a good slogan for our posters.'

'It might just have been used before,' replied his friend with a knowing wink – for she was a cat who had walked in the world and knew its ways.

17

Madame Lulu's First Day

Madame Lulu woke at dawn next day, her head buzzing with plans. It was still much too early to call anyone, so she set a pan on the cooker to make a comforting cup of sweet, hot chocolate.

Her temporary quarters were five flights up, at the very top of an old warehouse – a hard climb, but boasting a view that was worth every step. From her windows, she could see right across the town to the brightly striped Big Top and the green, rolling hills beyond. She poured her hot chocolate and stood for a while, sipping it and admiring the scene before her. *I was so right to come!* she mused. *Now I shall be doing what I love best – and with such superb artistes! This is going to be fun!*

As Madame Lulu set to work, the Animal Rescue vet arrived at the Big Top to give the Happy Days performers their annual health check – for without a veterinary certificate the circus wouldn't be allowed to carry on. Chia hovered anxiously behind her as she did her rounds. Lion was persuaded to have his teeth scaled, much to Tiger's relief; Dancing Dog's flea injections were brought up to date; and Irma had some ointment for her shoulder, where her harness had rubbed a sore patch. It was nearly midday before the vet finished.

'Congratulations. They're in fine shape,' she told Chia as she was leaving. 'Come by my office in a day or two. I'll have your certificate ready.'

Chia hurried off to Madame Lulu's with the good news. As he hauled himself up the last of her many stairs he could hear her busy on the telephone. 'Yes! That's right!' she was saying, 'I assure you this horse really can tap dance. Yes! The animals most certainly do own the circus themselves. Yes! We'll be glad to add your town to our tour.' Chia came in and shut the door and plopped down into a chair to catch his breath.

'Animal Rescue has cleared us for another year,' he puffed as Madame Lulu put down the phone.

'Then there's nothing to stand in our way,' she replied. 'Before I'm through, every family in the land will be lining up to see the Happy Days Circus.'

'That's wonderful news,' beamed Chia.

'And there's more,' Madame Lulu went on, pleased with herself. 'This morning I landed the biggest scoop of all. "Dray Horse World" wants Dylan for their centrefold.'

'Do you mean the glossy equestrian magazine?' Chia enquired.

Madame Lulu nodded. 'Their photographer is coming this very afternoon. I can see the headline now! "The de Polka Family Does It Again – Desiree de Polka's Foal Becomes Megastar!"'

Chia clasped his hands together in excitement. 'Dear Madame,' he cried, 'you are *so* talented! I think this calls for a toast.' The tantalizing smell of hot chocolate had been tickling his nose ever since he'd arrived.

'It certainly does,' Madame Lulu agreed and poured out two brimming mugs. 'To the Happy Days Circus!'

'Indeed!' replied Chia. 'And to the world's finest impresario!'

Madame Lulu smiled. 'Now, Ringmaster,' she went on in a more serious tone, 'it's back to work.' And, before nightfall, bookings were pouring in from near and far.

Almost too soon, opening night arrived. The road that led to the field where the Big Top stood overflowed with eager families, impatient to see the remarkable Happy Days Circus with its new star. 'Fancy!' they told each other, 'a circus owned and run entirely by its animals. And who in the world ever heard of a tap-dancing horse?'

'Guess we can't ask him for an autograph,' someone quipped.

'Maybe he'll give us a hoof print,' chuckled another.

Press and television reporters were out in force, and Madame Lulu, like the thoroughly professional person she was, thanked each one individually for coming. Chia stood at the Big Top entrance, bellowing through his huge megaphone. 'Roll up!' he cried. 'Roll up! Roll up! Our show is about to begin!' The audience surged past him and clambered enthusiastically into their places.

'Just listen to that crowd,' Tiger gasped as the troupe waited nervously backstage.

'We're full right up for the whole of this week,' Irma confided.

'If *I'm* to be full right up for the whole of this week, I'm going to need a bunch more bananas,' cracked Marmaduke.

'No, no,' Irma protested, missing Marmaduke's brave attempt at a joke. 'I meant all the tickets are sold.'

'Musicians, take your places,' called Chia, who had nipped backstage from his spot by the entrance.

The lights in the Big Top dimmed. A hush fell over the crowd. Bandmaster Sea Lion raised his flipper and the band launched into a lively overture.

The music set off another flurry of nerves and the mood of the waiting animals turned sombre. This was it. The first rung on the ladder of true success. It was now or never. There could be no turning back.

'We must make them like us,' Charlie muttered. 'We *have* to.'

'You've got that right,' agreed Tiger.

'We dare not fail,' said Lion, his great voice unnaturally quiet.

'Not if we are to stay free,' agreed his striped companion gravely.

'Performers, take your places,' interrupted Chia.

'Good luck, Dylan,' whispered Red Tabby.

'Keep safe up there, please!' Dylan replied.

Out in the darkened Big Top, a single spotlight shone down into the ring. Chia, superb in his shiny top hat, red and gold tailcoat and gleaming boots, strode boldly out into the brilliant circle of light. *What a fine figure he cuts,* thought Madame Lulu from her seat in the stands. And she felt her heart give an unexpected jump.

Ringmaster Chia bowed to the crowd then lifted his megaphone. 'Ladies and gentlemen, and little people,' he proclaimed. 'Kindly welcome to your town the unique and never-to-be-forgotten Happy Days Circus. And, leading our Grand Parade, the one, the only, the matchless talent of this evening's show – Dylan de Polka!'

Ranga blew a royal fanfare on his silver trumpet, Marmaduke's lithe fingers crashed out a resounding chord on his keyboard, and the 'March of the Grand Parade' began. The crowd craned their necks, all eagerness and expectation, and when Dylan appeared at the head of the parade he was met by a tidal wave of applause. Madame Lulu had certainly done her job well.

Just as Prudence had predicted, pre-show nerves swiftly melted away and all those painstaking rehearsals paid off as each fresh act drew ever more laughter and cheers. Dylan's spectacular act brought the show to a rousing conclusion and, as the troupe took its final bows, the crowd rose to its feet, stamping and whistling with all its might.

When the bustle and excitement was over and the very last of the rapturous families had dispersed into the night, Dylan and Red Tabby climbed wearily into their trailer. As they settled down to sleep, Dylan gave a quiet whinny. 'I wish my mother could have seen this day,' he said wistfully.

'She'd certainly be proud,' Tabby agreed. For a moment, a worrying twinge flitted across her mind, but she pushed it away and burrowed deep into her snug basket.

18

Chance Encounter

With the triumph of their opening night behind them, the Happy Days Circus went on to give one dazzling show after another. But at last, their busy schedule allowed a welcome day off.

Dylan woke late that morning to find the others already busy with their various plans. Irma was hard at work polishing her tuba. A 'DO NOT DISTURB' sign hung on the door of Lion and Tiger's quarters. Charlie and Ranga were off fishing. Red Tabby was nowhere to be seen. And Chia had gone into town with his usual long list of errands.

Dylan mooched about with no idea what to do with himself. He had just decided he might take a nap when Red Tabby appeared unexpectedly from around the corner of their trailer. 'Dylan! You're awake at long last!' she exclaimed. 'Let's get a move on! I'd really like to find a way into that mysterious park with the high wall around it.'

'What? Right now? This morning?' asked Dylan.

'Why not?' asked Tabby, her eyes gleaming with the prospect of a fresh escapade. Dylan couldn't think why not, so he held still while his friend clambered up to her usual spot behind his ears. 'Besides,' Tabby went on as she settled down, 'we're moving on quite soon. This may be our only chance.'

Early rain had given way to warming sunshine, and Dylan's spirits lifted at the thought of the fun that lay ahead. They climbed the hill behind the Big Top and wandered across the flower-sprinkled fields beyond. Now and then they'd pause – whenever Dylan spotted a tasty clump of grass, or Red Tabby found a mouse or rabbit hole to nose into.

With the mighty old oak acting as a helpful beacon, the two adventurers easily found their way back to the borders of the great park. As before, its imposing pink stone wall seemed to run on forever in both directions, but somewhere, surely, there had to be a way in. 'Which way shall we try first?' Dylan asked Tabby. 'Up the valley or down?'

Tabby looked around from her spot on Dylan's back. 'Down,' she suggested. So 'down' they went.

Before long, they reached a place where a part of the park wall had crumbled away, creating a tempting gap. 'I can jump that,' Dylan offered.

'Maybe so,' Tabby said, 'but you'd better not. Look! There's a long drop on the other side. You might sprain an ankle – or worse.'

Ahead of them, the wall turned and ran along the side of a noisy highway. A big coach flashed by, dangerously close to them, as they tried to carry on.

'We'd better turn back,' Tabby advised, and, retracing their steps, they soon left the busy road behind them.

Barely a dozen miles further down that same busy road, Dangerous Dennis eased his old truck to a stop in a dusty lay-by where a wayside snack bar offered refreshments. Beside him, his tubby assistant, Clumsy Golightly, dozed fitfully. The two horse dealers were making their way from one livestock fair to another, and the journey had been long and wearisome.

Dennis climbed stiffly from the cab and went over to get a much-needed cup of tea. Clumsy woke with a start to find himself alone and, not being one to turn his back on a snack, climbed down and hurried after him.

Nothing had gone right for Dangerous Dennis after Dylan and Red Tabby had escaped his grasp the summer before. Not a day had passed since without him vowing to take revenge. But neither he nor Clumsy had any idea where to find them.

Clumsy blew loudly on his tea and watched his boss on the other side of the table thumbing moodily through the latest issue of Dray Horse World. He had just decided that the tea was cool enough for a first cautious sip when he saw Dennis stiffen in his chair, eyes agleam. Without warning, a fist came down hard on the table, splashing Clumsy's tea into his saucer.

'Gotcha! Gotcha at last!' the horse dealer cried. 'Look at this 'ere,' he went on, his voice shaking with excitement. 'Tell me what 'orse that is.' And he thrust the magazine under Clumsy's nose.

Clumsy peered at the magazine's centrefold. 'Yoo-neek dan-sing horse woos ... er, no, wows holiday crowds,' he mouthed slowly. 'That horse, there, Boss, that's Dylan! Don't you recognise him?'

'What d'yer think, you fool? Of course I recognise 'im!' Dennis snatched back the magazine and ran a grubby finger down the page.

'Ah ha! 'Ere we are. Show Dates. Page 42.' He flipped to the page and deftly ripped it out. 'Where and when to see the unmissable Happy Days Circus and the amazing Dylan de Polka.'

Dennis scanned the long list of scheduled performances printed on the list.

Clumsy pulled the discarded magazine across the table towards him and gazed intently at the centrefold headline. 'Desiree de Polka's Foal Now Megastar,' he read. 'Look Boss! They're saying something here about Dylan's mum!'

Dennis's smothered the centrefold with a broad hand, his nose within an inch of Clumsy's. 'I've told you before,' he rasped, 'that mare's no business of yours.'

'But, Boss, there's a picture of her right there. She's real pretty, she is,' the little man pressed on innocently.

Dennis's eyes took on the pained and secretive expression that Clumsy had seen once before. Slowly, the centrefold crumpled in the horse dealer's clenching fist. ''Ow often do I 'ave to spell it out for you? That mare ain't none of your business!' And he flung the magazine violently across the room. 'It's that Dylan we're after. 'E's mine by rights and we're gettin' 'im back – and a lot more besides.'

'But what about the horse fair, Boss?' Clumsy protested.

'Forget it,' snapped Dennis. 'We've got bigger fish to fry. Giddy up, Clumsy!' and he made for the door of the snack bar. Clumsy scooped up a generous fistful of biscuits and hurried out after him. His boss's sudden change of mood, he feared, meant long days and hard nights ahead.

The old pink stone wall meandered on and on. Try as they might, Dylan and Red Tabby could find no way into the great park that lay behind the silent ramparts. The sun shone down from a cloudless sky. By now, the chill that had marked the morning had gone, and the air felt close and hot.

Red Tabby, ever the slave to her curiosity, jumped down from Dylan's back onto the wall and went skittering ahead. Dylan, feeling deliciously lazy, dawdled idly along behind her. After a while, he came upon an old stone water trough set against the park wall. Under a sprinkle of floating leaves, the water in the trough smelt cool and tempting. Nosing the leaves aside, he took a long, refreshing drink.

Near the trough, the trunk of an immense fallen tree offered welcome shade. The carpet of leaves beneath the fallen giant looked invitingly soft. 'Tabby?' Dylan called. 'How about a little nap?' But Tabby, far ahead, was well out of earshot. Dylan prodded the ground with his hoof until he found just the right spot, and settled himself down with a contented sigh.

When Tabby returned to look for her friend, she found him lying beside the fallen tree, his legs curled neatly under him, sound asleep. 'Some adventurer you are,' she purred in amusement. All the same, she tucked herself up under Dylan's chin and soon, she too, drifted off.

The morning had flown past by the time Chia finished his errands in the town. Whistling cheerfully, he headed towards Madame Lulu's and a tasty mug of hot chocolate. But as he climbed her stairs something seemed to be amiss for he could hear her arguing furiously down the telephone. As he reached the top landing, the phone was slammed down noisily.

'Three cancellations!' Madame Lulu complained, looking up from her desk as Chia came in. 'Three!'

'Cancellations? You mean cancelled reservations?' Chia asked, looking bewildered.

'No. I mean bookings. Three towns have cancelled their bookings just in this last half hour.'

'But how could that be?' Chia demanded.

Before Madame Lulu could answer him, the phone rang again. Chia could hear an aggressive voice on the other end of the line.

'We're on to you!' the voice grated. 'Don't think we don't know your game. You lot make all your cash bein' cruel to animals.'

'Not true!' Madame Lulu protested. 'Our animals have the last word around here. It's their own circus, after all!'

'You can't fool anyone with that tall tale,' the caller retorted in an ugly tone. 'Animal Rescue's gonna shut your rotten show down, and the sooner the better.'

'Now just you listen to me, whoever you are …' Madame Lulu began, but the caller had hung up.

'What's happening to us?' Chia asked.

'I don't know,' replied Madame Lulu. 'But whatever it is, I don't like the sound of it.'

At a crossroads not far from the town, Dangerous Dennis stepped out of a telephone box and hurried back to his truck. Clumsy saw his boss coming. He stuffed the last of his biscuits into his mouth and wiped his lips free of crumbs with a sleeve.

'I'll wager that puts the cat fairly in with the pigeons,' bragged Dennis as he climbed into the driver's seat beside his helper.

'What cats? What pigeons?' managed Clumsy through his mouthful of biscuit. 'You don't even like cats, let alone pigeons.'

'Leave it,' Dennis grunted, and he pulled a screwed-up piece of paper from his pocket. It was the Happy Days Circus tour schedule. He marked it with the stub of a pencil, threw the truck into gear and stepped on the accelerator.

'Ringmaster Chia and his Lulu Lady can't 'alf be wondering what's up with all their bookings goin' up in smoke,' he chuckled as the old vehicle lumbered out onto the road. 'And while they're sortin' out that riddle, we can push on with savin' those poor, ill-treated circus animals.'

'But, Boss,' Clumsy protested. 'What are we doing with circus animals?'

'That's our trade: buyin' and sellin' livestock,' Dennis snapped, 'just in case you've forgotten.'

'But we trade in horses, Boss. Horses!' Clumsy pleaded. 'Not wild animals and 'specially not *those* ones! That rotten Lion took against me last summer, I know it.'

A sharp elbow landed on Clumsy's ear.

'You're a fool, Golightly, and you always were,' spat Dennis. 'We're grabbin' the lot of 'em, and sellin' 'em on. It'll make us a fortune.'

Red Tabby woke from her nap and sniffed the breeze. *What a mouth-watering smell,* she thought. *It has to be fish!* She climbed onto the great fallen trunk and looked around her. On the far side of the field a small river flowed. Beside it, a long-haired figure tended a fishing rod propped up on the bank. He wore a tattered emerald green jacket trimmed with purple braiding, and flared, silver trousers. Close by, a large frying pan sat over a lively fire. Red Tabby jumped down and prodded Dylan on his great soft nose.

'What's up?' Dylan mumbled drowsily as he woke up.

'It's him,' Tabby urged. 'The man from the park who we saw before. Let's go over and say hello.'

Dylan looked knowingly at Tabby's twitching nose. 'You're just after those sausages again,' he grumbled. 'What's in it for me?'

'It's not sausages today, Dylan. It's fish!' pleaded Tabby. 'And what about all those carrots I've dug up for you in my time? Anyway, I bet *he* could show us a way into the park.'

'You might be right!' said Dylan, and he scrambled to his feet. But Tabby had already bounded off across the field towards the stranger. Dylan gave himself a thorough shake and hurried after her.

'I'm Red Tabby, ship's cat and aerial artiste extraordinaire,' Tabby was saying as Dylan trotted up. 'And this is my best friend, Dylan de Polka. He's the star of the Happy Days Circus, you know.' Dylan felt a bit awkward, but the stranger just smiled and nodded as he carefully turned three newly-caught fish in his pan with a large fork. 'Please don't think me rude,' Red Tabby persisted, 'but may we ask who you are?'

'Oh yes! Of course!' the man apologised. 'Being on my own so much makes me forget my manners. Stomper's the name – Lord Stomper.'

'Do you live near here, Lord Stomper?' asked Dylan.

'That's my place over there,' Lord Stomper replied, and waved his fork in the direction of the pink stone wall. 'Great Park, it's called. Didn't I see you two gawking over my wall the other day?'

'That was us all right,' Dylan agreed. 'Tabby waved, didn't you, Tabby?' But, by now, Red Tabby's nose was practically inside the sizzling pan.

Lord Stomper hid a smile. 'Join me, won't you?' he asked. 'There's lots to go round!' Red Tabby licked her lips hungrily.

It's all very well for Red Tabby, thought Dylan, *but I don't eat fish!* Lord Stomper caught Dylan's expression and dipped a hand into his haversack.

'You might enjoy a nibble of these,' he offered, drawing out a large bunch of carrots. 'Very sweet. I grow them myself.' With such a fine, unexpected lunch on offer, Dylan and Red Tabby couldn't resist.

19

Mealtime & Mayhem

'Listen up,' ordered Dangerous Dennis. He and his tubby assistant sat in the cab of their truck, parked in the high street of the nearby town. 'See that ironmongers over there?'

Clumsy looked across the road and nodded.

'Right then,' said Dennis. 'You go in and buy a can of white paint – see it's good paint, too – and a brush. Don't forget the brush.'

'What's all this stuff for?' Clumsy asked.

Dennis glared at him and pulled a folded sheet of paper from his top pocket. 'See these letters? You copy them out, painted nice and large on both sides of the truck.' He shoved the paper at Clumsy. 'And try to do somethin' right for a change,' he added.

'But how do I get paint and a brush without some "readies"?' Clumsy protested.

Dennis impatiently drew some cash from his pocket and slapped it down on the seat between them. 'And Clumsy,' he went on, prodding his assistant with a long, bony finger, 'while you're writin' up them letters, be sure you're parked some place where you can't be spotted.'

'Where are you off to then?' Clumsy whined as Dennis jumped down from the cab.

'To 'ire some 'elpers of the sort what know these parts and can keep their mouths shut, if you must know,' Dennis answered. 'Don't want to 'andle that fierce lion on yer own do you?' Dennis fixed Clumsy with a hard eye. 'Be back 'ere at four o'clock,' he ordered. 'Mind you're not late.' And he strode away.

Clumsy watched until Dennis was out of sight, then carefully counted up the cash. He stuffed the money into his pocket and smoothed out the sheet of paper his boss had given him. 'A-N-I-M-U-L R-E-S-K-E-W,' he spelt out and scratched his head. 'What's his game now?' he wondered. With a shrug, he climbed down from the truck and made his way across the road.

He was just about to push through the ironmonger's door when he caught sight of a faded sign propped on the pavement further along the street. 'The Dog and Duck,' it announced. 'Home Made Pub Food. All-Day Carvery.'

Clumsy fingered the cash in his pocket and his mouth began to water. Then he remembered Dennis's stern warning. *First things first,* he thought with a sigh, and went inside to buy his paint.

To start with, the ironmonger was helpful when asked for the cheapest white paint money could buy. But as Clumsy began to dither, the man grew annoyed. 'If regular paint's too dear for you, sir,' he said sharply, 'perhaps you should consider using whitewash.' Clumsy's eyes lit up. Five minutes later, he emerged from the shop with a large bucket of whitewash in one hand and a paintbrush in the other. In his pocket jingled more than enough change to buy a big, juicy plateful of roast beef and Yorkshire pudding.

Clumsy drove the truck to a quiet lane and set to work. One by one, he copied the letters as large as he could onto each side of the truck. The bucket of whitewash was completely empty by the time he had done. He carefully checked the letters against those on the sheet of paper.

'A-N-I-M-U-L R-E-S-K-E-W,' he spelled out again. 'He won't find nothing wrong with that.' His stomach gave a loud rumble as he stood back to admire the finished job. *Better let that paint dry for a bit,* he thought and jiggled the change in his pocket. *Could be there's still time for a bite of lunch.* The rare treat of an hour to himself, and the prospect of succulent roast beef made him hum with joy. He threw the brush and the empty bucket into a hedgerow and set off happily to the Dog and Duck.

On the stream bank, Red Tabby lay sprawled beside Lord Stomper's glowing fire. Close by, Dylan nibbled luxuriously on the soft grass. By now the frying pan was scraped clean and all the carrots gone.

With lunch over, Red Tabby's curiosity got the better of her. 'Are you a musician by any chance?' she ventured. Lord Stomper leant back on his rucksack, his hands clasped behind his head, and gazed up at the sky. 'Yep!' he said. 'I used to have my own pop group once.'

'That would explain your beautiful coat and trousers,' said Tabby.

Dylan felt confused. What could Tabby mean?

'Trouble was we were *always* touring; always on the road. It was all hotels and planes and mobile phones ringing day and night. In the end I called a halt. The rest of the guys went off to America and I bought this place. It's the simple life for me now. Growing my own food and just an old motorbike to get around on.'

Dylan could stand it no longer. 'Tabby,' he whispered, 'what exactly is a pop group?'

'A sort of musical act,' Tabby told him.

Lord Stomper shot Dylan and Tabby a keen glance. 'You two seem to be close mates,' he observed. 'How come?'

He listened carefully as his two guests told how they first met and about their escape from Dangerous Dennis and Clumsy Golightly.

Stomper frowned. 'I've heard bad things about those two,' he said. Then he wanted to know all about Chia, Madame Lulu and the Happy Days Circus. Dylan and Red Tabby did their best to oblige, but, all too soon, it was time to go. The sun had already dipped low in the sky and dark banks of clouds hovered on the far horizon.

'If we were to visit you another time, Lord Stomper,' said Tabby as she scrambled onto Dylan's back, 'where might we find your gate?'

'Oh, that's a hard question to answer,' Lord Stomper replied evasively. 'But we're certain to meet again. And when we do I'll take care to have fish on the menu.'

'Then Tabby will be back for sure,' Dylan joked.

'And carrots for you, Dylan, of course!' Stomper added with a cheerful wink. He stood for a moment, waving them on their way, as Dylan trotted off across the meadow. 'Until next time!' Red Tabby heard him call. *But will there be a next time?* she wondered and felt a little pang of regret that, at daybreak, the Happy Days Circus would be moving on.

In the nearby town, at the Dog and Duck pub, a good fire danced and flickered in the grate. By now Clumsy's stomach was full to bursting with roast beef, potatoes and gravy-smothered Yorkshire pudding, topped off with custard-soaked treacle roly-poly. With a contented sigh, he settled himself into a comfy fireside chair. His eyelids drooped. His head sagged forward until his chin rested on his chest, and, before long, his snores were keeping gentle time with the ticking of the old grandfather clock at the corner of the hearth.

Suddenly an angry voice crashed into his cosy dreams and he felt himself lifted from his seat and shaken violently.

'Wake up! Wake up, you lazy piece of rubbish!'

Clumsy opened his eyes slowly. Dangerous Dennis stood over him, his mouth twisted in fury.

'I should 'ave known I'd find you 'ere! Get up! It's time!'

'T-t-time? Time for what?' the terrified Clumsy stammered. Dennis dropped the little man back in the chair and a strange look of elation flooded the horse dealer's cruel face.

'Like I told you, Clumsy. It's time.' The words hissed from his lips. 'Time for revenge!'

Dylan became quiet as he bore Red Tabby back towards the Big Top. Tabby guessed he was mulling something over in his own careful way and didn't intrude on his thoughts. 'The thing is,' Dylan began at last, 'do we believe what Lord Stomper says?'

'You mean about him being a pop star?' asked Tabby.

'About him being a pop star and a Lord,' Dylan answered. 'What is a Lord, anyway?'

'A Lord is a Peer,' Tabby told him.

'A pear?' Dylan responded. 'My favourite fruit.'

'Not a pear, Dylan,' Tabby corrected gently. 'A Peer of the Queen's Realm. I know, because I met one once when he came on board my ship.'

'The Queen, you say? Then why would such an important person fry his dinners out of doors when he knows the Queen and has a whole big house to cook in?'

'A good question, Dylan,' agreed Tabby. 'And he *did* say he grew his own carrots.'

'Then he could really be the gardener at the great park,' Dylan concluded triumphantly. 'Perhaps he could show us around.'

'Perhaps so,' Tabby agreed. 'But, for now, we'd better keep trotting. Look over there!'

Dylan turned to follow his friend's gaze. Behind them, dark thunderclouds were rapidly overtaking the dying afternoon sun. He quickened his pace, and they travelled the rest of the way in happy silence. Eventually, they reached the brow of the hill and gazed down on their own little trailer parked behind the Big Top. 'Home at last,' Dylan murmured contentedly.

'And not before time,' remarked Tabby as she cast another worried glance towards the gathering storm.

20

The Trap Closes

'Hold on tight, Tabby,' urged Dylan, shaking his thick mane. 'We don't want to get drenched.'

He was about to break into a gallop when Tabby held up a warning paw. 'Dylan! Shush!' she hissed. 'Something's wrong!'

As if to confirm her fears, a great trumpeting and growling broke out below them, sending echoes across the valley. Dylan came to a dead stop and Tabby slipped down from his back. 'Come on!' she whispered and beckoned to him to follow as she crept down the hill.

Dylan, who hadn't shared a year's adventures with his friend without learning a thing or two, moved cautiously after her. A little further down the slope, they reached a thick clump of trees from which they could watch without being seen. Below them, an enormous truck stood beside the Big Top.

'But we're not supposed to leave 'til tomorrow,' Dylan muttered.

'And that's not our transporter,' Tabby whispered in alarm.

As they watched from their hiding place, two burly men appeared from inside the Big Top dragging Lion between them on long ropes. A broad ramp led up to the doors of the truck and, to Dylan and Tabby's horror, up the ramp went poor Lion, still struggling to break free and roaring with all his might despite the nooses drawn tightly around his throat. A sharp prod from a barbed stick and he was in.

Dylan and Tabby could see that most of the Happy Days Circus troupe was already inside the truck and they could hear Tiger growling bleakly from the dark interior. Then the doors were slammed shut. Dylan tried to make out the name painted in bold white letters on the vehicle's side. 'An-im-ul-res ...' he began.

'Animal Rescue?' Red Tabby spluttered. 'But that makes no sense. We've got our certificate from the vet.'

A sudden flash of lightning was followed by a crack of thunder and the rain began to fall in earnest. Poor Dancing Dog, yelping piteously, was thrown roughly in with the others.

Red Tabby gulped as a short, plump figure stumbled out of the Big Top grasping two squealing meerkats by their necks. 'It can't be Animal Rescue,' she cried. 'They'd never treat anyone like that!' The frightened creatures were pushed inside and the doors banged shut again.

Dylan and Tabby watched in growing confusion as the huge letters whitewashed onto the sides of the truck began to melt and run together. In moments, only a few white streaks remained.

The driver stuck his head out of the cab window. 'Hurry it up back there!' he bellowed. 'With all this meat on board, I don't want to get stuck in the mud.'

'We're just loading the last one,' a second man shouted back, as Charlie, tightly bound, was shoved into the already bulging vehicle. The ramp was stowed, doors were slammed and bolted, the handlers climbed up with the driver, and the cumbersome truck, churning mud, ground its way out of the field and disappeared from sight.

The two friends looked at each other, dumbfounded. Who on earth could have done such a terrible thing? Then a dreadful suspicion began to take root in Red Tabby's mind. She turned to look at the deserted scene below.

'Come on, Dylan,' she said bravely. 'The coast's clear. Let's go and find Chia. He'll know what to do.' Wet through and bedraggled, the two set off down the rain-soaked hill towards the Big Top.

Just inside its entrance, two shadowy figures stood sheltering from the storm. The taller man busied himself as he waited, expertly forming a lasso noose at the end of a strong rope. 'We'll just sit tight 'ere in the dry and let them two come to us,' he said, and fingered the lasso.

'Suppose they don't?' squeaked the shorter figure miserably. His damp clothing clung to him uncomfortably, and he felt cold and hungry.

'Lookee there!' the tall man croaked and pointed past his companion with a bony finger. Through the downpour, they could just make out Dylan and Red Tabby, picking their way across the muddy field. The tall man's eyes glinted evilly.

'Do I know 'orses or what?' he gloated. 'You grab the cat and I'll take the nag.'

Half-blinded by the wind and rain, Red Tabby ran on ahead of Dylan, and as she blundered out of the storm into the shadowy dimness of the Big Top, she bumped with a thud into something soft and round. 'Ringmaster Chia?' she mewed doubtfully.

'Gotcha, you creepy little red rat catcher,' a familiar voice rasped in Tabby's ear. She felt herself yanked up by her tail.

'Dylan!' she cried, dangling helplessly in mid-air. 'It's CLUUUUUMSY!' Then everything went black as her captor stuffed her into a thick burlap sack and tied its top with a fat double knot.

Tabby's cry of alarm brought Dylan galloping towards the Big Top, but as he burst into the darkened tent a vicious 'swizz-swizz' sounded from the gloom. Something came flying over his head and encircled his neck, tightening cruelly.

'Mine at last!' shrieked another horribly familiar voice.

'Tabby,' neighed Dylan. 'It's DENNIIIIIS!'

Rooks, sheltering from the storm in the nearby trees, flew up in alarm at his desperate whinny.

Dangerous Dennis yanked sharply on the rope. Dylan's head snapped downward, his ear pulled close to the wily horse dealer's twisted, grinning mouth. 'Quiet, my beauty! Quiet!' said Dennis, his voice suddenly gentle. Over the rattle of the rain against the Big Top's canvas, Dylan could hear Tabby's frantic mewing as she struggled to escape from Clumsy's sack. He yearned to go to her rescue, but his limbs felt strangely numb and powerless.

'Great lads like you aren't born to dance,' Dennis crooned. 'You're born to obey. Born to obey.' The horse dealer's murmurings seemed to weave an invisible web around Dylan. As if hypnotized, he stood obediently, eyes downcast, while the whispered words swam round and round in his bewildered brain. *Born to obey. To obey. Obey.* Then, very lightly, Dennis began to stroke his captive's forehead. Despite his fears for Red Tabby, Dylan felt himself slipping into a dreamlike trance.

'Ow! You red devil!' cried Clumsy.

Tabby had torn a hole in the sack and sunk a sharp claw into Clumsy's chubby hand.

Dennis turned on his hapless assistant. 'Shut it, will you?' he hissed fiercely. 'You'll break the spell.'

'Oooow!' howled Clumsy again as Tabby managed another stinging swipe. 'But, Boss, what can I do with this ginger-furred banshee?' He held the violently-heaving sack at arm's length and thrust it towards Dennis. Once more, an angry claw flashed through the rent in the burlap, coming within a whisker of the horse dealer's nose. Dennis stepped back hastily.

'Shove a rock in the sack and chuck the 'ole lot in the nearest river,' he ordered. 'That should do for 'er.' The cruel orders, sealing Red Tabby's fate, sent a shiver of dread coursing through Dylan's helpless body.

'There, there, my pretty one. Born to obey …' Dennis's silky tones droned on once more. As if from far, far away, Clumsy's howls and Red Tabby's ever more defiant cries began to pierce the mists enveloping Dylan's mind. The power of the trance was weakening and, all at once, it shattered completely.

Dylan raised his head and looked his adversary full in the face. *Not born to obey! Not born to obey!* His thoughts raged in a torrent through his fast-awakening brain. *Not born to obey! Born to dance!*

Dennis's lip curled contemptuously. 'Don't think you're goin' to defy me, my lad!' he hissed. 'No 'orse ever beat Dangerous Dennis!'

Dylan's eyes flashed his defiance. *Oh, no? Just you watch me!* 'Clip-clippity, clop' his front hooves began. 'Clop-cloppity, clip' his back hooves replied. Out from the Big Top and into the heavy downpour he danced, with the horse dealer hanging on grimly to the end of the rope.

Round and round went Dylan, tearing up the sodden grass with his beating hooves, churning the wet earth beneath into a thick, oily mud. And everywhere Dylan went, Dennis was forced to follow. Struggling to keep both his balance and his grip on the rope, Dennis ducked and dived. But, twist and turn as he might, Dylan was always beyond reach, dancing for all he was worth.

Dennis felt the muddied rope slipping through his fingers. 'CLUUMMSY!' he bellowed. 'Get over 'ere and 'elp me!'

Still clutching the wriggling sack with its hissing, seething contents, Clumsy came racing across to Dennis as fast as his short legs would carry him. One step into the sea of mud churned up by Dylan's dancing hooves and up went his feet. Down he went on his back with a loud 'Oomph!' The sack flew from his hands and out burst Red Tabby, fighting for her life.

In a single well-judged bound, Tabby landed squarely on Dennis's back. Claws, long, unsheathed and sharp, dug deeply into his skin.

Dennis yelped and, keeping hold of the rope with one hand, he tried to grab his attacker with the other. Clumsy struggled to regain his feet, but Dennis, staggering backwards, tripped over him.

As the villains sprawled full length in the slimy, oozing mud, Red Tabby jumped clear. 'Run for it, Dylan!' she yelled, and streaked off, full pelt, up the hill. 'Come on, Dylan,' she called again as she disappeared into the undergrowth. 'Make for the ...' Her words were drowned by the sound of the storm and the shouting of the two men, but Dylan felt sure she had said 'park'. He reared into the air, frantically pulling against the choking noose that encircled his neck.

21

Cawt!

The cruel rope had become entangled in Dennis and Clumsy's flailing legs, and Dylan's hooves skidded on the slippery ground as he tried to pull himself free. With a final, determined wrench, he yanked the line loose and galloped off up the hill after Red Tabby. Dennis, burning with anger, scrambled to his feet and, dragging the mud-caked Clumsy after him, stubbornly gave chase.

Far ahead, Red Tabby fought her way through the tall, wind-tangled grasses and across the drenched fields where, less than an hour before, she and Dylan had shared their happy adventure. Dylan pushed on after her as best he could. The rope, heavy with water, whipped against his flanks and its thick noose tightened further as, now and then, its trailing end snagged on a branch or bush.

In the lashing rain, Dylan couldn't see Red Tabby anywhere, but, not far across the fields, a parliament of rooks had set up a riotous squawking, and there, he could just make out the ancient oak that stood in Lord Stomper's park. *I've made it,* he thought. But, as he turned towards the great tree, the dragging rope went taut and the noose closed chokingly around his neck. Held fast, Dylan reared and tugged, but it only made things worse.

'Cawt, Cawt, Cawt,' screeched the rooks, swirling above the great tree. 'Cawt, Cawt, Cawt.'

Caught am I? thought Dylan. *We'll see about that!* And he swung round to confront his pursuers. To his surprise, he found himself alone, the rope-end not in the hands of Dennis or Clumsy, but hopelessly entwined in the branches of a stout gorse bush. He battled once more to break free, but it was of no use. The noose now cut so painfully into his skin that he could scarcely breathe.

'Cawt, Cawt, Cawt,' the rooks screamed again. Over the raucous cawing of the birds came a harsh shout.

'It's 'im! Across there! Get after 'im, Clumsy!'

'Red Tabby!' Dylan whinnied. 'Dear, dear Red Tabby. If you are anywhere near, help me.'

'I see him, Boss! We've got him!' came another yell, much closer this time. With the last of his strength Dylan tried to fight the stubborn rope, but his trembling legs gave way beneath him and he fell heavily to the ground.

'*Someone* help me! Please!' he gasped, and the world began to turn black around him.

'Hold on, Dylan! Hold on!' The voice sounded right by his ear. 'It's all right! It's me! Stomper!'

Stomper quickly cut through the painful noose and Dylan drew in a welcome gulp of air. 'Quick!' said Stomper. 'You must stand up. We've got to get you away.'

'But, Red Tabby! What about Red Tabby?' Dylan croaked.

'I'm right beside you,' came Red Tabby's urgent voice. 'Hurry, Dylan, or it'll be too late.'

With Lord Stomper's help and Tabby's urging, Dylan stumbled to his feet. Stomper led the two animals straight up to the familiar high, pink stone wall that circled Great Park.

At the sight of the wall, Dylan's heart sank. He knew he was far too weak to jump over it. What could Stomper be thinking? But then he heard a rumbling sound and a small section of the wall swung inward. Stomper hustled them through the gap, and the opening rumbled shut behind them.

'Nobody move!' Stomper raised a cautionary finger to his lips. 'Sshhh!'

They could hear the horse dealers thrashing about in the bushes just on the other side of the wall.

'What do you mean, "you lost 'em"? You thick-'eaded fool!'

'But, Boss! I saw them. Really, I did. They went straight through that wall.'

'Any more of yer tall tales and I'll 'ave *you* straight through that wall, me overfed little friend,' raged Dennis.

Clumsy muttered something bleak in reply. The grumbling voices faded into the distance and were lost in the rushing noise of the storm.

Safe inside Lord Stomper's park, Dylan nuzzled Tabby with a muddy nose. 'Thank goodness you're all right,' he breathed.

'And you,' replied a weary but overjoyed Red Tabby.

Dylan's long mane hung heavy with mud and his legs shook under him from exhaustion. Red Tabby's fur was stuck to her sides, her fine tail reduced to a long, matted spike. Stomper's heart went out to the bedraggled pair and he found himself gazing at them fondly as the rain poured in rivulets from the wide brim of his leather hat. Tabby gave a big sneeze.

'Let's get out of this storm,' Stomper declared, and he led them away from the wall and up towards the big house with its rambling outbuildings. In no time, the exhausted animals found themselves clean and dry and left to settle in a snug stable filled with fresh straw and comforting smells. Before long, Stomper returned, bearing a large wicker basket and a fat nosebag, golden oats spilling generously over its rim.

'Anyone for a bite of dinner?' he asked cheerily as he came in, but Dylan was already snoring gently. Red Tabby's nose caught the scent of fresh cream and tuna but even as she licked her lips, she shook her head.

'Oh, thank you, dear Lord Stomper,' she said. 'We're grateful, really we are. But we daren't waste another moment. We must find the others.'

'Others? What others?' asked Stomper.

'The rest of the troupe,' explained Tabby. 'They've been kidnapped, each and every one.'

Stomper's eyebrows shot up in disbelief. 'Kidnapped?' he repeated. 'By Dangerous Dennis?'

Red Tabby nodded. 'And Clumsy Golightly. And a whole crew of villains. Dylan and I saw it all. Only Chia can help us now. We have to find him!'

Stomper raised his hands in protest. 'Hang on,' he said. 'It's pitch black out there and the storm is still raging.'

'But there's no time to lose!' Tabby cried in dismay.

Stomper squatted down beside the worried cat. 'Believe me, Red Tabby, I can see that,' he assured her. 'But let's just think about this. After all you've been through, you must get some rest or you'll be no use to anyone.'

Red Tabby looked over at the sleeping Dylan and sighed. 'I suppose you're right,' she admitted. 'Maybe we should stay a little longer. At least until this storm is over.'

Lord Stomper pulled the wicker basket closer. He ladled a generous portion of tuna into a bowl and poured out a saucer-full of rich cream. Tabby needed no further invitation and tucked in with a grateful 'mew'.

Stomper hung the nosebag on a convenient nail. 'Dylan can have his dinner when he wakes up,' he said. 'Meanwhile, Tabby, suppose you and I make the best use of our time?'

Stomper settled himself on a bale of hay, pulled out a notebook and opened it to a fresh page. 'Now then,' he went on, 'why don't you tell me exactly what happened?'

Between mouthfuls, Tabby described the horrible scene she and Dylan had stumbled upon that evening when they returned to the Big Top. Stomper carefully wrote down all she said, asking a question here and there where needed. When the tale was told, he looked back over his notes and shook his head. 'It's not a lot to go on,' he said, 'but it will have to do. We'll get busy the second it's light. More cream, Tabby?'

But despite her concerns, Red Tabby had already dropped off, her dinner half-eaten in the bowl beside her. Lord Stomper quietly shut his notebook and tiptoed out, leaving the two exhausted animals to their much-needed sleep.

Outside the windows of Madame Lulu's home the stormy evening had faded into night. It had been the worst ever day of her eventful career. She had started the morning with enough bookings to keep the Happy Days Circus in work all season long, but now her list was nearly empty. While she had been busy on the phone, Chia had been dashing off letter after letter begging the towns to reconsider and let the circus visit them after all. At last, he licked and sealed the final envelope.

'Thanks for your help, Chia,' said Madame Lulu in a tired voice. 'I don't know if our efforts will do any good, but at least we've tried.'

Chia pulled out his grandfather's old fob watch. 'Oh my! Look at the time!' he gasped. 'I must get back to the Big Top. Everyone will be starving.'

'I'll drive you over,' Madame Lulu offered, but she remained seated at her desk, head in her hands.

'You've had a terrible day,' Chia replied gently. 'Best not.'

'But you can't walk there,' she protested, 'it's still pouring. Why not take my car?' She pushed the keys towards him and he took them gratefully.

The circus site lay under a blanket of darkness as Chia arrived. Through the rain-spattered windscreen, he could just make out the looming shape of the Big Top. As he pulled up, he felt the back of his neck tingle. Something didn't seem right. In fact, something had to be badly wrong, for not a glimmer of light shone anywhere.

Taking a torch from the glove box, he stepped from Madame Lulu's warm vehicle out into the relentless rain and made a mighty dash for the Big Top.

'Hellooo!' he called into the gloom and flashed his torch into the farthest corners of the great tent. Nothing. With a worried shake of his head, he left the shelter of the tent and sploshed his way across the field to look in the trailers. Still nothing.

Everywhere, doors hung open with the rain sweeping into once cosy quarters. Windows banged in the wind. Chia looked about him in alarm. Where had everyone gone? Had the old owners returned to claim what was no longer theirs? But that would be impossible seeing that he and Red Tabby had taken all the proper legal steps.

By now Chia was wet through, yet still he searched on. Ahead of him, his torch beam picked out a wide patch where grass had been churned and trampled into a sea of mud, as if in some terrible struggle. Beyond that, he came across deep tyre tracks across the muddy earth, suggesting that a great truck, heavily laden, had ground its way out of the field. Heartsick, he climbed back into Madame Lulu's car and drove straight to the police station.

22

After the Storm

All night, the thunder had echoed and banged against the walls and roof of the big corrugated iron building in which the Happy Days troupe found themselves held captive. Nobody had any idea where they were. It had been getting dark when the great truck's doors had finally opened and they had been roughly shoved down the ramp into their draughty prison.

There was nothing to eat or drink, and no bedding. Only by following Irma's suggestion and huddling together had they managed to keep warm during the long hours. By dawn, they were desperate for food and water, but the two ruffians guarding them seemed unconcerned about their plight.

'Let us out!' yelled Ranga, banging uselessly at the great sliding door.

'I must look dreadful. I need my rollers. My rollers!' moaned Lion over and over.

'And I need my dinner or my breakfast. I don't much care which,' chimed in Marmaduke.

Tiger called for calm. 'Getting ourselves into a panic won't change anything,' he said. 'Chia and Madame Lulu are bound to come looking for us. They can't be far away. After all, we weren't in that horrible truck all that long before we were dumped in here.'

'But how will they know where to find us?' Lion protested.

Tiger was stumped at that, but he didn't want the others getting more downhearted than they already were. 'Dylan and Red Tabby will help them,' he answered a little bleakly.

'But suppose they've both been captured too?' Lion persisted. Tiger glowered at him and Lion decided not to say any more.

'I know!' Bandmaster Sea Lion broke in, 'Music! That's what we need!'

'Music? At a time like this?' wailed Prudence.

'Good idea, Bandmaster!' declared Marmaduke. 'We'll show 'em they can't get the Happy Days Circus down!' And he grabbed a piece of old plastic pipe that was lying on the floor, put it to his lips, and gave out a loud, resounding blast. 'How's that for a trumpet?' he asked.

'Almost as good as mine!' agreed Irma, raising her trunk over her head and sounding an ear-splitting note.

'I'll be the drummer,' announced Dancing Dog. Picking up a stick of wood in his mouth, he ran back and forth along the corrugated iron walls, clattering out a lively rhythm.

By now, everyone had found something with which to make a noise, and soon the cavernous building was echoing with cheery bangs, yelps and squeaks. Outside, in the first glimmering of dawn, the two shifty guards looked uneasily at each other and threw a few rocks at the hangar doors, hoping to silence their charges.

'Storm's passed,' said Stomper as he woke Dylan and Red Tabby. The damp flagstones of the stable yard steamed in the morning warmth. 'There's fish in the pan for you,' he told Tabby, taking his multi-coloured, patchwork-leather overcoat from its hook. 'And oats and sweet apples for you, Dylan.'

Dylan looked up, his eyes still bleary from his long sleep. 'Where are you going?' he asked as Stomper wheeled his dilapidated motorbike from the back of the stable.

'To get on the trail of your friends, of course,' Stomper replied. 'Someone in town must have seen something.'

'But what about us?' Tabby pleaded. 'Can't we come with you?'

'You two get a good breakfast inside you. It's going to be a long day.' Stomper plonked a gaudily painted crash helmet on his head and, mounting the bike, kicked its engine into life. 'I'll be back before you know it,' he said.

'Try to find Chia!' Tabby called after him.

'I promise!' Stomper shouted back, and disappeared round a bend in the drive.

As he nosed out onto the main highway, a huge old truck laboured past splashing up great sheets of water as it ploughed through the roadside puddles. Stomper pulled in behind it and hovered, waiting for the chance to overtake.

'Come on!' he muttered. 'Give me a break!' His moment came and the motorbike surged ahead with a roar.

As he sped past the truck, Stomper caught a glimpse of wide, smeared streaks of whitewash running down its sides. Tabby's account of the 'A-N-I-M-U-L R-E-S-K-E-W' letters melting in the rain flashed through his mind. In his side mirrors, Stomper could see two figures sitting in the cab. *I'll bet that's Dangerous Dennis and his mate,* he told himself. *What luck!* He slowed the bike a little to keep the men in view.

The truck clattered into the high street and lurched to a halt in front of 'Ye Olde Greasy Spoone', the local café. Stomper stopped a short way along the road and watched as the two men climbed down from the cab and disappeared inside.

Wasting no time, he wheeled his motorbike out of sight, stowed his helmet and quickly crossed over to the parked truck. A few sharp taps on its side reassured him that the kidnapped circus troupe was no longer within. He hastily jotted down its registration number in his notebook and crossed the street to the café.

Through the front window, he could see the two men just starting their breakfast, napkins tucked under their chins. Stomper slipped in and sat at the counter. The owner of the café, who knew Stomper well, turned to greet him. Stomper put a finger to his lips. 'Coffee and a newspaper,' he whispered, 'and, please, pretend I'm not here.' The owner gave Stomper a questioning look but did as he was asked.

Stomper watched over his newspaper as the two men scoffed their brimming plates of eggs, chips and beans. After a while, the taller one threw down his napkin on his empty plate, got up from his place, went over to the payphone by the café door and dialled a number. 'It's me, Dennis,' Stomper heard him say. At that moment, the little man bellowed rudely for a fresh pot of tea and the rest of the phone conversation was lost in a rattle of teacups. Dennis's face wore a satisfied grin as he hung up the receiver and rejoined his companion. From behind the paper, Stomper strained every nerve to listen.

'Clumsy, me lad, the deal's done,' Dennis gloated. 'All signed and sealed. All we 'as to do now is deliver.'

'How much, Dennis?' asked Clumsy eagerly.

'Fifteen thousand, right on the old 'orse's nose,' came the reply.

Clumsy whistled with pleasure, his eyes shining greedily. 'When do we get our hands on the loot?' he asked.

'Once that miserable lot are on the boat,' Dennis answered.

'Waaahoooo! We're in the money! We're in the money!' Clumsy whooped.

'Shut it, Clumsy!' hissed Dennis. 'Stop shooting your mouth off.'

Stomper lowered his paper to get a better view of the two men who had brought so much grief to his friends, and found himself looking straight into Clumsy's eyes.

'Wot you gawping at, pasty face?' Clumsy demanded. Stomper quickly ducked behind his newspaper again. 'You're a peculiar sort and no mistake,' Clumsy persisted.

'Leave it out, Clumsy,' Dennis warned. 'We've got to load those brutes double quick or we'll miss the boat. No delivery, no cash.'

While Dennis was busy paying the café owner for breakfast, Stomper slipped quietly from his stool and out of the door. As he straddled his motorbike, he heard the big truck's engine grumble to life. There wasn't a moment to lose. He threw on his helmet and sped off to fetch help.

23

The Hunt is Up

'Where do you think I can find bail money at this hour of the day?' fumed Madame Lulu as she paced back and forth before the duty sergeant's desk. 'The bank is shut!'

'It'll be opening soon enough, madam,' the sergeant replied, his smooth tone making the agitated impresario seethe.

'And what does poor Ringmaster Chia do in the meantime?' she demanded.

Before the man could open his mouth to reply, the 'putt-putt' of a motorbike and the squeal of brakes sounded in the street outside. The door of the police station burst open and in came a tall figure wearing a colourful leather overcoat and highly decorated crash helmet. The sergeant's face broke into a welcoming smile as the helmet came off.

'Ah! Lord Stomper, sir!' the man exclaimed, 'and how, pray tell, may we be of assistance to you so early this fine morning?'

Madame Lulu stared curiously at the striking newcomer with his colourful clothes and golden, flowing hair. The sergeant beckoned Lord Stomper over to his desk and, leaning towards him, addressed him in confidential tones. 'We got the message you left last night, sir,' he said. 'Frankly, we found it a bit of a riddle at first. Zoo animals, you mentioned? And kidnapping was it?'

'Not zoo animals, Sergeant,' Stomper corrected him. 'An entire troupe of professional performing animals kidnapped and about to be sold abroad.'

'Kidnapped? Sold abroad?' shrieked Madame Lulu.

The sergeant scowled at her. 'This is between this gentleman and me, madam,' he warned her. 'Private, like.'

Madame Lulu's face flushed with frustration, but she held her peace and listened while Lord Stomper completed his report.

'You'll find it all in here,' he said and plonked his notebook in front of the sergeant. 'Witness statements. Names and whereabouts of the two kidnappers. Registration number of their truck. The whole story.'

'Very kind of you, Lord Stomper, sir, but there's no need for all that,' the sergeant assured him smugly, and pushed the notebook back across the counter. 'The culprit's locked up right here! We nabbed him last night, soon after we got your message.'

'Rubbish!' Madame Lulu protested. 'Ringmaster Chia a criminal? Impossible! Whatever you may think, you're holding him on a trumped-up charge.'

Stomper turned to her in surprise. 'Did you say "Ringmaster Chia"? Then you must be Madame Bombazine!'

'Thank goodness!' exclaimed Madame Lulu. 'Someone's making sense at last! Yes! I'm Madame Bombazine and I've been trying for the past hour to get poor Chia bailed out of here.'

Stomper fished out his wallet. 'How much?' he asked, and began counting bank notes into a little pile.

The sergeant began to feel decidedly uncomfortable. 'Well, Lord Stomper, sir,' he muttered, 'I think we can overlook bail this time if you can vouch for the rascal – I mean for Ringmaster Chia as you call him.'

'That's really decent of you, Sergeant,' said Stomper, discreetly slipping the notes back in his wallet. 'We'd better get after those kidnappers though. We'll lose them if we don't act fast.'

'No can do, sir. Well, not until the next shift.' The sergeant smiled ruefully. 'At this hour, there's only me on. Now, if you'll excuse me, I'd best fetch the culprit – I should say, Ringmaster Chia – from his cell.'

Madame Lulu was bursting with questions for Lord Stomper, but the duty sergeant reappeared almost immediately with his 'culprit' in tow. Chia's face lit up with relief when he saw Madame Lulu waiting for him. Lord Stomper stepped forward, his hand outstretched in greeting.

'I'm Lord Stomper,' he said. 'I've heard all about you, Ringmaster, from Dylan and Red Tabby.'

'They're safe then?' Chia asked clearly relieved.

'Perfectly,' Lord Stomper reassured him. 'But we need to hold a council of war about the others. If I'm right, we've not got much time. May we use your office, Sergeant?'

The sergeant nodded approval and waved them towards the back of the police station.

'First of all,' Stomper began when they were settled around the sergeant's tiny desk, 'Dylan and Red Tabby are back at my place.'

'But what about Lion, Tiger and the rest of the troupe?' demanded Chia. 'What can have happened to them?'

'Kidnapped!' exclaimed Madame Lulu. 'Isn't that right, Lord Stomper? They're to be sold off and shipped abroad.'

'That's disastrous!' said Chia. 'Who would do such a thing?'

'Red Tabby described the kidnapper's truck,' Stomper explained, 'and I passed it on my way into town earlier. I followed the drivers into 'Ye Old Greasy Spoone'. They turned out to be Dylan and Red Tabby's old enemies, Dangerous Dennis and Clumsy Golightly.'

'Those two again?' gasped Chia in dismay.

Madame Lulu gave the Ringmaster a sharp look. 'Dear Madame, it's a long story,' Chia said, 'and I fear it will have to wait.' He turned back to Stomper. 'The others. Are they still in the truck?'

'No,' Stomper assured him. 'I checked it myself a short time ago.'

'But they're nearby, certainly, or the kidnappers wouldn't still be in the town,' said Madame Lulu.

'You're absolutely right!' agreed Stomper. Madame Lulu and Chia waited hopefully as Stomper shut his eyes and drummed his fingers urgently on the sergeant's desk. 'Nearby? *Nearby?*' he mused. 'It has to be a large building and a large building nearby.' At last, he thumped his forehead with his fist. 'I've got it!' he cried.

'Got what?' asked Madame Lulu and Chia together.

'There is only one likely spot hereabouts – and it's not far from my place either. Come on! Let's try it!'

Lord Stomper jumped to his feet, dashed past the startled sergeant and disappeared out of the door of the police station. By the time Madame Lulu and Chia had reached the pavement, Stomper's helmet was back on his head and he was revving up his motorbike. 'Follow me!' he shouted and shot off down the high street.

'I only hope this fellow knows what he's about,' Chia said as Madame Lulu nosed her sunshine-yellow car out onto the road and set off after the fast-disappearing motorcycle. 'This is no moment for a wild goose chase.'

'Dylan and Red Tabby seem to have become friendly with him,' Madame Lulu said. 'If they trust him, perhaps we should too.' She glanced at the ringmaster shrewdly. 'And now Chia, suppose you tell me all about these "old enemies" you spoke of.'

Chia's brow puckered. 'It all happened long before you joined us,' he began. 'After the last encounter – well, we really thought we'd shaken them off for good.'

By the time Chia had finished his account, the would-be rescuers had driven well clear of the town and out into the countryside. Up into the surrounding uplands they went and along narrow, winding lanes. Eventually Stomper came to a stop where a lane rose to the crest of a low hill. Chia and Madame Lulu pulled up beside him and he pointed through a gap in the hedge to the rolling valley beyond.

'This'll be it,' he told them. There, beyond the next field, loomed a timeworn corrugated iron building, its walls and roof stained with years of rust.

'An old aircraft hangar!' exclaimed Chia.

'There used to be a military airbase here,' Stomper explained. A sturdy chain-link fence encircled the hangar and behind it two scruffy figures could just be made out, lounging inside the hangar's compound near the closed gate. 'See those men?' asked Stomper. 'This place is usually deserted. I'll bet they're guards and I'll bet it's our friends they're guarding.' To prove his hunch right, the sound of trumpeting reached their ears.

'That's Irma!' cried the ringmaster. 'I'd know her voice any-where!' As they watched, one of the guards picked up a rock and threw it hard against the hangar door. A chorus of trumpeting, roaring and whooping followed, echoing faintly across the fields.

'They're in there all right!' exclaimed Madame Lulu. 'What's our plan?'

Chia was all for marching straight up to the guards and demanding that they let the captives out, but Stomper was more cautious. 'We'll stand a better chance if we rally our troops.'

'What troops?' asked Chia blankly.

'Dylan and Red Tabby, of course. Can you two keep a look-out while I go and fetch them?' Chia and Madame Lulu nodded. Stomper turned his motorbike and, without starting it, rolled silently away down the hill. As he reached the foot of the rise, Madame Lulu and Chia heard a muffled 'putt, putt'. The motorbike sputtered to life. Stomper waved an arm and was gone.

24

Wonder Woman

'While we wait, we might as well see what we can find out,' Madame Lulu suggested. 'But we'll need to get closer than this.'

Chia swallowed a protest and followed her along the lane towards the hangar. 'What if they catch sight of us?' he whispered.

Madame Lulu pressed a silencing finger to her lips, left the lane and plunged through the hedge. Chia shut his eyes and plunged after her. For a moment he thought the brambles would tear the very coat from his back, but at last he broke free into the open. Ahead of him, Madame Lulu crouched at the edge of a wide sweep of dense gorse bush that stretched away towards the hangar fence.

What can she be doing? Chia wondered as he saw her wave frantically in his direction. Then he realised the meaning of her signal and dropped to his knees to be out of sight of watchful eyes. He crawled towards her across the hard ground, but no sooner had he reached her than she moved on and disappeared into more thick bushes. Cautiously, the two edged forward until the chain-link fence loomed ahead of them. Sharp spikes poked up along its top and they could see its gates held fast by a heavy padlock. Loud whoops, cries and thumps still echoed from inside the hangar. The two guards eyed the building warily from their post nearby. Madame Lulu and Chia crept yet closer.

'How much longer before Mr Dennis is supposed to get here, anyway?' they heard one of the guards ask, and saw his companion check his wristwatch. 'Three o'clock give or take,' the second man answered. 'About twenty minutes or so.'

Chia and Madame Lulu looked at each other anxiously.

'I hope he makes it snappier than that,' the first man grumbled. 'That menagerie is hell-bent on breakin' out – and if it does, there's not much you and me can do to stop it.'

Madame Lulu beckoned for Chia to follow and retreated into the cover of the gorse bushes. 'This changes things,' she whispered. 'We can't wait for the others. We have to act now!'

'There's not much we can do on our own,' protested Chia. 'What with that fence and that gate and that padlock. Not to mention the guards.'

A fierce and determined light that Chia had not seen before flickered in Madame Lulu's big, green eyes. 'Leave this to me,' she commanded. 'You stay put and keep watch. Even when Stomper gets back with Dylan and Red Tabby, do nothing until you hear from me.' And before Chia could protest further, Madame Lulu was gone.

For a long, long, agonizing moment she was lost to sight. Chia dared not break cover to get a better view for fear of attracting the attention of the guards. He held his breath in a fever of suspense. Then there she was again, standing upright for all to see.

In a panic, Chia looked towards the guards, but Madame Lulu must have been well out of their line of sight, for the two men lounged idly at their post as before.

Chia looked back to see Madame Lulu take a few measured paces. She paused for a moment, staring intently at the barrier before her. Then, as he watched, she made a sudden run forwards, vaulted up and over the towering fence, to land neatly on the other side. It was all Chia could do to keep from bursting into applause. *Wherever did she learn to do that?* he wondered.

Madame Lulu ran lightly across the open ground to the hangar. Still the guards failed to notice her. When she reached the big hangar door, she studied it carefully. Then, to Chia's horror, she signalled a huge 'thumbs up' and walked right out into the open and up to the guards. 'I've come to collect my animals,' he heard her announce boldly.

The men hesitated. 'Mr Dennis never mentioned no woman,' said one, glaring at her suspiciously. 'Anyway, where's your truck?'

'How did you get in?' asked the other.

'I don't like the look of this,' said the first man. 'Best shove her in with the beasties 'til Mr Dennis gets here.'

From his hiding place in the gorse bushes, Chia looked on helplessly as the guards grabbed Madame Lulu and dragged her, kicking and protesting, towards the hangar. One of the men unlocked a small access hatchway in the big sliding door. But, even as they were bundling her out of sight, Madame Lulu managed another thumbs up and, to Chia's bewilderment, flashed him a big grin.

The Happy Days troupe blinked as bright sunlight came flooding through the little door into the dimness of their prison. 'Tie her up and throw her in the lock-up,' someone rasped. A door banged, a lock clicked, and before the captives' eyes could adjust to the glare, the small hatchway slammed shut plunging them once more into darkness.

From his hiding place, Chia saw the men emerge from the hangar, secure the little door and return to their positions. He pulled out his fob watch. Already a precious ten minutes had passed. In another ten, Dennis and Clumsy would be here and it would all be too late. Unable to bear the suspense any longer, Chia frantically clawed his way back through the gorse bushes and tore off down the road in search of help.

Inside the hangar, the Happy Days Circus troupe had fallen silent. Their eyes had again grown used to the gloom and all seemed just as it had been before the guards had burst in. But now a strange scuffling sound came from a far corner. 'There,' whispered Marmaduke in Tiger's ear. 'It's coming from over there.' He pointed to a tiny room set in a corner of the hangar near the access hatchway.

Tiger padded silently across the hangar floor, the others following him on tiptoe. 'Who's in there?' he demanded, but the scuffling only grew louder.

'Come on, who are you?' asked Charlie as boldly as he could manage. Then came a slight 'click click.'

'I'm going in,' Ranga declared. He was just about to take a run at the door when it swung open of its own accord.

'Good morning, everybody,' said Madame Lulu. She flicked a small nail file back into her bag and smiled calmly as if nothing whatsoever had happened.

'Good morning, Madame Lulu,' chorused the surprised troupe in reply. Then they all began asking questions at once, and a deafening babble of barks, squeaks, yelps and hoots echoed around the hangar.

'Now then,' said Madame Lulu when the commotion had quietened down. 'Gather round, if you will, and I'll tell you what we're going to do.'

At a petrol station on the edge of the town, Dangerous Dennis stood seething by the cab of his truck while a hangdog Clumsy stood at the pump, filling the truck's huge fuel tank. It was taking an awfully long time.

Dennis squinted at his wristwatch. 'Can't you do nothin' right?' he fretted. 'You should 'ave filled 'er up before breakfast! If we ain't loaded and on the road in an hour, we'll never make the docks before the boat sails.' At last, Clumsy pulled the nozzle from the fuel tank and returned it to the pump. He secured the petrol cap, but began to hop from one foot to the other, looking even more hangdog than usual. 'What's the matter now?' barked Dennis

'I need a wee, Boss.'

Dennis raised a fist. Clumsy flinched. 'Sorry, Boss,' whined the little man plaintively. 'I'll be as quick as I can.'

Once out of Dennis's sight, Clumsy made a beeline for the food counter. There was a long drive ahead, and, late as they were, there would be no hope of a meal on the way. By the time Dennis had finished paying for the petrol, Clumsy was back in the cab — a comforting secret stash of cakes, biscuits and fizzy drinks stowed away under his seat. With an angry screech of tyres, Dennis wheeled the truck off the forecourt and out onto the road.

25

A Brilliant Idea

When Chia got back to Madame Lulu's car there was still no sign of Dylan, Red Tabby or Stomper. He pulled out his fob watch yet again. If what the guards had said was right, then Dennis and Clumsy were due at any moment, and he knew he couldn't tackle them alone. Once the troupe was loaded back into Dennis's truck, Chia feared he might not see any of them or Madame Lulu ever again. Just as he began to despair, the rattle and roar of a motorbike and the swift thud of galloping hooves reached his ears.

Around a far bend in the lane came Stomper's old machine, sporting a sidecar in which perched Red Tabby, her fur flying in the wind. Following them, mane streaming out behind him, came Dylan at a gallop.

'Sorry I took so long,' Stomper called as he braked to a stop. 'Darned sidecar refused to hitch on, and we'll need it for the rescue.'

'They've locked up Madame Lulu!' Chia interrupted wildly. 'And the guards said Dangerous Dennis would be here in twenty minutes, and that was a good fifteen minutes ago!' The others listened keenly while Chia told them, as briefly as he could, how Madame Lulu had come to be captured.

'Perhaps she meant to get caught,' Stomper suggested. 'So she could get inside the hangar.'

'Yes, maybe she's got a plan,' added Red Tabby.

'I certainly hope so,' said Chia.

'But what plan?' asked Dylan, who'd been quiet up to now because he'd needed to catch his breath.

'That's what we have to find out,' replied Stomper. 'And fast!'

Stomper tucked the motorbike and sidecar out of sight behind a hedge and the four of them made their way swiftly back up the lane. When they reached the gorse bushes, they crept forward until they were close enough to see the lounging guards.

'What happens now?' asked Chia. Before Stomper could reply, an urgent 'Psst!' came from the other side of the fence.

'There you are at last!' hissed Madame Lulu.

'But I saw you captured!' gasped Chia. 'How on earth did you manage to escape?'

'I'll tell you later,' Madame Lulu replied. 'Now listen! I've unlocked the big hangar door and the troupe's ready to run for it when I give the signal. But first we have to deal with the padlocked gates. They have to be opened. Any ideas?'

'We could ram them with your car,' Chia suggested eagerly. Madame Lulu stared at him, alarmed.

'That wouldn't work,' whispered Stomper. 'We can't be sure we'd break through. We'd only risk capture.'

Madame Lulu looked relieved. She was determined to save the troupe, but she did love her sunshine-yellow car. 'Perhaps we can trick them into opening up for us,' she said.

'But how?' asked Chia.

Red Tabby turned to Madame Lulu. 'If Dylan agrees, I think I know a way,' she said. 'We can be the bait. After all, we're the ones those villains most want to get their hands on.'

'Let's do it,' nodded Dylan.

'Brilliant!' said Stomper.

'The very thing!' agreed Chia so enthusiastically that Madame Lulu had to shush him.

'It's the perfect strategy, Tabby,' she whispered admiringly.

'We'll need your car up near the compound,' Stomper told her. She pushed the keys to him under the fence and he slipped away.

Madame Lulu turned to Chia. 'Do you have your watch?' she asked. The ringmaster nodded. Madame Lulu smiled. 'Give me three minutes to get back inside the hangar to alert the others.'

'But how?' asked Chia.

'There's a small window high up at the back. Awkward, but manageable,' she informed him.

Lost in admiration, Chia watched as Madame Lulu slipped out of sight around the big, rusty building. Then he drew his grandfather's fob watch from his waistcoat pocket. Dylan and Red Tabby waited silently behind the gorse bushes while Chia watched the second hand of the timepiece sweep round its large face – once, then twice, then three times. Slowly, he raised his free hand. 'Ten, nine, eight, seven,' he hissed. 'Six, five, four, three, two and one!' He dropped his hand.

On the signal, Dylan and Tabby stepped from their hiding place and out into the lane. They sauntered casually up to the gates and, as Madame Lulu had done before them, placed themselves in full view of the guards. 'Well, I'm blessed,' exclaimed one of the men. 'If it ain't the horse and the cat.'

'Mr Dennis's missing pair, no less,' said his companion. 'This should be worth a nice fat bonus.'

'Come to fetch your friends, have you?' the first guard asked mockingly, his face twisting in an unpleasant sneer.

The guards grappled eagerly with the padlock on the gate. Over the men's shoulders, Dylan and Red Tabby saw a tall dark crack appear on one side of the big hangar door. The crack widened as the great door slowly slid open. There was a faint screeching as its rusty metal protested, but the guards were too busy with their task to hear.

After what seemed like forever to Dylan and Red Tabby, the padlock clattered to the ground, and the gates swung wide in welcome. At that precise moment, there came a shrill whistle from Chia, followed by a loud 'Run for it!' from Madame Lulu.

Instantly, the Happy Days Circus troupe thundered out of the hangar towards the open gates and freedom. Faced by a charging wall of animals, with Tiger and Lion roaring in the lead, the two guards abandoned their posts and fled in terror out of the compound and down the lane towards the town.

26

Breakout

Dazzled by the sunlight, everyone milled excitedly about in front of the hangar. 'All keep together,' Chia warned them. 'We don't want anyone left behind.'

'We'd better get a move on,' called Stomper, pulling up in Madame Lulu's car. 'I thought I saw a big truck turn off the main road down in the valley. It could be theirs.'

'But where are we to go?' asked Madame Lulu. 'The Big Top isn't safe. They'd be on to us right away.'

'To Great Park, of course,' said Red Tabby. Chia and Madame Lulu looked blank.

'Lord Stomper's place,' explained Dylan. 'It's got a high wall. We'd be safe behind it.'

Red Tabby looked imploringly at their new friend. 'May we?' she asked.

Lord Stomper answered at once. 'My home is your home,' he told them, for, in a funny sort of way that he didn't quite understand, he had felt happier since meeting Dylan and Red Tabby than he had done for a long while.

'We are deeply grateful to you,' Chia told him, bowing courteously.

Stomper beamed and ran back for his motorbike while Madame Lulu and Chia bundled the sea lion family into her car.

'I hope you don't mind, Celia,' apologised Chia to the pups' mother, 'but we have to hurry and you sea lions can't – well – gallop quite the way our Dylan can.'

Red Tabby swiftly made sure that everybody who needed one had a ride. Half the meerkat family scrambled onto Lion's back and the rest onto Tiger's. Irma raised Charlie and Prudence onto her shoulders with her trunk. 'You can act as lookouts from up there,' Red Tabby suggested.

Lord Stomper came churning through the gate with his motorbike and sidecar. 'Anyone else for a lift?' he called. Marmaduke, Dancing Dog and Ranga were all that were left.

'Can we really ride with you?' asked Marmaduke. He had never been on a motorbike before.

'Climb aboard!' Stomper laughed, and Marmaduke and Dancing Dog quickly took their places in the sidecar.

'You ride pillion, Ranga,' Stomper urged, and the orang-utan clambered up behind him, wrapping his long arms around Stomper's waist. With the whole troupe accounted for, Red Tabby made a fast run up onto Dylan's back and took a firm grasp of his mane, ready for the 'off'. With the last of the sea lion family now in the car, Chia jumped in beside Madame Lulu and slammed his door.

They were just moving off when Charlie gave an urgent call from his lookout spot atop Irma. 'Something's coming over the hill,' he called. The others craned their necks to see where he was pointing. Sure enough, a large cloud of dust and diesel exhaust fumes could be seen rising beyond the lane that led to the hangar.

'Follow me! I know a shortcut!' yelled Lord Stomper as his sturdy old motorbike and sidecar bounced away across the fields. Madame Lulu put her foot on the accelerator and shot after him. Somehow, Lion and the others managed to keep close behind.

Trailing its tell-tale cloud of exhaust smoke, Dennis's battered old truck lumbered heavily along the narrow country lane towards the hangar.

'Not long now,' smirked Dennis, 'and I'll 'ave me own back on that rotten dancin' 'orse and that miserable scrap of ginger fur that's 'is pal.'

'Not long now and we'll be rich!' hummed Clumsy, rubbing his chubby little hands together in glee. An instant later, Dennis slammed on his brakes and Clumsy jolted forward, cracking his shin against the dashboard. 'Owww!' he yowled. 'What did you do that for?'

'It's them blasted guards!' shouted Dennis. He jumped down from the cab and ran ahead along the lane where the two frightened guards were flying towards him. 'Where do you two think you're goin'?' Dennis yelled.

The guards skidded to a stop, took one quick look at the horse dealer's furious expression, and climbed over a handy stile.

'Stop! Stop! You useless articles!' shrieked Dennis, waving his arms in frustration, but the two men wisely paid him no heed and, running as hard as their legs would carry them, were soon lost to view.

'Get in the cab!' Dennis yelled at Clumsy who, despite his bruised shin, had clambered down to see what all the fuss was about. Clumsy had barely managed to do as he was told before Dennis, back at the wheel, sent the truck racing towards the hangar and his profitable cargo of animals.

As they careered through the open gate and into the deserted compound, the wide-gaping door and the empty space within told the full story 'They've escaped!' Dennis screeched in fury. 'They've all escaped!'

There was little the fleeing troupe could have done to hide the way they had gone, and Dennis was quick to pick up their tracks. He reversed out of the gate, swung around and drove full speed ahead, straight across the fields.

The truck lurched and swayed alarmingly over the bumpy ground. It was all Clumsy could do to unwrap a comforting sweet while hanging on for dear life.

The shortcut Lord Stomper had taken should have provided the Happy Days Circus with a fast getaway route, but he had reckoned without the stream that ran from Great Park out into the valley beyond. The angry storm of the night before had swollen its waters beyond its banks, and the little bridge that spanned it was now all but submerged under the surging flood.

The troupe hovered at the water's edge, uncertain of what to do. From his perch high on Irma's back, Charlie shouted an urgent warning. 'Hurry!' shrilled Prudence from beside him. 'They're closing in on us!' Over the hill came the enemy, heading relentlessly towards them.

'Hold onto your hats,' Madame Lulu yelled. Gritting her teeth, she drove her precious sunshine-yellow car over the submerged bridge, throwing up a great spray of water as she went.

'Youch!' barked Sea Lion as he and his family were tumbled about in the back. Dylan followed at top speed with Red Tabby clinging on for dear life, while Tiger, who rather liked a swim, waded in bravely and 'doggy-paddled' through the racing water to the other side.

Stomper revved up his motorbike and shot across the bridge. The old machine ploughed up a big wave that swamped the sidecar and drenched Marmaduke and Dancing Dog. 'Whoops!' yelled Ranga, 'I'm glad I'm riding pillion!'

Lion, who hated getting his magnificent mane wet but didn't want to be thought cowardly, took a deep breath, closed his eyes, and plunged in. 'Oh dear!' he wailed as he swam valiantly after Tiger. 'There goes my perm!'

Irma, afraid that the bridge might not take her weight, lowered herself carefully into the swollen creek. The water swirled menacingly around her belly, but Charlie and Prudence, high on her shoulders, stayed safe and dry as she made her way through the racing current and up the other side.

'Where are our meerkats?' Red Tabby asked anxiously. She was counting heads and the little clowns were missing.

Marmaduke pointed. 'Oh, goodness! They're still on the other side!' he cried. Sure enough, the meerkats were huddled together on the far bank, chattering forlornly. Lion and Tiger looked at each other and gulped in dismay. 'They must have jumped off before we swam over,' Tiger muttered guiltily.

Stomper tried to wheel his motorbike around to rescue the meerkats, but its sidecar was so full of water it could barely move, and Madame Lulu's car was facing in the wrong direction. The troupe looked on helplessly as Dennis's truck closed in on the frightened band of stragglers.

Suddenly, to everyone's astonishment, the drowned bridge appeared to rise all by itself out of the rushing stream. The water level, in fact, was falling rapidly, and in moments the bridge stood clear of the flood, glistening in the sun.

'It's Irma doing it! It's Irma!' Charlie yelled excitedly. Everyone turned to see, and there – a short way upstream where the creek grew narrow and its banks were high – lay Irma, her determined body forming a dam.

Red Tabby raced back over the bridge to where the meerkats stood, glued to the spot. By now, the truck was so close that, even from the far bank, the troupe could see Dennis grinning through the cab window and a petrified Clumsy clinging on beside him. Irma strained with all her might to hold back the relentless water. 'Come on! Come on!' shouted Ranga. 'Irma can't hold on much longer.'

'Across the bridge! Move it! *Now!*' Red Tabby screamed, treating the meerkats to her scariest mouse-frightening face. The tiny clowns obeyed instantly, tumbling headlong over each other as they ran, with Tabby urging them on from behind.

'Okay!' yelled Charlie to Irma. 'They're across!' Relieved, Irma heaved herself to her feet. The surge of dammed-up water almost swept her away, but she grabbed a nearby tree with her trunk and clambered up to safety.

Down the streambed towards the bridge raced the wall of floodwater. Down the bank towards the stream lumbered the great truck. Too late, Dennis saw the deluge rushing to meet him. He slammed on the brakes, and the truck skidded, reaching the bridge just as the tidal wave struck.

Over went the great vehicle into the foaming water. Moments later, Dennis and Clumsy bobbed to the surface, gasping and spluttering. Clumsy's precious bags of sweets went floating away unnoticed in the commotion.

'Look! Look!' Marmaduke cried out. 'Here come the police!'

And, sure enough, hurtling down the hill came the sergeant on his bicycle with three of his constables pedalling furiously behind him. Dennis and Clumsy saw them too. With never a backward glance, they clambered hastily up the bank and took off across the fields at a run. The last the Happy Days Circus saw of their tormentors, they were disappearing over the horizon with the men in blue in hot pursuit. Safe at last, everyone heaved a huge sigh of relief.

The sun, as if to celebrate their narrow escape, emerged from behind the clouds. Its golden rays, reflecting in a late-afternoon shower, painted a brilliant rainbow in the sky high over Lord Stomper's estate. The luminescent arc of colour seemed like a glittering entranceway, welcoming the tired adventurers home.

Irma helped Stomper tip the water out of his sidecar. Then, with the rainbow beckoning them on, the weary-but-happy band set off once more. Before long, they arrived at the very place that Dylan and Red Tabby had come to know so well: Great Park's pink stone wall, close to the ancient oak.

27

Settling In

Stomper hopped off his machine, reached up, and gave a sharp rap on a small stone near the top of the wall. Once more there was a low rumble as part of the wall swung smoothly inward.

'So that's how it's done!' exclaimed Red Tabby. 'I'd wondered.'

Stomper grinned. When everyone had filed through, he rapped the stone again. 'Very handy in an emergency,' he said as the wall swung back into place. 'Besides, it saves going miles along the road to the main gate.'

Once inside the park the Happy Days troupe gradually recovered their wits. Prudence's knees stopped knocking; the Meerkat Clowns began chattering again; and the sea lion pups honked with delight when, from the back of Madame Lulu's car, they glimpsed Lord Stomper's sparkling stream.

'Well, this is it, everyone,' cried Stomper cheerfully. 'Great Park!'

The troupe followed him thankfully up the broad drive towards the big old house with its stabling and outbuildings.

Once there, Stomper bustled around hospitably. 'Let's build a fire,' he suggested, 'and get everyone warm and dry.'

The idea of getting warm didn't appeal to the sea lion family. They flopped off to the chilly stream and dived in joyfully. While Madame Lulu helped Stomper start dinner, Irma, Ranga, and

Marmaduke went into the woods to collect some sticks. Before long, with the help of Chia, they had a huge bonfire going.

'Make yourselves right at home, folks,' Stomper invited as the weary troupe warmed up beside its crackling flames. 'Wander wherever you like. And feel free to choose your own sleeping places for tonight.'

Dylan turned to Red Tabby. 'Shall we keep our old spot in the stables?' he asked.

'Good idea!' she agreed. 'It's cosy in there. But, for now, suppose we take a stroll until it's time to eat?' And so, at last, the two friends fulfilled their long-held wish – wandering freely across the flower-strewn meadows and through the silent glades of Lord Stomper's estate.

Red Tabby and Dylan weren't the only ones who were curious about Great Park. It was his sprawling stately home that interested Lion and Tiger most. The more the two ambled about its crumbling grandeur, the more intrigued they were. On a colonnaded terrace that fronted the west wing, a pair of wide French doors hung invitingly open.

Lion and Tiger padded through and found themselves in a long room, its walls painted to represent a jungle. They gazed about them in awe. Tiger only knew the circus and had never actually seen the jungle. But he'd heard it described when he was a cub and he found himself breathless with excitement. 'Superb,' he muttered, his whiskers twitching. 'Truly superb!'

A tall, gilt-framed mirror stood propped in a corner of the room; the tangled vines and shrubbery of the jungle scene reflected in its silvered glass. 'Ugh!' Lion exclaimed as he caught sight of himself. 'Did you ever see such a mess?'

Tiger eyed a pair of cushion-strewn couches positioned under a grove of painted palm trees. 'I think this should suit me nicely,' he declared. His mighty jaws opened in a wide yawn. 'Very nicely indeed!' And he climbed onto the nearest couch for a snooze.

It wasn't long before a huge and tasty feast had been laid out on the terrace. Madame Lulu rang an old dinner gong she'd found inside the house and the Happy Days Circus troupe gathered for a badly needed meal. Lord Stomper came bounding out to join them, a big grin creasing his face. 'Good news!' he cried. 'The police have just phoned. Our sergeant and his constables have caught Dangerous Dennis and Clumsy Golightly.'

Charlie gave a joyous hoot and the troupe broke out in a loud cacophony of yelping, barking, and trumpeting.

Stomper clamped his hands over his ears. 'Wow!' he exclaimed. 'What a racket! You must all be feeling a lot better!'

'But what's to happen to them?' asked Tiger when he could make himself heard.

'They'll be charged with kidnapping and cruelty to animals,' Stomper replied. 'It wouldn't surprise me if they were locked up for quite some time.'

A moment of silence followed, for the thought of their enemies behind bars reminded everyone how close they had come to suffering the same fate. Stomper glanced around at his new friends as they encircled his bonfire, and wondered afresh at their brave hearts. 'Anyone for chow?' he asked brightly. Spirits rose at his welcome invitation, and soon everyone was tucking into a delicious meal.

After dinner, the Happy Days Circus settled down around the bonfire and began to piece together the remarkable events of the past two days. Tales were told and retold. Mighty tales of great danger and supreme courage; of perilous escapes and of pulling together to win through. Lord Stomper's rooks gathered in the eaves to listen, and the tawny owl perched nearby, keen to catch every word.

'Irma's our heroine,' declared the meerkats after the brave elephant had explained how she got the idea to dam up the stream. Irma blushed right down to the tip of her trunk.

'I'm voting for Dylan and Red Tabby,' announced Prudence. 'We'd all be caged up without them!' Lion shuddered at the thought.

'And what about Madame Lulu?' Chia asked, and looked at the renowned impresario with undisguised admiration.

'Each of us has played our part,' Madame Lulu replied in her warm, melodious voice.

'Lord Stomper's our hero,' declared Dylan and Red Tabby together. 'For where would we all be without him?'

'Well, you are *all* my heroes, each and every one. And that's a fact,' Stomper declared. The troupe glanced round at each other, greatly pleased.

'But, Lord Stomper, there's still something I can't make out,' said Dylan. 'When I got caught in the gorse bush, how did you manage to find me?'

'Oh, that was easy!' answered Stomper. 'It was my rooks you see. I heard them calling "Cawt, Cawt". I came out to learn what the fuss was about only to find an exhausted, soaking wet, mud-caked cat stumbling towards me. It was Tabby, of course, and she led the way to you.'

As everyone reflected on Dylan and Red Tabby's narrow escape, Chia turned shyly to Madame Lulu.

'Dear Madame,' he ventured. 'In order to rescue our circus, you vaulted the high mesh fence that stood in your way. You escaped from the ropes that bound you. You scaled a building to reach a high window. And you opened every lock that defied your purpose. Tell me, please … where did you acquire such admirable skills?'

Madame Lulu's beautiful green eyes sparkled. 'The answer is simple,' she replied. 'Like most of you, I grew up in the circus.' Dylan's ears twitched forward with interest. 'My father was a respected acrobat. My mother was known as "The Female Houdini". I am in fact …' Madame Lulu paused dramatically, '… an escapologist!' Chia gazed at her, entranced.

Overhead, a bright moon rose high in the night sky. The bonfire burned low as the gentle evening drew to a close. With the entertainment over, the rooks flew home to their rookery. Tiger stretched and yawned. 'I'm for bed,' he announced, and he and Lion padded off to their soft couches in the jungle room.

Dylan and Red Tabby ambled over to their stable. The meerkats settled comfortably in the embrace of the curled up trunk of their heroine, Irma. The rest of the Happy Days troupe settled down for the night in their chosen spots. Lord Stomper carefully banked up the fire and then he too went to his bed. For his part, the tawny owl set off on his night's hunting, well satisfied with the adventures he'd heard told.

Dylan, tired though he was, spent a few moments at the stable door – watching the starlit sky, listening to the sigh of the wind, and wondering where his mother might be living now. Above him, tiny dots of light winked and blinked in the infinity. The moonlight bathed the silent countryside in pale light, and the deep glow of sunrise spread upwards from beyond the trees on the farthest hill. *Moonlight and sunrise?* Dylan wondered.

'Tabby!' he whispered, and gently prodded her with his muzzle. 'Tabby! The sun is coming up in the middle of the night!'

Red Tabby opened a sleepy eye. Through the top of the stable door, she could just make out the red glow on the horizon. But it had been a long day and she was very tired. 'That's not a sunrise,' she managed. 'There must be a fire somewhere. Look, Dylan, it's late – why don't you try to get some sleep?' Dylan gladly took his friend's advice.

28

A Dreadful Discovery

Early next morning, the Animal Rescue vet drove up to Great Park to check the troupe over. 'Here's some medicine for Dancing Dog's sniffle,' she told Chia when she'd finished. 'He may have caught cold from getting soaked in the creek, but, all in all, they seem to have survived their ordeal extremely well.'

Chia thanked her for driving all the way from the town to see them. 'Glad to be of help,' she replied. 'There's one more thing though,' and she drew the ringmaster away from the others. 'Lion's mane,' she whispered. 'He's putting a brave face on it, but the sooner someone untangles it for him …!' She left the sentence unfinished, but Chia understood and nodded gravely.

'It shall be done,' he promised. 'Just as soon as we're back under the Big Top.'

Once the Animal Rescue van had driven off, Madame Lulu turned to Chia, eyes shining. 'Did I hear you say "Back under the Big Top"?' Chia nodded, and Madame Lulu grinned. 'Back under the Big Top, and back in business!' she cried, and, in her excitement, found herself hugging him.

After breakfast, Lord Stomper drove Chia back to the circus to fetch the transporter while Madame Lulu busied herself on the phone. The others mooched about feeling unexpectedly glum. No one, it seemed, wanted to leave this magical place quite so soon. Irma went down to join the sea lions for a goodbye dip in the stream; Charlie and Prudence wandered hand-in-hand through the endless rooms and corridors of the sprawling old house; Tiger and Lion padded off to take one final look at their beloved jungle room; and Dylan took Red Tabby for a farewell ride around the park.

After everything Lord Stomper had done for them, the two friends felt sad to move on and leave him behind. Such a lot had happened between them, and he now seemed an important part of the Happy Days Circus family.

Chia crouched in Lord Stomper's sidecar, holding on tight as Stomper steered his old motorbike along the country lanes towards the Big Top. Ever since they'd turned off the main road, the acrid reek of burning had grown stronger. 'Do you smell what I smell?' Stomper asked Chia as they bounced down the track that led to the circus field.

Chia frowned and sniffed. 'Smoke,' he answered uneasily. 'That's smoke.'

As they wheeled around the last bend in the lane, a scene of such unbelievable destruction lay before them that they could scarcely trust their eyes. Scarlet fire trucks sat in the far corner of the field. Everywhere, water hoses criss-crossed the ground. The Big Top was gone, its canvas reduced to ashes. Only its great poles, charred by the fire, still stood, harshly spearing the hazy air. Firemen with axes poked here and there amid the steaming ruins.

'Dangerous Dennis,' Chia cried. 'This must be his work!'

'Lightning, more like,' said the fire chief when Chia and Stomper explained their suspicions.

'But that big storm the other night left everything so wet,' protested Chia.

'True,' agreed the fire chief. 'But not inside the Big Top. We reckon that during the storm, lightning must have struck your King Pole, sending sparks and embers down onto the dry sawdust. Then late last night, when the wind got up, it must have fanned the embers into a blaze. The rest, I don't have to tell you.' The fire chief swept his arms around the charred remains of the Happy Days Circus. 'Pity no one was here to raise the alarm,' he ended sympathetically.

Everything was gone. The Big Top had collapsed in flames onto the trailers, setting them alight too. Even the great transporter was left a burnt-out metal skeleton. Chia put his face in his hands. 'How am I going to break the news?' he groaned. 'How am I ever going to tell them?' Stomper put a comforting arm around the ringmaster's shoulder, led him back to the motorcycle, and drove him away from the heartbreaking scene.

A sombre Chia called a meeting as soon as he and Stomper got back to Great Park. From the look on his face, Madame Lulu guessed they were all in for a dreadful shock. Chia felt there was nothing for it but to be completely blunt. 'Lightning from the storm,' he began. 'It started a fire. The Big Top is burnt to ashes. We have nothing left. Not a single, solitary thing in the whole world.'

For a long time, no one spoke. 'Then what is to become of us?' ventured Prudence at last.

'A zoo,' Lion stated flatly.

'A cage,' added Tiger.

'Freedom gone,' added Marmaduke.

'Red Tabby will come up with another clever plan, I know it,' said Dylan a bit too hopefully. All eyes turned to Tabby as if she could solve their problems with the mere flick of a paw, but she could find nothing to say to the stricken troupe.

Marmaduke turned to Madame Lulu. 'You'll leave us now, I suppose?' he said in a tremulous voice, his lower lip starting to quiver.

'Leave you?' exclaimed Madame Lulu in a hurt tone. 'I most certainly hope not!'

'Oh! I'm so sorry,' mumbled Marmaduke. 'I didn't mean it like that.' And to everyone's dismay he began to snivel.

'It's not fair,' wailed Prudence, joining in. 'It's just not fair.'

'I'm getting too old for all this,' moaned Lion and, for once, Tiger had to agree with his friend.

For a moment there was just the sound of Marmaduke snivelling and Prudence softly whimpering, then Irma broke in. 'I know what!' she said. 'Why can't we all just stay on here at Great Park – for good?'

Lord Stomper, who had been gazing steadfastly at his boots during this distressing exchange, glanced up sharply.

'Here? With me? At Great Park? For good?' he echoed, an odd break in his voice. Irma felt suddenly dismayed at the boldness of her suggestion and hung her head in embarrassment. The others held their breath.

'You know, folks,' Stomper said after a while, 'perhaps that might be arranged.'

Dylan's ears shot forward. 'Do you mean we could live here and *perform* here, too?' He could hardly contain his excitement.

'Something along those lines, Dylan,' Stomper agreed with a grin.

'It would certainly solve our problem,' said Madame Lulu.

'And be more comfortable,' Tiger added with a thought for his jungle room.

'Stomper, are you really sure?' asked Red Tabby, wide-eyed.

'I wouldn't have it any other way,' Stomper replied firmly. 'I've been on my own long enough. And after all that we've been through together, we can't be parted now.'

Ringmaster Chia shot a keen glance around the troupe. 'May I put Irma's suggestion and your generous offer to the vote?' he asked. Stomper nodded. 'Those in favour?' cried Chia.

Once more Stomper had to clap his hands over his ears as the troupe broke into a roar. Suddenly, he felt like the luckiest man alive.

29

A Fresh Start

There was so much to do. Without a Big Top, the Happy Days Circus needed to create a new arena for their performances. Red Tabby and Chia, with Stomper as their guide, made a thorough inspection of the stately home and its grounds.

'This might work for now,' Red Tabby suggested as they stood in the spacious forecourt where the stables and outbuildings formed a large, U-shaped enclosure.

'I should think so,' Chia agreed.

'So long as we don't get more rain,' Stomper added.

'We're bound to think of somewhere weatherproof later on,' Chia answered, trying hard to sound positive. With that decided, the troupe set to work to make things ready.

Late that afternoon, Chia called everyone together once more. 'Dear friends,' he began, 'since we no longer have the magic of the Big Top to assist us, our future performances will need to be even more special than usual. Every idea you may have will be welcomed.'

The troupe burst out in its usual buzz of animated chatter – especially the Meerkat Clowns who were desperate to tell their news. 'Not all at once, dear friends. One at a time, please!' protested Chia.

'Lord Stomper wants to join the band,' Sea Lion broke in eagerly. 'And he's got some instruments!' A cheer went up from the others.

'And Dylan is working on a new routine,' Red Tabby announced.

'It's called "Duelling Hooves",' Dylan admitted, 'but it's not quite ready yet.'

By now, the meerkats were almost beside themselves with excitement. 'Ringmaster! Ringmaster!' they chirruped. 'We've got something to show!'

'All right! All right!' Chia laughed, 'It's your turn now!'

The little clowns turned to Irma. 'Can we show them? Can we?' Irma nodded and her eyes shone. She was quite enjoying being a heroine.

While Irma fetched a log, the meerkats rushed off and returned staggering under the weight of a long wooden board. With her trunk, Irma rolled the log into the centre of the forecourt and set the meerkats' board across it. The troupe formed a big ring round them, and the act began.

As each little clown clambered onto one end of the improvised seesaw, Irma brought a big foot down on the other end. One by one, the meerkats sailed high into the air, landing nimbly on Irma's ample back, until they all stood there in a wiggling line.

Moving carefully, Irma got down on her knees, with the meerkats chattering noisily all the while as they tried to keep their balance. Once down, Irma began to roll over very slowly onto her back, the meerkats following her every move. At last she lay with all four feet in the air with the meerkats all safely bunched together on her stomach. Then, to everyone's astonishment, the little clowns clambered up onto the soles of Irma's broad upturned feet and began somersaulting backwards from one foot to the next, going faster and faster until they resembled nothing so much as a furry spinning top.

'Bravo! Bravo!' the troupe cheered as the meerkats somersaulted clear and Irma lumbered back onto her feet. Then, with a final flourish, the little clowns lined up neatly along her outstretched trunk and took their bows.

'Well, that's a novelty for certain!' beamed Chia amid the stamps and cries of approval.

The next week saw the troupe endlessly busy with rehearsals. In between band practices, Lord Stomper roared about on his motorbike fetching this or that and feeling more and more light-hearted by the day.

'Cawr! Cawr! Cawr!' screeched the swirling rooks as Madame Lulu drove up in her sunshine-yellow car, her belongings piled up on the trailer hitched behind. No sooner had the renowned impresario unpacked in her new quarters than she got to work on Lord Stomper's phone. Already she'd given the newspapers the story of the Happy Days Circus kidnap and of their daring escape. Now she intended the world to know that they had a new and permanent home.

While Madame Lulu conjured up publicity, Chia borrowed her car and trailer and spent the better part of three whole days rummaging painstakingly through the ruins of the Big Top and the caravans, returning, at last, with all the things he had managed to rescue. The others gathered round expectantly as he carefully laid out each object for inspection.

'My pink hair rollers!' cried Lion in delight.

'My tuba!' exclaimed Irma.

There was Red Tabby's deep-blue velvet waistcoat, studded with the little winking mirrors. There was Irma's jewelled headdress, Bandmaster's music stand and Ranga's clown costume. Chia had even found Dancing Dog's drums and the meerkats' trick car.

'A touch of spit and polish and everything will be as good as new,' he proclaimed.

'Not my snare drum though,' protested Dancing Dog. 'Look! It's got a great big hole in its top.'

'Come with me,' invited Stomper. 'I may have just the thing.' And he led Dancing Dog off to poke around in the basement of the big house. They returned with a fine old drum-set left over from Lord Stomper's pop group days. With Dancing Dog happily taken care of, Stomper excused himself without explanation and disappeared off to town, the sound of his motorbike sending the rooks 'caw-cawing' into the air once more. By the time Chia's finds were safely returned to their owners, the sun had begun to dip away below the distant hills of the Westlands.

While Prudence and Madame Lulu prepared dinner, the meerkats began a furious game of tag around the tall columns that lined the terrace of the big house. Irma busied herself cleaning the soot from her tuba, the sea lion pups flopped down to their stream, and Dancing Dog went off to the east wing to try out his new drums. Altogether, the Happy Days Circus, despite their recent misfortunes, felt strangely content and at home in their new surroundings.

30

A Gift for Dylan

Red Tabby's comfortable basket had been among the precious things that Chia had managed to salvage. Dylan helped her carry it to their new home in the stables. With the basket safely in a corner near Dylan's stall, Tabby jumped in. She turned round and round several times, plumping up the soft cushion until she had it just the way she liked it. Then, with a contented sigh, she stretched out in it for a rest.

'Dylan!' she remarked. 'Lord Stomper's park is just as I imagined when you and I first caught sight of it.' Dylan made no reply. Tabby glanced keenly at her friend as he stood gazing out of the stable door. 'We could gallop round it all day and still have more to explore,' she pressed on cheerfully. 'It really is the purrfect place for us.'

Dylan turned to his friend. An unhappy cloud seemed to hover about his usually contented features. 'I wish Chia had found my mother's picture. Really, I do,' he admitted at last. 'It was all I had to remember her by.'

Oh dear! Red Tabby scolded herself. *I should have guessed.*

Ever since the day Tabby had snatched Desiree de Polka's photograph from Emlyn's dairy and sped with it to Dylan's rescue, the portrait had stayed with them on all their adventures. Now it was gone, destroyed in the fire. Naturally Dylan would be upset. But before Tabby could think of something comforting to say, they heard Irma trumpeting loudly. It was dinnertime. Dylan left Red Tabby's side and trotted out of the stables towards the terrace at the front of the big house. *Hmmm,* mused Tabby pensively as she followed after him.

As Lion, Tiger and the rest of the troupe gathered for the evening meal, it would have been hard to imagine a happier scene. But Tabby could see that, although the cloud of sadness had faded from Dylan's brow, it had not left his heart.

The 'putt-putt' of a motorbike announced Stomper's return some minutes before he came into sight, hurtling up the long drive. Curiously, instead of joining everyone, he scuttled away into the house clutching his colourful leather coat around him as if he was hiding something. When he reappeared for dinner, he was coatless and smiling a little sheepishly. *Stomper's keeping a secret,* thought Red Tabby, *or I've never been a ship's cat.*

A breeze came up as dinner was ending, and the sky darkened, heralding more rain. 'No point in a bonfire tonight,' Stomper remarked. 'Best we get under cover.' And he disappeared indoors again, whistling in an especially jaunty manner.

The troupe quickly bedded down for the night. Soon, all was quiet but for the patter of a gentle shower and the soft swish of a rising wind. With a watchful eye on her friend, Red Tabby climbed into her basket. Dylan, for his part, sighed deeply, and without even a 'Goodnight', flopped down in his stall. Red Tabby was just about to have the matter out with him when there was a sudden, sharp knocking at the stable door.

'Helloo! Anyone at home?'

The door creaked open and Lord Stomper poked his head in. He held a lantern in one hand and a square, brown paper parcel in the other. 'I know it's not your birthday Dylan,' he said, 'but here's a little something for you, anyway.'

Dylan lifted his head politely, but even the prospect of a gift could not dispel the unhappiness in his gentle brown eyes. Red Tabby's heart went out to him. 'Come on, Dylan,' she urged. 'It's not every day someone is given a present.' She hopped out of her basket and ran along the top of Dylan's stall to see what was in Stomper's parcel.

Stomper hung his glowing lantern on a nearby hook and sat himself on a bale of straw. 'You'll need to come nearer, Dylan,' he said, 'if you want to watch me unwrap it.'

Dylan got slowly to his feet and joined Stomper and Tabby in the warm circle of light the lantern cast across the stable floor. Carefully, Stomper untied the string and pulled away the crackly brown wrapping paper to reveal a plain wooden square. It had a short length of wire, fastened with hooks, strung across its width. Stomper held it up to the lantern light.

'Well, what do you think?' he asked, beaming.

'It seems a very nice piece of wood,' Dylan commented in a polite but baffled tone.

'Turn it over, Stomper,' prompted Tabby, who had begun to guess what it really was. With a grand flourish, Stomper did as he was asked, and there, before Dylan's amazed eyes, appeared the cherished picture of his mother – perfect in every way.

'Oh!' was all he could manage. 'Oh!' and again, 'Oh!'

'Do you like the frame?' Stomper asked. 'I thought your mother deserved the very best.' Dylan nodded.

'How did you …? I mean, I thought the fire …?' he gulped.

'It *was* a little damaged,' Stomper admitted, 'but I found someone who could put it right, and – well, it looks as good as new, doesn't it?'

'Better!' agreed Red Tabby.

'And it's bigger, too,' said Dylan.

'I hope you don't mind. I had it enlarged,' said Stomper.

Dylan pressed his soft muzzle against Stomper's cheek, and for a while there was silence. 'Can it hang above my manger like it used to do in my trailer?' he managed at last. Stomper fetched a hammer and rustled up a nail, and, in short order, Desiree de Polka gazed down once more on her son.

'I'll be off then,' said Stomper, unhooking his lantern. 'Happy dreams to both of you.'

For some time after Stomper had left, a greatly-contented Dylan stood listening to the gentle rain on the stable roof, going over all the events that had brought him into such fortunate circumstances.

He thought about the Happy Days Circus; about its boundless future made possible by Irma's inspired suggestion and by Lord Stomper's kindness. He thought about his closest friend, Red Tabby; of all that she meant to him, and how she would always be at his side through the good times to come. Then, as sleep came, his mind drifted back to his mother, who he had last seen when he was a foal. He lifted his head and could just make out her gentle face gazing down on him from within her elegant new frame. Since the dreadful fire at the Big Top, he had only been able to imagine her. But now, thanks to Lord Stomper, her true likeness was magically back to comfort him. 'You were right, Tabby,' he murmured into the warm darkness of the stable. 'This is the purrfect place!'

Tabby stirred in the warmth of her deep cushion. 'Sweet dreams, Dylan,' she mumbled.

In the dark night beyond the stable door, the handsome tawny owl, swooping silently over the trees, peered down at Great Park, his mind full of the newcomers who had settled within it.

Born to Dance

Dylan and Red Tabby's Great Adventure

Part III

In which hope and trust win out,
and fondest dreams come true.

31

The Disappearance

All summer long, eager crowds flocked to the makeshift outdoor ring set up in the stable yard of Great Park. 'Bring your brollies!' Chia's posters jauntily advised. And the audience did just that, for neither rain nor shower was going to keep them from seeing the Happy Days Circus and Dylan de Polka, the famous tap-dancing horse.

Dylan loved his new life: dancing for his adoring fans, wandering through Great Park with Red Tabby, and revelling in the company of Lord Stomper and the circus family. Yet despite his good fortune, he felt an unexpected melancholy nudging at his heart. As the days flew by, how ever much he tried to cheer up, the sadness only seemed to deepen.

Red Tabby, with her usual wisdom, guessed the cause and looked for a way to help him regain his usual high spirits. But before she could manage to do so, the busy summer ended and the circus season drew to a close. Almost at once, planning began for the year ahead.

One brisk autumn morning, Ringmaster Chia, Lord Stomper and Red Tabby trooped up the grand staircase of the old house to Madame Lulu's cosy sitting room. She handed Chia and Stomper mugs of rich, hot chocolate, and set out a bowl of creamy milk for Tabby. They settled down to their treat while she laid out the circus accounts. 'We've already saved some of the money we need to replace our Big Top,' she announced, 'but that doesn't leave much to spare for other things such as fresh costumes.'

Red Tabby took a rapturous last lick from her saucer. As she cleaned her whiskers with her paws, she looked up at the worried faces around her. 'I could try wearing my trapeze waistcoat inside out,' she suggested. 'Then people might think it was new.'

'Good idea, Tabby,' replied Chia, but he didn't sound very confident. 'I suppose,' he sighed, 'we'll just have to cut our coats to fit our cloth.'

'Speaking of cloth,' said Stomper, 'maybe I can be of some help in that department.'

'No! No! Please!' Madame Lulu protested. 'You can't keep riding to our rescue.'

'All the same,' Stomper replied, 'I'll bet you anything you'll like my idea,' and, without explaining himself further, he bounded out of the room.

'Now where's he off to?' asked Chia.

'Knowing our Stomper, we'll find out soon enough,' laughed Madame Lulu.

Making his way along a rarely-used passage on the ground floor, Stomper unlocked a small door that opened onto a well-worn stone staircase. Descending into the labyrinth of dark, spidery cellars that lay beneath his stately home, he worked his way carefully down the maze of corridors and soon reached the room he was looking for. There, lit by dim light filtering through cobwebby windows, sat a tall pile of heavy cardboard cartons tied up with string.

Stomper set to work at once, brushing aside the cobwebs, blowing off the dust, and hauling them into the corridor. Then, one by one, he carried them up to the main floor and along endless hallways, depositing them in his ballroom.

Madame Lulu's circus accounts were quickly laid aside when a breathless Stomper poked his head round her door to invite the troupe to join him.

'Can the others share in the mystery?' asked Red Tabby, as they made their way back downstairs.

'You bet, Tabby,' agreed Stomper. 'That's the whole idea!'

Tabby raced off and in no time everyone knew that Stomper had a surprise waiting for them – everyone, that is, except Dylan who was nowhere to be found. *Perhaps he's best left to himself,* thought Tabby as she headed back to the ballroom, *at least for the moment.*

Irma was having a lie-in, when Red Tabby roused her. She stretched and yawned. A burst of excited chatter reached her from across the stable yard and, through her window, she could see all the others hurrying towards the big house. By the time she got there, they had already vanished through the elegant glass doors that led from the terrace into the ballroom.

Irma paused. In all the time the troupe had been Lord Stomper's guests, she had never dared to enter the big house. As she hesitated, Stomper appeared, smiling, on the terrace. He held out a welcoming hand for her trunk and she found herself drawn gently into the glorious mirrored room.

A puffy cream sofa was set facing the massive fireplace. Piled all around it were boxes and boxes and yet more boxes. Red Tabby perched on the sofa's plush, velvety back, her eyes nearly popping out of her head with curiosity. 'Over here, Irma!' she called as Irma stood gazing at herself in the many reflections. 'Be quick or you'll miss all the fun!'

By now the others were gathered round Tabby's sofa. Before them lay the mysterious cartons. A ripple of eager anticipation ran round the troupe, making Stomper grin with delight.

'Did you drag all these in here by yourself?' asked Chia, raising an eyebrow.

'I wanted to keep the surprise, Chia,' Stomper confessed. 'Anyway, it was good exercise.'

Stomper knelt down and began to cut the strings from the nearest boxes. As he did so, the overfilled cartons burst their seams, disgorging pile after endless pile of glittering, glowing material that flowed like a river of rainbows across the carpet.

Gold and silver, sequined and pearled, striped, checked, spotted and plain. Red, green, purple and pink – and a shimmering leopard-skin silk that brought a gasp of delight from Madame Lulu. The onlookers gaped. 'It was all meant for band costumes,' Stomper explained. 'Take as much as you like. More use to you now than to me.'

'Why, we'll look more gorgeous than anyone in the whole wide world!' cried Prudence, pulling out a bundle of pink tulle. She held the fine material against her body and smiled at the image that gazed back at her from one of the great old mirrors.

'And all the colours imaginable,' Charlie exclaimed as he heaved a bolt of rich purple satin from another box.

'It's a good thing I'm handy with a needle!' laughed Madame Lulu.

'I'll help!' offered Prudence.

'And me,' chimed in Ranga.

'I call for a vote of thanks!' roared Tiger, and, once more, Lord Stomper had to cover his ears as the troupe stamped and bellowed their appreciation of his generosity. Irma, however, took care not to trumpet too loudly, for she didn't want to break the beautiful mirrors.

As the rumpus died away, the impatient honk of a car horn intruded on the cheerful scene. 'Someone's in a hurry!' Madame Lulu remarked, and everyone crowded to the windows to see what was going on.

Down in the drive, a spotless white stretch limousine gleamed in the morning sun. A black-clad figure slouched against its open door, pushing hard on the horn.

'Man, oh, man!' cried Stomper. 'Surely it can't be him! Not after all this time!' and he dashed out onto the terrace.

Noses pressed to the window panes, the troupe looked on as Stomper and the stranger threw their arms around each other. The two men jumped up and down and danced this way and that, finally disappearing from sight, their arms still wrapped around each other's shoulders. Red Tabby ran and peered through the farthest window, but there was nothing more to see.

'Perhaps we'd better get on,' Madame Lulu prompted. The troupe returned to their task and soon lengths of chosen material lay on the sofa. Madame Lulu and Prudence began placing the rest neatly back into the boxes.

They had just finished when the sharp honk of the limousine's horn sounded once more. Again, everyone rushed to the windows, in time to see Stomper waving his visitor off.

The mysterious vehicle glided away like a great white shark. No sooner was it out of sight than Stomper began to behave in a rather peculiar way, leaping all over the place and whooping and yelling with all his might.

'Yahoo-yippity-dee!' he bellowed. 'Yippity-do-da! And yip-yip-yip-yip-eee-ee-ee-ee-ee!' His gleeful antics set the meerkats squeaking with pleasure.

'Well!' exclaimed Tiger. 'What can that be about?'

Before anyone could say another word, Stomper came bursting into the ballroom, grinning from ear to ear. 'That was my old mate, Banjo, from my pop group days,' he announced. 'Banjo's become a big shot producer, and guess what! He wants to make a Christmas TV Spectacular with the Happy Days Circus!'

'This is bound to cheer Dylan up!' exclaimed Tabby joyfully. 'I'm going straight out to find him.' And she sped off towards the stables.

Dylan had woken that morning with the sadness that had haunted him all summer weighing heavily upon him. Red Tabby, he knew, was bound to notice and start asking questions, and he didn't feel like being quizzed just at the moment, no matter how gently. So, after breakfast, he had slipped away to take a quiet stroll by Lord Stomper's stream.

Its murmuring, chuckling sound comforted him as he wandered along its green banks. On and on he went, pondering the strange ache in his heart, until, at last, he found himself nearing Great Park's encircling high, pink stone wall. It was a part of the estate that he had never visited before. An old humpbacked bridge was set into the wall, and the sparkling water flowed under it and out of the park towards the green hills beyond.

Down at the water's edge, he drank deeply. Then, as he lifted his head, his gaze was caught and held by the distant, hazy scene framed by the bridge's graceful arch.

Those hills must be in the Westlands, he mused. Tabby has said as much, I'm sure. Then all at once, something he had overheard when he was a foal came drifting up from the depths of his memory. 'That's it! Of course!' he gasped. 'My mother! She was sold into the Westlands!'

Dylan felt his heavy mood fall away from him like a discarded horse blanket, and he knew exactly what he must do.

32

Red Tabby Plays Detective

Red Tabby was in a dreadful state. She had run to tell Dylan the thrilling news about the Christmas Spectacular, but he was nowhere to be found. She searched high and low in all their favourite spots, but with no luck. Fearing that something terrible had happened, she raced back to consult the others. 'Dylan's disappeared,' she blurted. 'Have you seen him today, Tiger?'

'Only at breakfast,' Tiger replied.

'Anyone else since then?' Tabby persisted.

'He was about a bit later,' offered Sea Lion. 'I caught a glimpse of him quite some way down the stream.'

'I'll have to go after him,' she told them. 'He's not been at all himself lately.'

'I'll come with you if you like,' Tiger offered.

'That's really good of you, Tiger,' said Tabby warmly. 'But perhaps I should go alone. Something's been bothering him all summer and it's time I got to the bottom of it.'

'Let me know how you get on,' Tiger replied, but Red Tabby was already racing off towards the stream.

When Tabby reached the spot where Sea Lion had last seen Dylan, she started a careful hunt along the high bank. The ground was hard and seemed to offer no clues, but every so often she came across a broken twig or two, or a place where the long grass had recently been crushed. Now and then, she stopped and looked around her, expecting at any moment to encounter Dylan. When, at long last, she reached the hump-backed bridge, her hopes rose; for there, where the stream bank sloped down to the water's edge, she spied two large hoof-prints in the mud. *It's him!* she thought. *It has to be! He must have stopped for a drink!*

She carried on searching along the bank, but all the ground in that direction lay undisturbed. *He must have crossed to the other side,* she decided, peering across the stream. But the red-brown mud of the far bank also lay untouched. The trail had grown cold.

For a while she sat on her haunches, carefully examining her surroundings. 'He can hardly have disappeared into thin air,' she muttered.

Through the arch of the old stone bridge, the far away hills seemed to beckon. *The Westlands. He can only have gone under the bridge towards the Westlands,* she determined at last.

No path ran beneath the bridge. Its steep sides were slimy and dank and covered with thick moss, which came away in great chunks when she tried to scramble up its stones. On her second try she got within a whisker of the top, but then the moss gave way again, and only a deft, mid-air twist saved her from plunging into the stream.

Great Park's boundary wall stretched away on each side of the bridge, high and imposing. Not a single tree, for as far as her eye could see, offered a convenient branch to help her over. Red Tabby groaned. She loathed the idea of getting her long fur wet, but she picked her way back to where Dylan had stopped for a drink, and, gritting her teeth, waded bravely in.

The icy waters made her gasp, but her spell on the tall ships had made her a strong swimmer. She cat-paddled well at first.

But the stream began to run deep and fast and, as it forced its way through the bridge's narrow arch, it dragged her beneath its bubbling, tumbling surface.

Red Tabby bobbed up from the rushing water only to be sucked down once more into the current. Again she broke the surface, thrashing about until she glimpsed a low willow dipping its limbs into the stream. Grasping at its trailing branches, she made one final desperate effort, and scrambled to the safety of the bank.

Exhausted, she shook herself off and flopped down on the sun-warmed track. She rolled to and fro to dry her fur, then stood up to stretch her aching limbs. She looked about her and saw that she was now well outside Lord Stomper's park and close to a sandy cart track that followed the course of the stream. It was obvious from the trail of wet hoof-prints leading off into the distance that her quest had only just begun.

'Bother that horse!' she exclaimed aloud, startling a small brown rabbit who had crept out to see what sort of creature had fetched up on his doorstep. 'Bother! Bother! And bother again!'

The rabbit ducked back into his burrow, thoroughly startled.

'Oh, Dylan,' sighed Tabby as she set off once more. 'Why on earth didn't you tell me where you were going?'

Far ahead of the bedraggled cat, Dylan clip-clopped along the cart track, the fallen leaves making agreeable crunching sounds beneath his hooves. The sun had dried his coat, and the fine weather, which had replaced the morning's chill, had raised his spirits. *Somebody, somewhere, must have news of an artiste as famous as my mother,* he assured himself.

Under the beaming sun, the Westlands looked more and more inviting, and Dylan quickened his pace to a trot. All along the verges, the grass grew rich and thick. Presently, feeling a bit hungry, he slowed once more to a walk. A particularly lush and juicy patch caught his fancy, and he settled down to graze. He had scarcely managed a second mouthful when he began to get an uneasy feeling that he was being watched.

'Where are you off to then, my lad?' The voice sounded close to his ear. Dylan looked up sharply to find a large man peering at him through a gap in the hedge. 'Wandering about all on our own are we?' the man went on in a kindly tone, and clambered awkwardly through the hedge, dragging a butterfly net after him. Dylan eyed the net warily. 'Lunchtime, I see,' the stranger went on with a smile. 'How would you fancy a treat?' He pulled a shiny green apple from a pocket, proffering it to Dylan on the flat of his palm.

Dylan looked at the apple, then at the net, and took two steps backward. 'Be cautious with strangers!' Red Tabby's warning words rang in his ears. *I'm not falling for the old apple trick,* he decided and quickly cantered away.

'Ah, well,' said the man and, taking a bite from the apple himself, he climbed back through the hedge, trailing his butterfly net behind him.

Looking back over his shoulder, Dylan saw that the track along which he had cantered was now deserted. No one was following him. He allowed himself to slow to a trot, and finally, to a walk. He began to feel a bit silly. The apple had looked tempting and the man's smile had seemed genuine. *It's always best to heed Tabby's advice,* he reminded himself firmly. But, at the thought of the crunchy green fruit, his hunger returned and he began looking about for another choice clump of grass.

By now, he had reached a spot where the track went wandering away from the stream, its hedgerows crowding in on either side. As he nosed about in search of an appealing tuft or two, the lazy clip-clopping of shod hooves reached his ears. Presently, around a bend up ahead, a brightly painted gypsy caravan came trundling towards him.

A young mare plodded indolently along between the shafts. The driver's seat was empty, and the slack reins flapped loosely against the mare's flanks. As there was no room to pass, the young mare came to a halt a few steps from Dylan, her head hanging down, eyes cast on the ground.

Dylan looked at her for a moment, then asked hesitantly, 'Excuse me, but do you come from the Westlands?'

The mare blew noisily through her nostrils and shook her head.

'I'm searching for my mother, you see,' Dylan went on. 'She was sold into the Westlands.'

The young mare looked up at him. 'You're a bit long in the tooth to be looking for your mum, aren't you?' she snorted.

Dylan would have blushed, but, at that moment, a chuckle sounded behind him. He turned abruptly. On the track, as if transported there by magic, stood a gypsy. The man smiled at Dylan from under a mop of tousled ginger hair, and sauntered towards him, hands clasped behind his back.

'You'll be that famous dancing horse I've heard talk of,' the man began in a jaunty tone of voice. 'Could I be right?'

Dylan whinnied, uncertain what to do.

'Lost, are you?' the man went on, drawing nearer. 'Why not let your Uncle Jack help you find your way home?'

But I haven't got an Uncle Jack, thought Dylan, confused. *At least, I've never heard of one.* And he started to feel decidedly uncomfortable.

Making a strange whistling noise between his front teeth, the gypsy took another step closer. His blue eyes bored into Dylan's like a pair of ice picks. Then his hands flew from behind his back and a thick coil of rope snaked upwards, aimed to encircle Dylan's neck. Dylan reared up in fear. With a wild leap he broke through the nearest hedge and galloped away across the newly turned fields. Only when he found his way barred by a broad canal did he come to a halt.

Luckily, there was no one about. He stood for a moment to catch his breath. *Where to now?* he wondered. Then, remembering what Tabby had taught him about making his way across country, he glanced up at the sky. The slant of the sun told him that the canal and its towpath led west. Blessing his good fortune, he set off along the path. But no matter how fast or how far he trotted, the distant hills appeared no closer than when he'd first set eyes on them.

For every step that Dylan took, Red Tabby, being that much smaller, had to take ten. So it was a while before she caught up with the caravan that Dylan had encountered earlier in the day. The young mare pulled her load along more slowly now if that were possible, ambling from one tuft of appetizing grass to the next. The gypsy lay on his back in the driver's seat, sound asleep, his snores adding a counterpoint to the caravan's creaking wheels.

'Have you seen a chestnut dray horse with a long blond mane?' Red Tabby burst out, as she ran up to the mare.

The mare looked up, her mouth full of grass. 'Who wants to know?' she mumbled.

'What do you mean "Who wants to know"?' Red Tabby shot back. 'I do, of course. I mean, who else is there about?'

'Oh, sorry!' said the mare. 'My boss always talks like that. I copy my boss sometimes, just for the fun of it. My boss …'

'Never mind your boss,' Red Tabby cut in. 'Please, tell me if you've seen my friend, Dylan. It's urgent!'

'There was a horse like that passed me some time ago,' the mare admitted. 'My boss made a grab for him, but he jumped through the hedge and made off towards the canal. A mile or so back it must have been.'

At that moment the gypsy sat up abruptly and rubbed his sleepy eyes with the back of his fists. Thanking the mare, Red Tabby nipped out of sight beneath the caravan. 'Made a big hole in the hedge when he jumped through, he did,' the mare called after her. 'You can't miss it.'

'What are you whinnying at, you useless nag?' Tabby heard the gypsy grumble.'

Red Tabby trotted along the cart track, keeping a sharp lookout for signs of Dylan's passage through the hedge. After a bit, she came upon the spot. The young mare had been right; the hole was certainly big. Red Tabby scrambled through it to the ploughed field beyond.

There, as far as her eye could see, were the unmistakable signs of Dylan's flight: a line of hoof-prints in the turned earth, leading away into the distance. But, when she finally found herself at the canal's edge, there was no sign of her friend, and the trail soon petered out on the hard gravel of the towpath.

So he came this far, Tabby mused, *but where did he go to from here?* She glanced about her, but there was no hint as to which direction Dylan might have chosen.

A piebald pony poked his head over a nearby stone wall and watched curiously as Red Tabby scoured the ground for clues. 'Looking for someone?' he called.

Red Tabby padded swiftly over to him. 'A chestnut dray horse. Did he pass by here?'

The pony nodded his stubby head. 'A good while back, too,' he volunteered. 'He was from some circus or other and bound, so he said, for the Westlands, whatever that is.'

The towpath stretched away from Red Tabby towards the place where, before too long, the slanting sun would dip beneath the hills. 'Ah! Then he must have gone that way,' she said to the pony, with some relief. 'Thank you. You've been a great help.'

Red Tabby hurried on along the towpath, but after a time its sharp gravel cut painfully into her pads. She tried walking on the soft verge, but the overlong grass hindered her progress. To make matters worse, she was famished.

Just as she had decided she could go no further, she heard the sound of an engine, and turned to see a narrowboat chugging its way along the canal towards her. *The perfect thing!* she decided. *Now, if only I can get aboard!*

Further along the towpath, a clump of alders had grown up by the bank, their slender branches overhanging the water. Running as fast as her sore paws would allow, Red Tabby raced towards the small thicket, clambering swiftly onto the outermost branch. As the narrowboat glided smoothly beneath her, she dropped lightly down from her perch onto its roof. Luckily she was unseen by either the helmsman or his mate, who sat chatting with each other in the stern.

Towards the bow, just forward of the galley funnel, Tabby found a bundle of old rope heaped carelessly on the roof. She made herself comfortable in its coils and settled in to scan the canal banks, right and left, for any sign of Dylan. On each side, the golden autumn countryside slid effortlessly past as the vessel bore her onward towards her lost friend – or so she earnestly hoped.

33

Tiger Raises the Alarm

Tiger opened an eye. On a big settee on the other side of the jungle room, he could see Lion still fast asleep. A wisp of the great cat's magnificent mane had fallen across his nose and it rose and fell in time with his snores.

'Bless my whiskers,' Tiger mumbled sleepily. 'Red Tabby must have found Dylan by now. I'd better run over and make sure they're all right.'

But when Tiger reached the stables, Dylan and Tabby were nowhere to be seen. Worse still, their lunch lay waiting for them, untouched. With a rising sense of concern, he went to break the troubling news to Chia and the others.

Chia clapped a palm to his brow. 'Both missing?' he exclaimed. Tiger nodded gravely.

'It's that blasted Dangerous Dennis,' fumed Chia. 'He's at it again! I'm going for the police!'

'No! Wait! It can hardly be Dangerous Dennis. He's still locked up!' protested Lord Stomper.

'Anyway,' said Tiger, 'Tabby told me that Dylan's been a bit moody lately. Maybe she's just taken him off somewhere quiet to try and find out what's wrong.'

'But if they haven't eaten their lunch,' said Stomper, 'it means they've been gone for over six hours! That's a long time, Tiger.'

'Without them, what will happen to our TV Spectacular?' asked Lion.

'One thing at a time, Lion,' protested Madame Lulu. 'Finding Dylan and Red Tabby is all that matters now.' An anxious murmur of agreement ran round the troupe.

'But what if we can't find them?' squeaked one of the meerkats.

'Yes!' cried Marmaduke. 'Suppose they're lost forever?'

Prudence's lower lip started to quiver. 'Oh no, Marmaduke! That would be too horrible!' she blurted. 'Why, I simply couldn't bear it!' Madame Lulu threw a comforting arm around the distraught chimp.

Ringmaster Chia raised his hands in a bid for silence. 'My dear, dear friends,' he said earnestly. 'Surely, what we must do now is keep our heads and make a plan!'

'Quite right!' growled Tiger. 'We'll start by searching Great Park. Ranga, you take the North. Charlie, you cover the South. Lion, if you will, take the East. I'll search the West. Dancing Dog, you and the meerkats scour the house and all the outbuildings. Bandmaster, can you and your family hunt along the stream?'

'What about us?' chorused Prudence and Irma. 'What shall we do?'

'Get yourselves up to the top of the ancient oak,' replied Tiger. 'Maybe you can spot them from there.'

'But, Tiger,' Irma protested, 'forgive me for pointing this out, but elephants can't climb trees! At least, not this elephant!'

'Of course not! Sorry!' apologised Tiger. 'What I meant was, Prudence should climb the ancient oak and you, Irma, you're to stay here.' Irma's face fell.

'Let me explain,' Tiger went on patiently. 'If anyone finds Dylan and Red Tabby or learns anything new, head straight back here to Irma, and she will trumpet for the rest of us to come.'

'Good thinking, Tiger,' said Chia. 'And while you're all doing that, I'll cover the police station, Animal Rescue, and anyone else in town who might have seen them.'

'Why don't I make the rounds of the nearby villages on my motorbike?' suggested Stomper.

'Good idea!' agreed Madame Lulu. 'And I'll get straight onto the newspapers.'

For a moment there was silence around the little circle and an exchange of worried looks. Then Madame Lulu pulled her keys from her bag. 'Take my car,' she told Chia. 'We'll need to make the best use of our time.'

'Listen for Irma's trumpet and meet back here at dinner if not before,' Tiger ordered as the searchers fanned out.

'And a late dinner it's likely to be, I should think,' remarked Charlie.

'How can you think of food at a time like this?' Prudence protested – and she made off for the ancient oak.

Back at the canal, Red Tabby's narrowboat wended its way along at a leisurely pace. Despite her urgent mission, she was enjoying being afloat again. Of course, it was nothing like being under sail, but it brought back fond memories nonetheless.

From her vantage point on the roof she kept constant watch for Dylan, thoroughly scanning both banks of the canal and the open countryside beyond. Her sharp eye missed nothing: sheep and cows, birds and dogs, people and ponies, she noted them all – but of her dearest friend and companion, there was still no sign.

Ahead of Red Tabby, Dylan trudged doggedly westward along the towpath. Of everyone he met, he asked the same question, but no one had even heard of Desiree de Polka, much less known where to find her. 'I'm only a yearling, you see,' one small heifer had explained. 'It's sort of before my time.'

For Red Tabby, there were no halts by the wayside to ask after Desiree, or stops to munch on succulent grass, so the narrowboat steadily gained on Dylan. By late afternoon, the distance between the two friends had shrunk to less than a mile.

As the sun lost its power, a sharp wind got up and Dylan began to feel the cold of the autumn evening. *I must find a safe place to spend the night,* he thought. Once more he followed Tabby's wise advice and looked about for a field with other horses where he could rest yet not stand out.

All afternoon, Irma sat patiently on the terrace of Stomper's house, but no one brought news. Then, one by one, the Happy Days troupe came trudging home, weary from their efforts and hoping against hope that, perhaps, someone else had had better luck. But by day's end, Dylan and Red Tabby were still nowhere to be found. They certainly weren't anywhere within the high, encircling wall of Great Park, and Chia reported sadly that no one in town had spotted them either.

Stomper's inquiries, too, had drawn a blank, but he was unwilling to return empty-handed. As dinnertime approached, he checked his remaining petrol. 'Just one more village,' he promised himself, but he found no one about to ask when he reached it.

He was turning for home when a rambling, thatch-roofed building, half-hidden down a narrow lane, caught his eye. Over its weather-beaten door hung a creaking sign adorned with a painting of a gnarled tree and the words 'Ancient Oak Inn' carved into the dark wood. *Worth a try,* he decided. He parked his motorbike and found his way into the public bar.

It was early yet, with only a few customers scattered about the long, oak-timbered room. A good log fire burned merrily in the grate, and an old man was hunched on the fireside settle, warming himself, a tankard of cider at his elbow. Behind the bar stood the landlord, neatly attired and with a brisk, no-nonsense air about him.

Stomper pulled off his crash helmet, sending his long hair cascading over his long, patchwork coat. The landlord's eyebrows shot up and he stared at the newcomer with some alarm.

Stomper knew only too well the effect his old band costumes could have on strangers. He smiled at the landlord politely. 'A half-pint of your finest ale if I may,' he said in what he hoped was a reassuring tone. Still eyeing Stomper suspiciously, the landlord took down a glass and began drawing from the pump.

'Has anyone come across a blond-maned, chestnut dray horse hereabouts?' Stomper asked, addressing the room at large. 'I've been searching all afternoon.'

A woman at a nearby table looked up as he spoke. 'This is horse country, laddie,' she laughed. 'Nags all over the place round here. They all look the same to me.'

'Well, this one might be with a long-haired, ginger tabby cat,' Stomper explained.

'I've seen a few pink elephants in my time,' joked a burly customer along the bar. 'You don't mean one of them, do you?'

Stomper gave a polite laugh and took a sip of his ale. 'This is a very special horse,' he explained. 'He's from the Happy Days Circus. Look, here's his picture.' And he pulled one of Dylan's publicity posters from his coat pocket.

The woman looked at the poster and shook her head. 'Too old for circuses, me!' she snorted. Stomper handed the picture round to the other patrons, but none seemed to recognise it.

When it passed to the old man by the fireside, he stared at it keenly for some moments, muttering 'de Polka – de Polka.' Stomper's hopes began to rise, but the old man gave the picture back with a shake of his head. 'Almost thought I was onto something there,' he said, staring intently at Stomper, 'but no, young fella-me-lad, I can't help you after all.'

Stomper thanked everyone, paid for his barely-touched drink, and left.

'Odd manner of person,' complained the landlord when Stomper had gone. 'For a moment I thought he'd come to rob the place.'

'Lord love you,' snorted the old man by the fireside. 'You don't have the first idea who the bloke is, do you, Landlord? Of course not. How could you when you've been here such a short while?'

'Only all of six years,' the landlord muttered under his breath.

'Calls himself "Lord Stomper",' the old man told him.

'Him! A Lord! Good Heavens!' gasped the landlord, rolling his eyes in mock wonder.

'Used to be a famous pop star,' the old man pressed on. 'Bit of a hermit now, I hear. Keeps himself shut up in that enormous park over east.'

The burly man at the bar gave a chuckle and leant towards the landlord. 'Need to know anything about matters in these parts, just ask Old Brock. He's been holding down that fireside settle for more years than the rest of us together can muster.'

'So I've been told,' replied the landlord with a sigh. 'So I've been told.'

By the time Stomper got home, the others were already eating. Everyone looked up expectantly as he joined them, but he only shook his head. They finished their meal in uneasy silence, and each nursed a growing fear that Dylan and Red Tabby might really be lost forever.

'We'll widen our search at daybreak,' suggested Madame Lulu. 'But for now, I think we'd all be wise to get a good night's rest.'

With the sun gone to warm the other side of the world, the ever-distant hills of the Westlands had fallen into shadow. Tabby, who hadn't moved for hours, began to feel cold and hungry.

She could hear one of the bargees clattering about in the galley beneath her, getting the evening meal ready. The narrowboat's funnel gave off a small puff, and then another. Before long, the smoke was pouring aft in a long streamer, and the little funnel glowed with the heat from the galley stove below.

Red Tabby felt a delicious warmth creeping over her. She shifted in her coil of rope to bring herself closer to the funnel and settled down again to watch for Dylan. But it had been a hard day, and it wasn't long before her head nodded forward. Now and then she jerked herself awake, fearing she'd missed her friend. But each time her eyelids would droop until, eventually, she slipped into a dream.

Just ahead, along the canal, Dylan stood concealed under some old and twisted willow trees. Their trailing branches pushed their way down towards the towpath from the corner of a likely looking meadow. One great withered branch, half-torn from its trunk, had fallen across the meadow's fence. Its weight held down the wire, offering him an easy way in.

Three young mares nibbled serenely on the pasture's lush grass. They had been moving steadily away as they fed, and Dylan had decided to wait until they were even further up the meadow before venturing over the downed fence. While he waited, a chugging sound reached his ears, and a narrowboat came into sight along the canal. Dylan stood unmoving, his chestnut coat blending with the shadows under the trees. Slowly, the narrowboat glided by, grey smoke billowing from its funnel. Then it was gone.

By now, the three mares were well up the field. With the coast clear, Dylan stepped neatly over the wire. Beneath the willows the ground looked soft, dry and inviting. *It's the perfect spot,* he thought. *Just the place Red Tabby would have chosen.*

His best friend, whose advice and wisdom he so often relied upon, slumbered peacefully on, curled up on the roof of the narrowboat moving steadily away from him into the distance.

The night had all but cloaked the sky when the vessel fetched up at a high lock. The bottom gates were open, and the dank stone of the lock's tall sides loomed ominously against the fading light. The helmsman put his rudder hard over, and his mate leapt ashore as the narrowboat bumped against a mooring close by the lock-keeper's cottage.

'Anyone at home?' he called. The door of the cottage flew open, sending a wide shaft of yellow light across the front path.

The lock-keeper came running out, a gleaming white napkin tied beneath his chin.

'Why can't you bargees keep decent hours?' he complained. 'You've taken me from my supper, and it's my mum's meat stew tonight.'

As if to bear out his words, a plump, elderly woman appeared behind him, brandishing a long serving spoon. A mouth-watering smell drifted out on the night air from the cottage. 'It'll be down to you if my boy's meal goes cold,' the plump woman scolded, and she followed her son down the path, her long, starched apron flapping about her knees.

Kicking his rudder to starboard, the helmsman revved his engine and the dark, cavernous mouth of the open lock soon swallowed up the narrowboat with the sleeping Red Tabby on board. On the bank, the lock-keeper and the bargee vigorously wound the handles of the windlass and the huge bottom gates lumbered shut.

The two men ran up the stone steps to the top gates that held back the waters of the higher canal. The lock-keeper's mother watched impatiently from the towpath as her son and the bargee set about opening the top sluices.

'Well, I don't know,' the plump woman grumbled on. 'There's another fine stew gone for nothing.'

Soon water began gushing into the basin, hissing and bubbling around the narrowboat's hull while the men shouted instructions over the roar. The commotion roused Red Tabby from her dreams with a start. 'Where am I?' she cried. 'What's going on?'

The inky black water gurgled and slapped against the narrowboat, making it bump back and forth between the high, slime-green walls as the lock began to fill. For a terrifying moment, Tabby thought the craft was sinking, but then she felt it start to lift up beneath her. Gradually, the dank walls fell away, and the roof of the narrowboat rose level with the side of the top lock.

Ahead stretched the upper reaches of the canal, shining in the moonlight and curving – Red Tabby saw to her dismay – far away to the south. The gushing water subsided, the top gates opened and the narrowboat, with the bargee back on board, began to nose forward.

'This is horrible,' Tabby mewed. 'How will I ever find Dylan now?'

She felt the boat gathering speed beneath her. Panic-stricken, she ran to the stern. The lower towpath, now in pitch darkness, lay far, far below her. There was only one thing for Red Tabby to do and she did it. She threw herself blindly, out into the ink-black void. The ghostly face of the startled lock-keeper flashed beneath her as down through the night air she flew.

For the briefest instant, as she plummeted earthwards, the tantalising aroma of savoury stew filled her nostrils. She landed with an unceremonious thud on something soft, warm, and scented overwhelmingly of lavender. A stifled squeal pierced the night's quiet. Then all was still.

34

The Search Widens

'You were right, Bandmaster,' said Stomper. 'Look at this!' Stomper had risen before daybreak and, as arranged the night before, gone to awaken Sea Lion. Together they had made their way downstream to the spot where Dylan had last been seen.

From there on, with Sea Lion sloshing along in the water and Stomper searching along the bank, they had traced the watercourse as far as the humpbacked bridge. Now, in the dim pre-dawn light, Stomper crouched at the water's edge pointing at a pair of muddy indentations.

Sea Lion swam over to take a look. 'Hoof-prints!' he declared. 'And Dylan's, too, by the size of them.'

Stomper waved a hand towards the bridge's stone arch. 'Could he have got through there?' he asked.

'The stream's deep enough. I've been through to the other side once myself,' Sea Lion confessed.

'Of course, if he made these prints yesterday,' said Stomper, 'he might be anywhere by now. All the same, great detective work, Bandmaster. At least we know he's left Great Park, and that's a good starting point.'

'Gong-gong-gong.' Stomper looked up at the sound. 'Gong-gong-gong.' 'Who's beating the gong at this early hour?' he asked. 'Something must be up.' And together, they turned for home.

The relentless sound of the gong reverberated through the big house, bouncing along the corridors and up into Ringmaster Chia's bedroom. The ringmaster sat up with a jolt and blinked in the bright dawn light. *My goodness,* he thought, looking in the mirror, *I must have dropped off to sleep in my clothes.* 'Gong-gong-gong.' Chia washed quickly then raced downstairs. Madame Lulu stood just outside the stately dining room beside the large brass dinner gong, its mallet in her hand and a mischievous smile on her face. 'I knew that would get you going,' she said as Chia blundered into the hall.

'But, dear Madame,' he spluttered, still groggy from his sudden awakening, 'I was already dressed!'

Madame Lulu had wrapped up warmly, and Chia noticed two large Thermos flasks poking from her bag. He hoped they held hot drinks, for he feared there would be no chance of breakfast today. But Madame Lulu, who could read Chia like an open book, led him to the kitchen where warm, buttered toast and a generous cup of hot chocolate stood ready and waiting. Chia gulped down his morning meal gratefully.

By the time they reached the stable yard, Stomper had already coupled an old horsebox to the towbar on the back of Madame Lulu's sunshine-yellow car. Now he knelt beside his motorbike, bolting on the sidecar, while Tiger looked on keenly. As Stomper worked, the rest of the Happy Days troupe appeared one by one and stood silently, watching the preparations.

'We're coming with you, Stomper,' Charlie announced as Stomper gave the last bolt a final turn.

'If Dylan or Tabby are hurt, you might need us,' Ranga added.

Stomper gave a vigorous nod. 'We need all the help we can muster,' he told them as he dropped his spanner into his toolbox.

Charlie threw on one of Stomper's ratty old sweaters and a pair of his cycling goggles that were hanging on a peg in the stables. Ranga dug up a thick, windproof jacket and slapped Stomper's old leather flying helmet on his head. When the two were ready, the sight of them made the meerkats titter, despite the gravity of the situation.

'All right, everybody,' Madame Lulu called. 'Let's go over our plan again.' The search party crowded around her car as she spread out a map on its bonnet. 'Chia and I will take the main roads while you, Stomper, with Ranga and Charlie, comb the back lanes and cart tracks, starting by the stream. Here's Stomper's Ancient Oak Inn,' she went on, and tapped a point on the map with a manicured fingernail. 'Come what may, we meet there at dinnertime. Any questions, anyone?' The others shook their heads. Just then, the sun poked above the horizon, and a radiant shaft of light bathed the Happy Days Circus troupe in its hopeful glow.

'We must be off,' said Chia gravely.

'Here, Charlie, your team can use this,' said Madame Lulu and handed him the map. 'I have another in the car.'

Chia drew Tiger aside. 'Can you manage without us today?' he asked.

'Leave rehearsals to me,' Tiger assured him. 'And Prudence can see to lunch.'

'What we'd do without you, I don't know,' Chia told him gratefully.

Stomper gave his starter a vigorous kick and the old motorbike sprang to life. Ranga clambered onto the saddle behind him, and Charlie vaulted into the sidecar, the map safe inside his jacket. Chia settled down beside Madame Lulu. 'You're the navigator,' she told him as they moved off down the drive.

'All right, everyone! Rehearsals!' Tiger called in his most commanding tone, and the rest of the troupe bustled off to get ready. There was nothing left to do now but carry on and hope.

Dylan had fallen asleep the night before screened by the curtain of trailing willow branches. He woke to find himself staring through a thicket of graceful, slender legs.

'It's Dylan de Polka,' said a tremulous voice.

'Dylan de Polka? Actually here in our pasture?' gulped another. 'It can't be true!'

'Clara's right! It *is* him!' cried the third. 'Whoever would have thought it?'

'Where am I?' mumbled Dylan. 'What's going on?'

A trio of young mares stared down at him, wide-eyed and dizzy with excitement. He quickly scrambled to his feet and the mares whinnied with undisguised admiration when they saw how tall he stood.

'And will you look at those eyelashes, Amanda?' the one called Clara exclaimed.

Dylan began to feel awkward. 'Who are you?' he asked shyly. But the mares were far too wound up to bother with introductions.

'Why! He's even more handsome than his poster,' sighed Kylie, the youngest of the three.

Amanda squealed ecstatically. 'I can't believe I'm meeting someone so famous.'

Since they seem to know who I am, thought Dylan, *maybe they'll want to help me.*

'I'm searching for my mother,' he ventured. 'Maybe you've heard of her? Desiree de Polka?' But any answer the star-struck mares might have given was drowned in a thunder of galloping hooves.

Down from the top of the meadow raced a black stallion, his neck stretched out to the full, ears laid back, teeth bared in a wicked grimace. The mares scattered as he charged in amongst them. 'Get away from that creature at once!' he ordered. 'How many times must I tell you mares not to go giggling after strangers?'

Amanda turned back to the stallion, petulantly. 'But he's not a stranger!' she argued. 'He's a celebrity! Why can't we talk to him if we want to?' By way of an answer, the stallion ran at her and nipped her smartly on the flank. With a frightened squeal, Amanda fled up the meadow after the others.

The stallion wheeled to face Dylan, but by now Dylan had wisely clambered back over the downed fence. The black horse rushed at him, but pulled up sharply before the fallen barrier, his teeth clicking savagely.

'Get out, and stay out,' he threatened.

Dylan stepped back onto the towpath, his heart beating a rapid tattoo against his ribs. Early morning mist hovered chill above the ground and he broke into a trot to try and warm himself up. But, a good mile further along the canal, he found he was still shaking. He'd never had much to do with other horses – except for those in his own family – and the stallion's hostile behaviour had left him badly rattled.

Stomper, Charlie and Ranga's day had got off to a flying start. The cart track, which skirted the high wall of Lord Stomper's park, forked when it reached the stream. One branch went on over the humpbacked bridge, and the other turned westwards along the course of the waterway.

'Look!' Charlie shouted from the sidecar as they approached the bridge. There, in a field close by, stood a brightly painted caravan. Not far off, a young mare grazed in the long, lush grass. The motorbike skidded to a halt.

'There's a pair of boots sticking out from under that caravan!' Ranga exclaimed.

'Why don't I go and talk to whoever's attached to them,' suggested Stomper, 'while you and Charlie see if that young mare knows anything?' And he strode across to where the caravan stood.

'What d'you want?' came a churlish voice. 'I don't take kindly to people poking round my 'ome.'

Stomper squatted by a back wheel where a man lay on his back on the ground busily greasing the rear axle. 'I'm looking for a horse,' Stomper began.

The man hauled himself out from under the vehicle and sat up. 'You can 'ave that one,' he said and waved a greasy hand at his mare. 'For a price, that is.'

'No,' replied Stomper. 'I'm looking for a chestnut dray horse.'

The gypsy laid a dirty finger against the side of his nose. ''orse flesh is easy to come by,' he replied, 'if you knows where to look, which I does.'

'I don't want to buy a horse,' Stomper protested. 'I'm trying to find one that's gone missing.'

'Missing, you say?' The gypsy's face took on a sneaky expression. 'Don't know nothing about no missing 'orse,' he muttered, and slid back beneath the caravan.

'But we're almost certain he passed this way,' Stomper persisted.

'Nothing to do with me,' said the man warily.

Stomper glanced across to where Charlie and Ranga were chatting with the mare.

'You're a couple of scruffy-looking specimens and no mistake,' the mare was saying, regarding Charlie and Ranga with an amused eye. 'I've never seen the likes of you before.'

'We're looking for a chestnut dray horse and a ginger cat,' Charlie told her. 'We're from the Happy Days Circus.'

She nodded. 'Oh! That would explain your hairdos! Never been to a circus myself. Not in my line of work.' And she went back to her grazing.

'Well, did you see our two friends?' demanded Ranga.

The mare lifted her head and slowly blinked at him. 'As it happens, I did,' she drawled. She was very much enjoying this unexpected attention. 'Only yesterday it was, too. Back a way up that cart track over there.' And she nodded towards the lane that ran alongside the bank of the stream.

'They've been here, Stomper!' whooped Ranga and Charlie, jumping up and down with excitement as Stomper came up to them. 'Dylan and Red Tabby have been here!'

'Mind you, they didn't come by together,' the mare went on. 'Horse first, about noon, and then the cat. Horse said he was looking for the Westlands. Cat said she was looking for the horse. Now, it seems, you're all looking for the both of them!' She whinnied in amusement. 'I never did see such a carry on!'

Before the young mare could say more, an angry shout interrupted her.

'You lot still 'anging around?' The gypsy had crawled out from under his caravan and was bearing down on them. 'If you ain't 'ere to do business, you can clear off,' he added menacingly.

223

Charlie turned back to the mare. 'Thanks a lot,' he said, 'but we'd best be on our way.' And the three searchers withdrew hastily to the other side of the hedgerow where Stomper's motorbike stood waiting.

'Why would Dylan head to the Westlands?' Stomper wondered aloud as they climbed aboard. Charlie and Ranga shook their heads, perplexed. 'Hold on tight,' Stomper warned. He revved the engine and the old machine careered off down the cart track in the direction the young mare had suggested.

A short time later, the bike and its riders flashed past the large gap in the hedge – but, in their haste, no one noticed it.

35

Imprisoned!

Red Tabby sat gazing out of the window of the lock-keeper's cottage. She'd been given a large breakfast, for which she was grateful, and she'd had a big, blue silk ribbon tied in a bow around her neck, for which she was not.

Every door of the cottage was shut tight and every window fastened. Red Tabby knew that for a fact. The moment the lock-keeper's mother had left the cottage, a shopping basket on her plump arm, the frantic cat had raced round and tried them all. There was no avoiding the dreadful truth: she was a prisoner – a prisoner in a big, blue bow. *Even if I do get out of this place,* she thought, *Dylan must be miles away by now. There's no way I'll ever catch up with him.* She yanked uselessly at the bothersome ribbon. 'Rats!' she cried aloud. 'Rats! Rats! Rats!'

Dylan stood in the concealing shelter of an old dry-stone wall that ambled untidily down to the towpath from the edge of a neighbouring field. Ahead of him, a looming lock interrupted the canal's course, and in its shadow nestled a cosy-looking cottage. The towpath appeared to end just beyond the cottage and Dylan had come to a halt, not knowing how to continue his journey west.

He had seen a plump woman coming out of the cottage gate carrying a shopping basket, but his recent misadventures had made him extra cautious so he waited a little longer in case anyone else was about. Luckily there were no narrowboats on the canal, and when, after a bit, no one else had appeared, he trotted forward.

Red Tabby was scratching half-heartedly at a window latch as he came by, and she nearly jumped out of her pelt at the sight of him. But her delight was short-lived for Dylan, without once looking her way, trotted straight on up the towpath.

When no fresh westerly path opened before him, the puzzled horse stopped in the shadow of the high lock and looked back the way he had come. The towpath ran away into the distance straight and unbroken for as far as the eye could see. *Maybe I missed a side road*, he thought and retraced his steps towards the lock-keeper's cottage.

Much to Red Tabby's relief, Dylan once more trotted past her window. Surely, he must notice her this time.

'Dylan!' she mewed. 'Dylan! It's me!' She clawed desperately at the window pane. 'Oh, please! *Please!* Look over *here!*' But Dylan, intent on finding his way, passed by again without so much as a glance in her direction.

Red Tabby was desperate. She raced from one window to another, frantically trying to keep her friend in sight. But it was useless. Heartsick and more dispirited than she had ever been in her entire, adventurous life, Tabby flopped down on the windowsill and buried her face in her paws.

Back and forth Dylan trotted, patiently tracing and retracing his steps along the towpath, but all to no avail. At last, he came to a complete halt before the cottage. In the window, he could see a ginger-haired cat lying flattened on the sill, her face buried in her paws. Had it not been for the wide, blue bow tied around the cat's neck, he could have sworn it was Red Tabby. He pushed open the gate to the cottage and trotted up the path for a closer look. *It certainly looks like her,* he thought, *but I must be dreaming. Tabby would never wear a bow around her neck and, anyway, how could she possibly be here? After all, I never told her where I was going.*

Suddenly, it dawned on him what a thoughtless thing he had done. 'Oh, no!' he exclaimed aloud. 'My poor Red Tabby! She must be worried sick.' At the sound of Dylan's voice, the ginger-haired cat with the big, blue bow lifted its face from its paws, and Dylan found himself staring straight into a pair of very familiar eyes.

'It *is* you!' he cried, overjoyed at the sight of his friend. 'Hang on,' he called through the pane of glass separating them. 'I'll get the door open and let you out!' Dylan nudged the latch with his nose, but the door had other ideas and refused to budge, even when he bumped it with his head. Red Tabby's window proved just as stubborn, as did all the others that Dylan could reach.

From inside the cottage, Red Tabby dolefully watched Dylan's valiant but futile attempts, but her rescuer was not about to give up. He trotted around behind the cottage and tried the back door. It, too, was firmly bolted. 'I'll just have to kick it in,' he told himself grimly.

He was about to lash out with his rear hooves when he noticed a milk hatch in the wall; the sort he remembered from his time with Emlyn, the dairyman. He turned its latch with his teeth and pulled open the outer door. Luckily, the inner door was unfastened. He eased it aside with his nose and called through.

'Tabby,' he whinnied. 'Come on! Back here! The kitchen! Quick!' He hardly had time to stand back before Tabby came hurtling through the hatchway, blue bow and all.

'Dylan!' she cried, 'Oh! Dylan!'

Above them, a window rattled open and they saw a dishevelled head poke out. 'What's going on down there?' called a sleepy voice.

'Rats!' hissed Tabby. 'We've woken the lock-keeper. Let's get out of here, or he'll lock us both up for sure.' The sudden clatter of running feet down the cottage stairs confirmed Tabby's fears.

'Get on my back and hold tight, Tabby,' Dylan ordered. Tabby was up in a flash, and in one splendid leap they were over the garden fence and galloping across the adjoining fields. They'd not gone far before Red Tabby, from her vantage point behind Dylan's ears, spied a crop of full-grown elephant grass, and the two friends were soon safely hidden from view amongst its lofty stalks.

'How on earth did you get locked in that cottage?' Dylan demanded when he'd caught his breath. Tabby told him about her trip on the narrowboat, and how she had fallen asleep and had needed to make the blind leap or be taken away far off to the south. 'Trouble is,' she confessed ruefully, 'I leapt off the narrowboat straight into the old lady's arms.'

'I think I saw her leaving the cottage. Is she the one who tied the ribbon around your neck?' asked Dylan with a slight twinkle in his eye.

'She thought I was a stray. Can you imagine?' Tabby admitted, shamefaced. 'But she meant no harm.'

'All the same, dear Tabby,' Dylan went on, 'I almost didn't recognise you in the window because of that bow.'

'I'd have had it off long since,' Tabby groaned, 'but each time I try, it gets into more knots.'

'Jump down and I'll nibble through it with my teeth,' said Dylan. 'I'll be really careful.' Very gently, he chewed away at the ribbon until, at last, Tabby was freed of her unwelcome fashion accessory.

'Oh, thank you, Dylan,' she breathed, and she looked up at him fondly. 'I can't believe I've found you again!' she exclaimed.

'But how did you know where I'd gone?' Dylan asked.

'Your hoof-prints at first,' Tabby told him. 'That's how I guessed you'd left Great Park by the stream. Just luck after that, really. And I was doing well, too, until I went and fell asleep on that narrowboat.'

With the sun warming their backs, the two friends wandered along through the tall rows of elephant grass in thoughtful silence.

'I expect you'd like me to tell you why I went off like that,' Dylan suggested after a while.

'I wouldn't mind,' replied Red Tabby, 'but it's up to you.'

'It's my mother, you see,' Dylan admitted. 'I remembered where she'd been taken to, so I came looking for her.'

'I was starting to guess as much,' Tabby said. 'That's what's been troubling you all summer, isn't it?'

'Well, yes,' admitted Dylan, 'But you see, I didn't realise that until yesterday. Oh, Tabby! We've had such adventures, you and I, and I just wanted her to be part of it all.'

'All right, then,' Red Tabby said briskly. 'We'd better get on with our search.'

Dylan could hardly believe his ears. 'You'll help me? After all the trouble I've caused?'

'That's what friends are for!' said Tabby, 'But we'll need to be quick about it. We can't miss too many rehearsals.'

'But we have all winter for rehearsals,' Dylan protested.

'Not any more,' Tabby replied, and she told him all about Stomper's friend, Banjo, and the Christmas TV Spectacular.

'You're our star, remember!' she finished 'So we've no time to lose. Now! What's your plan?'

'Just asking as I go along,' Dylan admitted. 'My mother is so famous someone is bound to have news of her, aren't they?'

Tabby nodded but, secretly, she had grave doubts.

36

Chia Loses Heart

It was well past teatime. Madame Lulu and Chia had driven down almost every route marked on their map. They had enquired at every village post office and posted notices on every village notice board. They had knocked on farmhouse doors and questioned local innkeepers, but all with no result.

'Someone *must* have seen Dylan,' Chia lamented. 'After all, he's big enough to be noticed even if Red Tabby isn't.'

'Well, we don't know if they're together, and besides, what if Dylan is meaning to keep out of sight?' said Madame Lulu. 'He was nearly kidnapped once before, remember.'

Chia nodded. 'I'm sure you're right, dear lady,' he sighed, and consulted his map for what seemed like the hundredth time.

'At the next fork, bear to the right,' he directed. 'I don't think we've tried down there.'

As Madame Lulu swung into the turning, there came a loud bang. The old horsebox lurched crazily on its towbar, nearly toppling over as the sunshine-yellow car skidded sharply. Chia shut his eyes, bracing himself for the crash.

'Burst tyre,' Madame Lulu remarked calmly as she expertly manoeuvred out of the skid. She braked smoothly and pulled to a stop at the side of the road. 'My poor car's had enough for one day,' she said as they examined the damaged rear tyre.

'But we daren't give up,' blurted Chia, alarmed. 'Dylan and Red Tabby can hardly stay out another night.'

'They're used to fending for themselves,' Madame Lulu reminded him.

'But what if they really are lost to us forever?' Chia cried and, giving way to despair, he hid his face. Madame Lulu took the ringmaster's trembling hands in hers.

'My dear man,' she reasoned. 'We owe it to Dylan and Tabby to keep steady. After all, if they are in trouble, they'll be depending on us for help.'

She gazed with sympathy at Chia, and for a moment the ringmaster found himself quite lost in the depths of her glorious green eyes. 'Come on,' Madame Lulu told him. 'We've got a tyre to change, and then we must get over to the inn or the others will be out looking for us as well.'

At a small crossroads where two leafy lanes met briefly before going their separate ways, and tall hedgerows crowded close, Stomper pulled his motorbike to a halt. 'Time for a council of war,' he announced as he dismounted. Charlie and Ranga jumped off too, glad of a chance to stretch their limbs. Stomper rummaged around in his pockets and shared out his last slab of cake and some fruit. The others joined him on the grassy bank under a hedge and munched hungrily while they reviewed the situation.

'We've searched all the lanes and cart tracks on this map,' Stomper said, 'not to mention the canal. We should have caught up with them by now.'

'But the gypsy's mare saw them both,' argued Ranga. 'So they must have gone this way.'

'But how far?' asked Charlie.

'Exactly! That's what we don't know,' Stomper replied.

'It must be near dinnertime,' said Ranga, whose stomach, despite the snack, was beginning to rumble. 'Maybe the others have had better luck.'

Stomper rose and brushed some bits of dry grass from his trousers. 'The Ancient Oak Inn's not far off,' he said. 'So, for that matter, neither is dinner.'

'Wait a minute!' Charlie broke in. 'The ginger stray! The one the lock-keeper said his mum took in. What if it was Red Tabby?'

'You know,' said Stomper, 'I've been wondering about that very same thing ever since we spoke to him.'

Ranga scratched his head. 'But the lock-keeper said that someone came and stole the ginger stray. Why would anyone want to steal Red Tabby?'

'Wait a bit,' said Stomper. 'What if it wasn't just "anyone"? Suppose it was *actually* Dylan? Maybe rescuing Red Tabby. Who knows? You've had a terrific idea, Charlie. Let's go back to the lock and try again.' And he swung a leg over the motorbike's saddle.

'Dinner can wait as far as I'm concerned,' Charlie agreed as he climbed into his seat in the sidecar.

Ranga clambered up behind Lord Stomper. 'Me too,' he broke in, 'if it means rescuing Dylan and Red Tabby.'

Stomper gunned the engine and, with a rattle and a roar, the motorbike sped off down the lane and disappeared behind the winding hedgerows.

Since the morning's rescue and their chat amid the elephant grass, Red Tabby and Dylan had tramped steadily westwards over the fields. Anyone who looked the least bit friendly was asked for news of Dylan's mother. But no one, it seemed, knew anything whatsoever about Desiree de Polka. The two friends were becoming thoroughly downhearted, and, by now, serious pangs of hunger were adding to their woes.

Red Tabby's large breakfast was long forgotten, and while Dylan enjoyed a tender mouthful of grass here and there and the occasional apple from an orchard, Tabby had not even had the sniff of a passing mouse. A dry-stone wall flanked the lane along which they were passing, and Tabby jumped up onto it, eager to scan the ground on the other side for a much-needed meal.

'Why not ride on my back for a bit?' Dylan suggested as Tabby padded along the wall level with his shoulders.

'While you keep an eye open for mice, you mean?' replied Tabby. 'I'm sorry Dylan, but if I'm to eat I'll need to hunt. Thanks all the same.'

Further along the lane, the outbuildings of a farm enveloped the wall, blocking Tabby's way. She was about to take up Dylan's offer of a ride when she stopped, head up, sniffing the air.

'What is it, Tabby?' asked Dylan. 'A mouse?'

'Something even better,' she answered. 'If I'm not mistaken, it's a dog's dinner.'

'A *dog's* dinner?' exclaimed Dylan. 'But you're a cat!'

'Dinner is dinner!' she replied and disappeared over the wall. Dylan craned his neck to peer after her. Against the side of one of the outbuildings stood a large kennel with the name 'Ripper' painted in rough letters over the doorway. Nearby stood a huge bowl overflowing with a generous helping of jellified meat. Luckily, Ripper wasn't at home, and in a flash Red Tabby was across the yard with her nose in the bowl.

Dylan looked on anxiously from his side of the wall, but Red Tabby was so famished that in a few moments the dog's dinner had disappeared. She was just licking the bowl clean when, around the corner, came the kennel's owner. Dylan gave a whinny of warning. At the same instant, Ripper caught sight of Red Tabby by his now-empty bowl. Realising he'd been cheated of his meal, he ran at her, his snarling jaws dribbling with rage.

'Run, Tabby! Run!' called Dylan, but it was too late – the burly mastiff was upon her. Tabby's back went up in a bristling arch. She puffed out her ginger fur until she appeared twice her normal size. Then, 'flick' went a wickedly sharp claw across the snout of the unfortunate attacker.

The dog dropped back on his haunches, a look of utter astonishment on his face. A ginger blur streaked across the yard and, the next moment, Tabby was tucked up safely on Dylan's back. But the deprived dog did not intend to give up that easily. Barking uproariously, he charged repeatedly at the wall.

'That fox after them pullets again, Ripper?' a deep voice shouted from the farmhouse. 'You keep that red devil at bay, boy, while I fetch my gun.'

Dylan whinnied again in alarm.

'I think we've rather outstayed our welcome,' Tabby remarked calmly as she licked the last of Ripper's meal from her whiskers. But the next thing she and Dylan knew, Ripper had jumped clear over the wall and was snapping and snarling around Dylan's feathered hooves.

'Bang! Bang!' The sharp reports of a double-barrelled shotgun rang out, echoing ominously off the stone outbuildings. Dylan galloped off down the lane as fast as his legs could carry him, with Red Tabby hanging on to his mane and Ripper in hot pursuit.

After some distance, the dog gave up the chase and, with a disappointed 'woof', turned and loped off home. Greatly relieved, Dylan slowed to a walk. He felt badly winded from the long run and it was some time before he could speak. 'You were so brave!' he gasped at last. 'Did you see the look on that poor dog's face?'

'Yes, but that was as close to actually being a dog's dinner as I ever care to get,' Tabby replied firmly. There was a moment's awkward silence between them, then Tabby spoke her mind. 'Dylan,' she began, 'I really don't think we can keep on like this. We're not getting anywhere. Maybe we should just go home.'

Dylan hung his head dejectedly. 'Then how will I ever find my mother?' he asked.

'The others are bound to help us look for her if we ask them,' Tabby responded.

'You're right as always,' he sighed. 'Let's be off then.' And he turned round, thinking they could go back the way they had come.

'We can't just retrace our steps, Dylan,' Red Tabby warned. 'Unless we want to run into that dog again, we'll have to find another way home.'

So Dylan trotted on between the tall banks that all but enclosed the lane. After a time, the distant hum of traffic reached their ears. Gradually, the hum grew to a roar and they saw a busy highway ahead of them.

'That road's too dangerous for us, I'm afraid,' said Red Tabby as cars and trucks whirred past at high speed.

'Then which way *should* we go?' Dylan asked.

'We've been walking more or less west all day,' Tabby reasoned. 'So now we just need to walk more or less east. It's really very simple.'

Dylan looked relieved. 'Good,' he said. 'So which way is east?'

Sitting on her haunches on Dylan's back, Tabby studied the overcast sky with care. Leaden clouds stretched from horizon to horizon. She peered hard at the surrounding landscape. In one direction, a huge, fenced cornfield bordered the highway, its orderly rows marching away into the distance. In the other direction a tangled wood pressed into and over the ditch that ran along the road's edge.

Neither tree nor fencepost cast so much as the hint of a shadow. 'It's no good,' she told him. 'Without the sun, I can't tell east from west.'

'Nor can I,' agreed Dylan as he scanned the grey clouds for even the smallest patch of blue. 'This whole thing's my fault,' he added gloomily, and hung his head.

'Not entirely,' Red Tabby corrected him. 'After all, it's me who ate the dog's dinner. It's my fault we got chased so far out of our way.'

Tabby was just considering where they might spend the night when the road before them briefly emptied of traffic and the din of rushing vehicles gave way to a temporary silence. Then came an oddly familiar sound. 'Putt-putt-putt.' Dylan's ears flicked forward.

'Do you hear that?' he asked.

Tabby looked along the highway and nearly tumbled off Dylan's back with joy as Stomper's motorbike and sidecar came into view. 'It's them!' she yelled. 'It's Stomper and Charlie and Ranga!'

'But they haven't seen us!' cried Dylan desperately as the motorbike swept up the road past them.

Just as he spoke, Charlie rose up in Stomper's sidecar. 'Stop! Stop!' he bellowed to Stomper. 'It's Dylan and Red Tabby. We've found them! We've found them!'

At the same instant, from the other direction, came a sunshine-yellow car with Stomper's tatty old horsebox rattling along behind it. 'It's them! It's really them!' yelled Chia to a delighted Madame Lulu.

Stomper swung his motorbike sharply to the side of the road and reversed while Madame Lulu turned at the next roundabout and drove up to join them. In moments, Chia had the horsebox open and the two weary adventurers climbed gratefully aboard.

'We're not far from the inn,' Stomper told Madame Lulu as he bolted the horsebox door. 'I think I know a quick way. Follow me.'

Stomper turned his motorbike into a twisting, overgrown byway close to where they had all met up, and everyone was soon gathered in the pleasant gardens of the Ancient Oak Inn enjoying a hearty meal.

37

Dylan Tells All

'Now then, Dylan,' began Chia once supper was done, 'what has this all been about?'

The others listened keenly as Dylan told once more how he'd been thinking about his mother all summer long, how he'd seen the Westlands through the bridge, and how he'd set out, on an impulse, to find her. 'I know she's somewhere in those hills, but I don't really know how I know. It's just something I overheard when I was a foal.'

For a while, no one spoke. 'I've put you all to so much bother,' he blurted out at last. 'Especially you, Red Tabby. I'm truly sorry. Really, I am.'

'The thing is, Dylan,' Charlie broke in, 'you're much more likely to find your mother if we all pitch in.' The others murmured agreement, and Dylan looked round at them in wonder, his eyes brimming with gratitude.

'We're going to stay here for the night,' Madame Lulu informed them. 'That way, we can start tomorrow's search at dawn.'

'Animal Rescue and the police need to know that Red Tabby and Dylan are safe,' advised Chia.

'Leave all that to me,' Madame Lulu told him. 'I need to bring the newspapers up-to-date anyway. It's only a couple more phone calls.'

'Perhaps our runaways would like to turn in,' smiled Stomper. 'The landlord should have the stables ready by now.'

'Can we bunk in with you?' asked Charlie and Ranga, eager to learn more about Red Tabby and Dylan's adventures. Dylan happily agreed, but the stables proved so warm and comfortable that, in no time, all four were lost in their dreams.

With Dylan and his companions attended to, Stomper returned to the inn to find Madame Lulu busily feeding coins into the payphone.

'Taking a little holiday, Lord Stomper, sir?' beamed the landlord as Stomper joined Chia at the bar.

'If only I were, Landlord. No, we're still searching for a missing horse.'

'But surely, sir,' the landlord protested, 'you found your horse only today. The ginger cat, too. Why, they're in my stables at this very moment if I'm not mistaken!'

'You're quite right,' agreed Chia, 'but now we are after another – a dray mare, and a famous one at that. Desiree de Polka, no less.'

'She was sold into the Westlands some time back,' Stomper added. 'Perhaps you heard about it at the time.'

The landlord shook his head. 'I can't help you there,' he said. 'But here comes someone who might.'

The old man whom Stomper had consulted on his earlier visit to the inn shuffled over to his usual place on the fireside settle. The landlord nodded in the new arrival's direction. 'Need to know anything about matters in these parts, Lord Stomper, sir, just ask Old Brock. Or so I've been told – time and time again.'

'Draw me a tankard of cider for the gentleman, would you?' Stomper asked, and when the landlord had done so, Stomper took it across to the settle by the fire.

'That's right kind of you, sir,' said Old Brock, taking a long swallow. 'Now then, what manner of thing do you need to know?'

When Stomper explained about Desiree de Polka, the old man's eyes lit up. 'That's what was tickling at the back of my mind last time we met, young fella,' he said. 'Desiree de Polka, the dancer! That poster you showed us when you were here last reminded me of her.'

'That was her foal, Dylan. Full grown now, of course,' Stomper told him.

'Her foal, you say?' said Old Brock and took a few more swallows from the tankard. 'There was a wealthy old coot in these parts took in a fancy horse a while back,' he went on at last. 'Some said it was a bit of a dancer. His place is a bit off the beaten track, mind.'

Old Brock pulled a grubby scrap of paper from his pocket, smoothed it out on the table, and, pulling the stub of a pencil from behind his ear, sketched out a rough map. When he had finished, he squinted at his effort critically then handed it to Stomper. 'See if that doesn't help you out,' he said and turned back to his tankard.

Early the next morning, the little cavalcade set off. Stomper, Charlie and Ranga took the lead on the motorbike while Chia followed behind with Madame Lulu in her car. Dylan rode in relative comfort in the old horsebox with Red Tabby curled up behind his ears.

With only Old Brock's crude map to guide them, Charlie worried that they might lose their way. But after many twists and turns, he looked up at last from his navigations and announced, 'This must be it!'

They turned in at a long, gravelled drive. Ahead of them lay a small manor house flanked on each side by stables and white-fenced paddocks lush with grass.

'My mother's been living in clover all along,' Dylan said to Tabby as he peered through the small window at the front of the horsebox. 'I needn't have worried after all.'

The front door of the house stood open and a young woman could be seen inside, busily pulling things out of packing crates scattered about the hall. She looked up as the searchers drew to a halt by her front step.

'Too bad we don't have a picture of Desiree to show her,' Chia said as the young woman came forward to greet them.

'We have Dylan,' replied Madame Lulu. 'And they're as alike as two peas in a pod.'

'What a fine creature!' the young woman exclaimed as Dylan emerged from the horsebox. 'And what a gorgeous ginger cat!' she added when she caught sight of Red Tabby sitting on Dylan's back.

When Chia explained the purpose of their visit, the young woman shook her head sadly. 'We've only just moved here,' she told him. 'The stables are empty until our own horses arrive next week.'

Dylan, who had been elated moments before, now felt downcast. The young woman shot him a keen glance.

'Come with me,' she said suddenly. 'There's something I want you all to see.' And she led the way towards the empty stables. 'Could that be the mare you are after?' she asked and pointed towards the back of one of the stalls.

'Why, it's a poster of you, Dylan!' exclaimed Chia.

'No!' cried Dylan joyfully, 'It's an old poster of my mother!'

'She looks so special,' the young woman went on. 'I couldn't bring myself to take it down.'

'Do you know who lived here before you?' Madame Lulu asked eagerly.

'A wealthy bachelor gentleman,' the woman replied. 'A bit of an eccentric, I think. We recently bought the property from his estate. He died some time ago.'

'What happened to his horses?' Stomper asked.

'Sold, I suppose,' came the bleak reply. 'I don't really know.'

'Then we're back at square one,' sighed Chia.

With a heavy heart, Dylan climbed back into the horsebox for the journey home. Even Red Tabby couldn't muster her usual optimism. 'We'll go on looking, Dylan,' she promised. 'Really, we will.' But Dylan would not be comforted.

As the old horsebox bumped along behind Madame Lulu's car, Red Tabby, perched on Dylan's back, watched the foliage lining the lanes flash past the small side windows. Several times the horsebox stopped, backed up, and changed direction. *This trip seems to be taking a long time,* she thought. *I don't remember quite so many twists and turns.* When the horsebox stopped yet again, Tabby heard the sound of concerned voices. The rear door opened and Chia poked his head in.

'I fear we've lost our way,' he admitted. 'Charlie tried his best, but we're right off Old Brock's map. You might wish to stretch your legs while we sort things out.'

Stomper and Charlie flattened the rough little map out on the bonnet of the car and studied it this way and that, while Madame Lulu pored over her own big map to see if she could find where they had got to. 'Why don't we just go back the way we came?' suggested Ranga.

'If only we knew which way that was, dear Ranga,' Madame Lulu smiled ruefully.

They had halted at yet another narrow crossroads. The landscape was hilly, and the deep and ancient trackways seemed to weave through it in every imaginable direction, with never a signpost to be seen. Stomper scratched his ear in puzzlement and there was a silence as everyone tried to think what to do.

Dylan stood by Madame Lulu's car, his head hanging down. Seeing him so miserable, Red Tabby leant forward and whispered in his ear. Without looking up, Dylan nodded half-heartedly. 'Dylan and I are going down the road a bit,' Tabby announced. 'Just to see if there are any landmarks that could help us.'

'Don't go too far,' Chia warned. 'We don't want you two getting lost a second time.'

'Are you sure this is a good idea?' Dylan asked as he and Tabby trotted off.

'We'll only go a short way,' Tabby reassured him. 'I'm just curious about what's round that next corner.'

'You and your curiosity!' said Dylan mournfully.

Curiosity doesn't come into it, thought Red Tabby. *I'm giving you something to do, my lad, to take your mind off your disappointment.*

The cart track ran down steeply into a leafy dell and then turned sharply at a high embankment. As Dylan and Red Tabby rounded the bend, they could see the high arch of a red brick viaduct.

'It's a railway line,' said Tabby. 'Let's find out what's beyond it.'

Dylan trotted on until they were almost under the archway. 'Won't the others be wondering about us?' he asked. But his worried words were drowned by a mighty roaring sound that grew and grew in volume until it set the very ground under their feet shaking violently. Above the heads of the startled pair, a sleek green and yellow object thundered over the viaduct and streaked away along the top of the embankment, its horn wailing deafeningly.

By the sunshine-yellow car, Ranga's jaw dropped in amazement as the train, half-hidden by a screen of trees, screamed past, not a stone's throw from where they stood. 'What was that?' he gasped as the roar died away into the distance.

'That was an Intercity Express,' Stomper told him excitedly. 'We must be right next to a mainline railway.'

Everyone gathered around Madame Lulu's map as Stomper traced the mainline route with his finger. 'Here!' he exclaimed after a moment. 'We're right here! Look!'

'Wait a bit, I just heard a whinny,' Charlie interrupted. The others looked up as the sound of hoof beats grew louder. Over the hill came Dylan at full gallop.

'Quick, everyone! Come with me!' he gasped.

Red Tabby was not in her usual place up on his back, and Chia felt a terrible sinking feeling in his stomach. 'What is it, Dylan?' asked Madame Lulu anxiously. 'What's wrong?' But Dylan simply turned and galloped back the way he had come.

Stomper revved up his motorbike and it was all Charlie and Ranga could do to scramble aboard before he was off down the road after the racing horse. As Madame Lulu threw her sunshine-yellow car in gear, Chia clasped his hands in dismay. 'Not another disaster,' he muttered. 'Please! Not another disaster!'

They reached the red brick viaduct to find Dylan standing under the arch, puffing heavily. Red Tabby was still nowhere to be seen. 'Follow me,' Dylan told them as they tumbled out onto the lane. 'But very, very quietly.' Everyone tiptoed through the gloom of the archway, not daring to breathe a word. As they emerged again into the light, they saw a scruffy, triangular paddock set into the shadowed slope of the railway embankment.

To Chia's immense relief, Red Tabby sat perched on the top rail of the fence that closed the paddock in. As they approached, she raised a warning paw. 'Sshh! Come and look, but don't make a sound!'

A painfully thin mare lay amongst the scrub that spilled down the embankment from the railway line above. She was shaking badly, her eyes blank with terror.

'We've found my mother,' said Dylan quietly. 'It's her. I know it.'

'Oh, Dylan, that's hardly likely,' Madame Lulu said gently. 'Remember, we've only arrived at this spot by total accident.'

'But you must admit she does look very like Dylan,' whispered Stomper. 'She has exactly the same colouring.'

The others peered across at the mare with growing wonder. Stomper was right. The likeness *was* remarkable. 'Well, whoever she is, she needs our help,' said Red Tabby firmly.

Charlie, who had made a swift inspection of the paddock fence, gave a low whistle. 'Over here!' he beckoned and, together with Stomper, he and Ranga wrestled open the rusty gate.

Hesitantly, Dylan crossed the dusty space to the emaciated mare and nudged her affectionately with his soft muzzle. 'Mother?' he whispered. 'It's me! Dylan!' But the mare only stared blankly ahead of her.

The rescuers needed all their strength to get the faltering creature upright. She could scarcely stand on her untrimmed hooves, even with Dylan supporting her on one side and Chia and Stomper on the other.

By the time they had managed to ease her into the horsebox and safely secured her beside Dylan, Madame Lulu had worked out their route home. With Stomper once more in the lead and Madame Lulu driving with great care, before too long, the pink stone wall of Great Park loomed up ahead of them. 'You get that poor creature into a stall,' Madame Lulu said. 'I'll call the vet.'

The mare had grown weaker from standing on the journey home and all but collapsed as Stomper, Chia and the others guided her from the horsebox to the stables. She sank into the soft, clean straw with a pitiful sigh and shut her tormented eyes. Dylan's heart nearly broke at the sight.

'She needs fresh water, lots of small meals, and absolute quiet,' advised the vet when she had examined the mare and seen to her hooves. 'She's very lucky you got to her when you did.'

Later, at Red Tabby's tactful suggestion, everyone agreed, for Dylan's sake, to presume that the sick animal was indeed his mother – unless later events should prove otherwise.

38

Trying Times

'Well done, Tiger!' cried Chia as he and Madame Lulu watched the Happy Days performers run through their routines for the coming TV Spectacular. 'Everyone's come on splendidly while we've been away. They truly have!'

'Time for a break,' Tiger called to the troupe who were scattered about in the stable yard that had been their performance arena all summer.

'We've got one major problem, though,' warned Stomper. 'Banjo says we can't hold the Spectacular here.'

'Why ever not?' exclaimed Chia.

'He says outdoors won't do in case it rains.'

'Don't they have brollies?' asked Irma, who had joined the little circle.

'They probably do, Irma,' smiled Madame Lulu, 'but I expect they're more worried about their television equipment.'

'If only we had enough money to buy our new Big Top,' sighed Lion who had sidled up to see what the conference was all about.

'Even if we did, I doubt it would be ready in time,' said Chia.

'I know what!' cried Irma. 'How about that old empty hangar? The one we were locked up in, remember?'

'Do I remember?' Lion groaned.

'Well, it's certainly big enough.' Tiger agreed.

'And it's waterproof,' added Marmaduke.

'I wonder who the owner is?' mused Chia.

'Suppose I find out?' offered Stomper. 'There's a solicitor pal of mine down in the town. I could ask him to look into it.'

The days that followed were full of hectic preparations. Between rehearsals, Dylan spent all his time with his mother, coaxing her to eat and drink what little she would. With Stomper and Chia's help, Red Tabby and Dylan moved Desiree to a stall at the far end of the stables so the sound of rehearsals wouldn't disturb her peace. They shifted their own sleeping quarters too, in order to stay close to her. Each morning Dylan woke with the fervent hope that perhaps today his mother might recognise him. 'Please get well again,' he would beg. 'I have so much to tell you and so many questions to ask.' But Desiree would only lie listlessly, gazing at the wall.

The Happy Days Circus troupe did their best at rehearsals, but it was hard to stay cheerful knowing that Desiree was weakening with each passing day. 'She can't go on like this,' the vet warned. The troupe had gathered round to hear the report, and the news was not good. 'It's not simply an illness, you see,' the vet explained. 'It's as if her spirit is broken. She must have suffered terribly.' Dylan turned his head so the anguish that he felt might not show.

'But someone, somewhere, has to be able to help her!' Chia insisted.

'I'm afraid the only one who can help Desiree now is Desiree herself,' the vet replied.

'You mean that she herself must decide to get better?' Madame Lulu asked.

The woman nodded. 'That's exactly it,' she agreed. The others looked at each other in dismay.

'But how can she when she's so weak?' blurted out Tabby.

'I fear you're right,' the vet admitted, thoughtfully. 'You know, perhaps what we need is a horse-whisperer.'

Late that night the telephone at the foot of the grand staircase rang. Everyone was already in bed, except Madame Lulu who was coming from the kitchen with milk for hot chocolate. She grabbed the receiver on the second ring. It was the Animal Rescue vet.

'Sorry to call so late. I've made some enquiries,' the vet told her. 'There's only one horse-whisperer worth the name in these parts, and I had a difficult time tracking him down. By the sound of it, he's fallen on hard times. But there's no question he's the man you want. He was once the best in the business.'

Madame Lulu searched about for a pencil and scribbled down the address the vet read out to her. 'Thank you,' she said. 'A thousand times, thank you.'

She had just hung up when Ringmaster Chia came padding down the grand staircase in his dressing gown and slippers. 'I heard the phone,' he said. 'Any news?'

'Yes,' Madame Lulu replied. 'Our vet's found the horse-whisperer.'

'Thank goodness for that!' said Chia, hugely relieved. 'We'll call him first thing in the morning.'

'Can't do that,' said Madame Lulu. Chia's face fell. 'No phone,' she explained. 'We'll have to go in person.'

Parked in the corner of a muddy field, the old railway carriage presented a mournful picture. The paint of its once-bright livery hung in great, peeling flakes. Torn, filthy curtains hung at its windows. A clutch of mangy-looking red hens pecked about in the mud outside its door, while patched and mended clothing fluttered on a nearby sagging clothesline.

'Oh, what a forlorn scene!' cried Chia in dismay. He, along with Red Tabby, Madame Lulu and Stomper, had risen early that morning and, following the vet's directions, had just arrived at the home of the horse-whisperer.

'She did say the man had fallen on hard times,' Madame Lulu reminded him.

'Let's hope he hasn't lost his knack,' said Stomper.

Chia looked round at the others. 'Well, nothing ventured, nothing gained. Are we agreed?'

Dylan had remained behind with his mother, and everyone knew he was counting on them to succeed in their mission. They all nodded. Chia pushed open the gate that led into the muddy field.

The hens, clucking indignantly, scattered in all directions as the little party made its way up the path towards the carriage. There appeared to be no one about. Chia knocked vigorously at the carriage door and waited. Nobody stirred.

Stomper pointed to a faint wisp of smoke rising lazily from a little stump of a chimney. 'Look!' he said. 'Someone must be in.'

Chia knocked again, but still nothing moved. 'Is anyone at home?' he called in a loud, clear voice. 'We need the horse-whisperer. We've a mare in a very bad way.' There was silence except for the clucking of the hens.

'What on earth are we going to do?' asked Red Tabby, her disappointment reflected in every face. Chia shrugged helplessly.

They were about to turn away when there came a rattle and scrape, and the door of the carriage edged cautiously ajar.

'What've you come disturbing poor folk for?' came a harsh and eerily familiar voice.

They stared up in alarm at the worn and haggard face peering down at them from the doorway. Red Tabby was the first to regain her composure. 'Dangerous Dennis!' she breathed. Chia's eyes flashed and his face flushed.

'Snakes alive,' whispered Stomper. 'Look at the state of the man!'

'*You're* the horse-whisperer?' gasped Madame Lulu.

At that moment, the gaunt man caught sight of Red Tabby and recognition flooded his worn features. 'I know you lot! Get away from me,' he rasped. 'Push off!'

Chia swallowed hard. 'You've got to help us. We're desperate.'

'If you really are the horse-whisperer, you're our only hope,' added Stomper.

'So that fancy dancer needs me now, does 'e?' asked Dennis with a bitter laugh. 'Why should I 'elp 'im after all 'e's put me through?'

'But it's not Dylan,' protested Madame Lulu. 'It's his mother, Desiree de Polka.'

Dennis reeled back as if struck. For a fleeting instant he stared with fear-haunted eyes at his visitors. Then the door slammed shut and they heard a loud 'click' as the bolt shot home.

Chia stepped back in dismay and there was anguish in his voice when next he spoke. 'There's no help for us here,' he said. 'I'm afraid we've come on a fool's errand.'

They had already reached the gate when the sound of running footsteps made them pause. A short, tubby man came hurrying towards them. He was running so fast that his fat little body got ahead of his stumpy legs, and he sprawled full length on the muddy ground. 'It's Clumsy!' cried Red Tabby, amused despite herself, by the comical display. Clumsy picked himself up and, with a final spurt, reached the gate and skidded to a stop.

'Ssshh! Not a sound!' he hissed, and he ushered the astonished foursome out through the gate and down the road until the railway carriage was well out of view.

'If he catches sight of me speaking to you, he'll just turn more stubborn,' said Clumsy. Totally mystified, they could do nothing but stare at him. 'I was pegging out the washing when you came knocking, Mr Chia, sir,' he went on. 'Couldn't help overhearing, you see, from behind my clothesline, like. I knows he turned you down, sir, but leave him to me. I'll get him to help you, I promise.'

'But why? How? I mean what's in it for you?' Chia burst out, completely bewildered.

Clumsy eyed his visitors nervously and gathered his thoughts before replying. 'Here's the thing, Mr Chia, sir,' he began haltingly. 'You only knows one side of Mr Dennis. Not a pretty side, I'll grant you, but he was a good boss once, long, long ago. Could be again, for all I know. Now, if he was to get that sick mare of yours back up on her feet, maybe he could look the world in the eye again. Get back to his old self. Not the old self you were acquainted with, mind you,' he blundered on, 'but his proper old self, see? That's if you follows me, sir.' It was the longest speech the little man had ever made in his life, and he shifted anxiously from one foot to the other as he waited for Chia's response.

'So Dangerous Dennis was once a horse-whisperer. Who would ever have thought it?' Chia said half to himself. He recalled the haggard face that had glared at them through the carriage doorway and shot Clumsy a keen look. 'He looks a broken man. Is he still up to it?'

'He will be or my name isn't Clumsy Golightly,' Clumsy replied earnestly.

'Give us a minute, will you?' said Chia and he drew the others aside.

'By rights we should go back and ask Dylan first,' advised Madame Lulu.

'And you, Red Tabby,' added Stomper. 'After all, it was you two who suffered most at Dangerous Dennis's hands.'

Sitting on her haunches at the road's edge, tail curled neatly round her paws, Red Tabby looked thoughtfully from one anxious face to another. 'Well,' she began slowly, 'Dangerous Dennis gave a big start when he heard the name "Desiree de Polka". Did anyone else notice?'

The others nodded. 'Just as if he'd seen a ghost,' agreed Stomper.

'If we only knew what made him do that,' Tabby went on, 'maybe we'd know if we could trust him – after all, he is our one hope.'

'You've hit the nail on the head, Tabby,' said Madame Lulu.

Clumsy looked at the ground and shuffled uncomfortably when Chia put Tabby's question to him. 'I don't know all the ins and outs of all that,' protested the little man.

'Tell us what you can, then,' said Madame Lulu firmly. 'Desiree is seriously ill and we've no time to waste.'

Clumsy took a deep breath. 'It was all many years ago, see? Seems there was this grand young mare. The mare what made Mr Dennis *want* to work with horses in the first place, or so I've heard.'

'And was that grand young mare Desiree de Polka?' asked Stomper.

'That's what he won't let on about, your Lordship, sir,' replied Clumsy. 'What I *does* know is that whenever Mr Dennis hears that name, he comes over all peculiar, like. Only happened a few times, but it's the name what does it.'

The foursome stared at the little man standing there on the road before them, nervously wringing his chubby hands, his expression a strange mixture of hope, fear and resolve. Red Tabby gave a slight nod to Chia. 'If you can get him to help us,' Chia told Clumsy finally, 'we'll hope to let bygones be bygones.'

A look of relief crossed Clumsy's face. 'You won't regret it, Mr Chia, sir. I promise you,' he said, 'but I'll need a night to bring him round.'

Chia nodded. Everyone watched in silence as Clumsy scuttled away down the road.

'I hope he succeeds for Desiree's sake,' sighed Chia when Clumsy had turned in at the gate and disappeared from view.

'And for Dylan's,' added Stomper.

'Well,' said Red Tabby solemnly, 'we've got nothing to lose by finding out.'

39

Fresh Pastures

The phone at the foot of the grand staircase was ringing off the hook as they got back to Great Park. Stomper dashed in to answer it while Ringmaster Chia and Madame Lulu went off to find Tiger and see how rehearsals were going.

Red Tabby sought out Dylan in the stables and broke the awkward news about the horse-whisperer and how he'd turned out to be Dangerous Dennis, now fallen upon hard times. At first, Dylan loathed the idea of letting his old enemy come anywhere near his mother. But then Tabby told him of the remarkable effect Desiree's name had had upon Dennis.

'And after all, Dylan,' she went on, 'the vet did say he was once the best in the business.'

Dylan was still unconvinced, but before he could say more, there came the 'putt-putt-putt' of Stomper's motorbike.

'My solicitor friend's got news about the hangar,' Stomper called as he rode off past the stables. 'Tell Madame Lulu I've gone to see him, would you?' And he set off for the town.

Dylan remained quiet for a moment, gazing towards the stall where his mother lay, and then he turned to Red Tabby. 'You are always so wise,' he told her. 'If you really think we should give ...' He paused, finding it hard to even *say* the name.

'… give Dangerous Dennis a try,' he went on, 'I won't say "no". But it scares me all the same.'

In the forecourt of his solicitor friend's office, Stomper pulled his motorbike to an abrupt stop and raced inside.

'I've got some answers for you, old chum,' the man announced as Stomper threw himself into a chair before the old mahogany desk. 'Terrific!' said Stomper. 'What's the story?'

Aubrey Winsome peered owlishly over a pair of trendy spectacles. 'I've dug up all the old paperwork from the Land Registry, and – well – I think you're in for a bit of a surprise.'

Stomper leaned forward eagerly. 'You mean you've found the owner? Great work! Do you reckon they'd let us use it for our Television Spectacular?'

'That depends,' said his friend with a mischievous twinkle.

'On what?'

'On you, old pal,' came the breezy reply.

'Why me?'

'Because it's yours. Not just the old hangar, but the land too. The whole lot.'

'Hangar? Land?' blurted Stomper.

'A very great deal of land.'

Stomper let out a whoop.

'A long time back, the Ministry of Defence leased it all from the former owner of Great Park for use as an air base,' Winsome explained. 'You bought the place when? Ten years ago?'

Stomper nodded. Winsome checked his notes and went on. 'The lease was still in force then, but it recently expired.'

He pushed some paperwork towards Stomper. 'It's all set down in here in black and white,' he said. 'The hangar and the land. To do with as you please.'

When Stomper got home, he found the Happy Days troupe huddled together in the stable yard.

'Hi, everyone! I've got some incredible news!' he called as he pulled to a halt on his motorbike. 'Banjo can use the hangar for the TV spectacular. Aubrey says it's ours, with all the land around it.' But his cheery announcement met with only sombre looks and silence. 'What's wrong? What's happened?' He asked, looking anxiously around the circle of solemn faces.

'It's Desiree,' explained Tiger. 'She's taken a turn for the worse. Madame Lulu and Chia have gone to fetch the vet.'

No one felt able to return to rehearsals. Instead, they hung about the stable doors, whispering together in little groups. When, at last, the vet arrived, she remained with Desiree and Dylan for a long time. 'She's losing strength,' the vet said when she came out of the stables. 'It's almost as if she's starving herself on purpose. I only hope that man, Dennis, agrees to help.'

'We won't know until tomorrow, I'm afraid,' Chia told her despondently.

The night hours seemed to crawl by and it was a bleary-eyed Chia who took his place in the sunshine-yellow car with Madame Lulu early next morning. Everyone was out to wave them off – everyone, that is, except Dylan, who dared not leave his mother's side, and Red Tabby who, by now, dared not leave Dylan's.

Once the car had disappeared down the drive, Tiger stepped forward briskly. 'Now, now,' he said, 'moping about won't help Desiree get better. We have a TV Spectacular coming up and we have to be ready.' As the troupe got back to work, the big striped cat turned to Lion. 'I'm worried, I don't mind telling you,' he confided. 'If Desiree doesn't recover, I fear for poor Dylan's mind.'

'Then bang goes the Spectacular,' said Lion.

'That too,' agreed Tiger gravely.

The sea lion pups were too small to understand what was happening to Desiree, but they were upset just the same. 'Let's take them down to the stream,' Bandmaster Sea Lion suggested to their mother, Celia. 'A good swim and a bit of juggling practice will soon take their minds off it all.' Sure enough, they hadn't been in the water long before their usual cheerful spirits returned.

While Celia watched from the bank, Sea Lion and the pups formed a wide circle in the sparkling water and soon coloured balls were flying back and forth from one shiny nose to the next. Every so often, their mother batted in another ball until more than a dozen were whirling from nose to nose.

'Whoopee!'

The sudden shout from behind her made Celia wheel around in alarm. There, in the undergrowth, a small brown animal hopped up and down clapping madly.

'Whoopee!' the creature shouted again. 'That's what I call juggling!'

Balls tumbled off noses and into the stream as all heads turned towards the unexpected and enthusiastic audience. The sea lion pups stared transfixed at the stranger. They had never seen anything like it before and scarcely knew what to make of its long tail, short front legs and long ears.

'Are you a giant rabbit?' the youngest pup asked. The stranger laughed merrily.

'Why! You must be a kangaroo!' exclaimed Celia, who had spotted the stranger's pouch.

'Right on!' came the reply, and the young kangaroo hopped from the bushes to the stream bank in one single hop. The pups' mouths fell open in surprise. 'I'm Roo,' she announced in a broad Australian accent. 'Don't blame me. I didn't choose me name, sport. There's some bear or other called "Pooh" and they named me after his old pal Kanga's joey.'

'Then why aren't you called "Joey"?' one of the sea lion pups piped up.

Roo let out another burst of laughter. 'Joey's just another word for pup or cub. You know … offspring! Kind of funny, isn't it? Naming a kangaroo after someone's offspring, what with kangaroos always springing off and all.' By now, the pups were thoroughly confused. 'Oh, don't mind me,' said Roo, and she laughed her merry laugh again.

'But what made you come here?' Sea Lion wanted to know.

'The rooks,' Roo explained. Sea Lion was mystified. 'They're telling everyone,' Roo went on. 'Spreading the word, like.'

'The word about what?' asked Sea Lion.

'About this being a good place to come,' Roo explained. 'If you're homeless, that is.'

'Don't you have a home?' asked one of the pups in a small voice.

'I did, but they got bored with me, or so I heard them say. Took me for a drive not long back and dumped me out on the road – and me only a teenager, too.'

'That's terrible!' said Celia, her large eyes brimming with concern.

'And it's not like I didn't do my best,' Roo went on. 'I even taught myself to juggle just to keep them entertained.'

'You can juggle?' asked Sea Lion in wonder.

'I'll show you if you like,' Roo offered, and fished about in her pouch. Before long, she had a swirl of little balls spinning in the air. With a deft flick she sent one, then another, flying towards the surprised sea lion pups. Without missing a beat, one of the pups caught the first ball on his nose, then the next and the next, passing each ball along to the next waiting nose. In no time a flurry of balls were flying to and fro between Roo and the sea lion family. Celia slapped her flippers together in delight. Then, one by one, Roo caught the balls again and popped them back in her pouch.

'Is that a pocket?' asked one of the pups.

Again, Roo laughed. 'Sort of, mate!' she said.

Sea Lion suddenly realised that, in the excitement, all their own big coloured balls had floated off down the stream, and he and the pups swam off to retrieve them. 'So do you think they'll let me bunk down then?' Roo asked Celia.

'Well, Lord Stomper is very generous,' she replied.

Roo's face fell. 'Don't have much truck with lords and such where I come from,' she said.

'Oh! I'm really not sure if he's that sort of lord,' Celia told her. 'All I know is he's a famous pop star, or used to be at any rate.'

'Well that's right enough then,' said the young kangaroo, and her sharp little face brightened.

Sea Lion and his pups came splashing back, pushing their juggling balls ahead of them. At the same moment, the sharp beep of a car horn sounded from the direction of the big house.

'That's Madame Lulu's car,' cried Sea Lion. 'They're home!'

'Who's Madame Lulu?' asked Roo. But in their eagerness to find out if the horse-whisperer had arrived, the sea lion family rushed off, leaving Roo staring after them.

40

The Enemy Within

The sound of Madame Lulu's horn brought the whole Happy Days Circus troupe hurrying to the big house. Everyone wanted to know if Clumsy had managed to persuade Dangerous Dennis to come and save Desiree's life. Only Dylan and Red Tabby were missing, for they were still by Desiree's side watching over her.

The Meerkat Clowns chattered nervously amongst themselves as the sunshine-yellow car pulled up. Its front doors opened and Chia and Madame Lulu climbed out. Without a word, they reached over and opened the back doors. Lion and Tiger tensed; Ranga and Charlie exchanged uneasy glances; and Prudence hid her face behind Irma's trunk.

For a moment, time seemed to stand still. Then, Clumsy emerged, blinking in the sunlight, followed slowly by Dangerous Dennis. An apprehensive gasp went up from the assembled troupe at the sight of their arch-enemies actually standing inside Great Park. But painful memories swiftly gave way to pity as they saw how ragged and run-down the two villains had become.

'Even so, I never thought I'd see the day,' whispered Tiger.

'Nor me,' muttered Lion.

Dennis and Clumsy stood in the drive, warily eyeing the watching troupe – Lion and Tiger in particular.

'We'll just get your things inside then I'll take you straight to our patient,' said Chia. As he opened the boot of Madam Lulu's car, a bundle of feathers engulfed him and squawking chickens flew in all directions.

'Where did all these come from?' asked the startled Chia.

'I shoved 'em in, last minute like,' Clumsy bleated. 'I couldn't leave 'em on their own, now could I, Mr Chia, sir? You know. In case of foxes.'

Chia shook his head wearily and led Clumsy and Dennis towards the big house, feathers trailing in their wake.

'Kind to chickens now, is he?' remarked Ranga.

'Maybe he and Dangerous Dennis really have turned over a new leaf,' said Prudence, who was always ready to find the best in anyone.

'Maybe so,' said Tiger, doubtfully. 'All the same, we'd better keep a sharp eye on them while they're here. I'll take the first watch, Lion, if you'll take the second.' Lion nodded.

'I must be daft 'elping this lot,' Dangerous Dennis grumbled as he and Clumsy settled into their quarters. He had made it clear to Chia and Madame Lulu that it might take time for Desiree to get well. Since the old railway carriage lay too far away to get back and forth from each day, Lord Stomper had agreed to let the two men stay at Great Park for as long as was needed.

'This is nice,' said Clumsy, looking around the neat little room. It was high up under the eaves and two tall dormer windows looked out over the woodlands of Lord Stomper's estate. 'This and three square meals a day can't be all that bad, Boss.'

Dylan felt a shiver run through him when the stable door opened and Chia ushered in his old enemies. Stretched out on a rail above the manger in Dylan's stall, Red Tabby looked down on her trembling friend and held her breath. Dennis shot a furtive glance at Dylan, then turned to Chia.

'Where is she then?' he asked gruffly. Chia pointed silently to the stall next to Dylan's. The mare lay on the clean straw, her eyes fixed dully on the back wall, her sides heaving in and out with the effort of breathing. 'Get me a low stool,' Dennis muttered, his voice cracking strangely. Chia rummaged about and came back with a small wooden crate.

'Will this do?'

Dennis took the crate brusquely and for a long moment stood clutching it to his chest, looking down at the mare. Then he shook his head as if to break off a train of thought. 'Clear out all of you and let me get on with it,' he demanded without looking around.

'Come with me, Clumsy,' said Chia. 'We'll find a proper spot for all those chickens.'

'You'd better come away too, Dylan,' suggested Red Tabby and she jumped down onto his back. The stable door closed behind them and Dennis was left alone in the stall with the sick mare. High overhead, Tiger's steely eye gleamed through a knothole in the loft floor.

Dennis gently set the little wooden crate down in the straw at the back of the stall. With infinite care he settled himself on it, his elbows resting on his knees, eyes fixed on his patient's suffering face. For a long while, except for the mare's laboured breathing, the two figures remained as still as statues.

''Allo again, old girl,' Dennis managed at last. His voice sounded hauntingly tender. 'Remember me?' He waited. Slowly, very slowly, Desiree lifted up her head and looked at him.

Forever after, Tiger swore that when Desiree turned her head towards Dennis, a bright tear glistened in the horse-whisperer's eye and rolled silently down his craggy cheek.

In the hours and days that followed, no one in the Happy Days troupe crossed the stable yard without wondering and worrying about the drama unfolding behind the closed stable doors. But there was nothing whatever they could do except get on with their rehearsals for the Christmas TV Spectacular.

'Ringmaster Chia, I'd like to present Roo,' announced Sea Lion one morning. Chia bowed and shook the little newcomer by the paw.

'Bandmaster tells me you're a dab hand at juggling, Miss Roo,' he said courteously.

'Too right! Watch this!' said Roo at once, and she began plucking the little balls from her pouch and flinging them into the air until there was nothing but a blurred circle of colour spinning from her flashing paws. 'I've been practising ever since I got here,' she boasted, hopping from one foot to the other as she concentrated on the whirling spheres. 'I can keep twenty in the air at once now.'

'Twenty?' marvelled Chia.

With a flourish, Roo held open the mouth of her pouch and the little balls streamed in like a string of pearls into a bag. Chia clapped in delight, but Roo hadn't finished yet. 'I shadowbox too,' she announced proudly. Up went her front paws, clenched into two tiny fists. Round and round she danced, feinting and jabbing at her own shadow until Ringmaster Chia and Bandmaster Sea Lion became quite dizzy watching her. Faster and faster she went, bobbing and weaving, until it seemed that her shadow really had become another Roo – matching blow for blow with its twin. Then, with a mighty swing, the 'shadow' landed Roo a huge wallop on the jaw. Down she went at the feet of the astonished ringmaster.

'Roo! Roo!' cried Sea Lion. 'Are you all right?'

Roo opened one eye and a grin cracked her sharp little face. 'Not too shabby, eh, sport?' she asked, and scrambled to her feet. 'Mind you, it works best on a really sunny day,' she added with a squint at the hazy sky.

'I think it will do admirably, sunshine or shower,' beamed the ringmaster. 'Tiger should be here any minute. Why don't you two go along and see him? I'm sure, if everyone agrees, Miss Roo can be fitted into the Spectacular somewhere.'

The sun streamed in at the ballroom's tall windows. Its rays bounced off the long, gilded mirrors and flooded the space with golden light. On the floor lay a rumpled sea of glowing material. Prudence knelt amongst rainbow waves of cloth, carefully cutting along the outlines of a paper pattern with a huge pair of scissors. A long rack, set against a far wall, held numerous costumes in various stages of completion. Madame Lulu came bustling in, her arms loaded down with yet more items of wardrobe.

'Irma will look like the Queen of Sheba in her new cape!' Prudence exclaimed, her eyes dancing with enthusiasm.

'Has Red Tabby seen her new waistcoat?' asked Madame Lulu.

'Not yet,' answered Prudence, 'but she's due any minute.'

'And here I am!' announced Red Tabby as she padded through the glass doors that opened from the terrace. Prudence eagerly held out the waistcoat for Tabby to try on.

'Oh, it's so stylish!' Tabby purred happily and turned this way and that to catch every angle in the long mirrors.

'We're working on another one for the second act. One with tails,' said Prudence with evident pride.

'Can I see?' asked Red Tabby.

'So far we only have the sketch,' Madame Lulu admitted. 'I have it somewhere.' And she began rummaging through piles of patterns and papers on the big cream sofa.

Red Tabby cocked her head to one side and listened intently. 'What's that noise?' she asked. From somewhere behind the long mirrors came the rhythmic 'boom-boom' of a drum and just the faintest hint of a melody. 'It seems to be music.'

'Well, that'll make a change,' Madame Lulu remarked wryly. 'We've had to suffer it all week long, and for the most part it's just sounded like a lot of squeaks and bangs.'

'It's coming from the old billiard room,' said Tabby. 'Let's go and look. Maybe our bandmaster has found a new place to practise.'

The big door to the billiard room was fastened tight shut. Peering in through the glass side-panels, Tabby could just make out some tall black boxes piled up at the far end. An urgent murmur of voices now replaced the peculiar musical noises they had heard a moment before. Tabby's curiosity could bear it no longer. She knocked loudly. Almost at once, the door opened a crack and Marmaduke's head poked out.

'Tabby! Prudence! Madame Lulu!' he exclaimed in surprise. 'What are you all doing here? This is supposed to be a secret rehearsal.'

'It can't be all that secret if we can hear you back in the ballroom,' Tabby countered.

Stomper loomed up behind Marmaduke, a big grin on his face. 'Well, Marmaduke,' he said, 'If we were going to get found out, it was bound to be by Red Tabby. What do you say we let them in?'

Dancing Dog poked his little head out between Stomper's long legs. 'Yes! Yes!' he cried. 'They can be our first audience.'

Stomper opened the doors wide and ushered the three intruders into the room. The place was a tangle of wires. The old billiard table stood stacked high with reams of sheet music. Beside the imposing red-marble fireplace, the shiny chrome of Dancing Dog's drums winked and gleamed. Bandmaster Sea Lion, half-hidden amongst black amplifiers and loud-speakers, was studying one of the music sheets, humming and beating time with his flipper. Stomper cleared his throat politely.

'Oh!' Sea Lion exclaimed, and hastily tried to push the sheet out of sight.

'I'm afraid it's too late for that,' Lord Stomper laughed.

'Just what are you four up to?' asked Madame Lulu, whose sense of curiosity could be almost as great as Red Tabby's.

'Well, the thing is,' Sea Lion began, 'Lord Stomper and I have … well, that is to say … well, we all wanted to do something to cheer Dylan up, and so, well, along with Dancing Dog and Marmaduke …'

'We've written a tune for him,' said Stomper coming to Sea Lion's rescue. 'Would you like to hear it?'

A chorus of 'yes-es' and 'oh please-es' assured him that they would. Stomper picked up his electric guitar from its stand, Marmaduke took his place at the keyboard, and Dancing Dog settled in behind his drums.

'The fingering's quite tough on this number,' admitted Stomper as he fine-tuned a string on his instrument.

'Bandmaster's had me practising to get me limbered up.' He looked round at his fellow musicians and smiled. 'I'm ready when you are, Bandmaster,' he said, and Sea Lion raised his flipper.

'In a-one-and-a-two …' and away they went.

The little audience watched open-mouthed as Stomper's fingers flew over the frets. 'Now that's real talent!' hollered Marmaduke, his long fingers pounding out the accompanying rhythm on his keyboard.

'Play it again! Play it again!' begged Red Tabby when the tune was done, and the little band gladly obliged – not once, but twice more, right through.

'Dylan must hear it as soon as possible,' Madame Lulu enthused. 'You're right! It's exactly the tonic he needs.'

That night, the whole troupe crowded into the billiard room. 'Ladies and gentlemen,' cried Sea Lion, in an imitation of Chia's best centre-ring voice, 'it is my great pleasure to welcome this evening, as the newest member of the Happy Days Circus Band, the one and only Lord Stomper!' A volley of honks, barks and trumpetings greeted his announcement. When the excitement had died down, Sea Lion continued in his own voice. 'It's a brand new song,' he told them, 'and we've only ever played it right through three times, so please forgive any mistakes.'

Stomper's eyes sought out Dylan, standing at the back. 'This is for you, Dylan,' he said simply. 'It's for your tap routine – so we've called it "Duelling Hooves".'

Madame Lulu had been right. Stomper and Sea Lion's 'Duelling Hooves' proved exactly the tonic Dylan needed. Next morning,

Red Tabby was not at all surprised to find him off by himself, humming the new tune and fitting his dance steps to its rhythms. Dylan looked up shyly when she came in, but Red Tabby merely smiled her encouragement and went on her way.

41

The Fight to Save Desiree

Right from the start, Dangerous Dennis had scarcely left Desiree's side. Night after night he'd bring his blankets into the stables and sleep on the straw close to her. In the loft overhead, Tiger kept silent watch through the long hours, relieved from time to time when Lion, padding on silent paws, arrived to take his turn at the knothole. It had taken Dennis four days of patient effort before he could get Desiree to her feet, and now she stood in her stall trembling and panting from the effort.

'She's bin lyin' down for too long,' he complained gruffly when Chia praised him for his achievement. 'You should've called me sooner.' But by week's end, Desiree could be seen with Dennis, walking slowly round the stable yard in the quiet of an evening.

Keeping well out of view as Chia had instructed, the Happy Days troupe marvelled at the sight of the mare tagging after Dennis – her head nodding close to his as he murmured in her ear.

By the start of the second week she had even been persuaded to go as far as the paddock, but the horse-whisperer was still far from happy. 'Trouble is,' he confided to Clumsy, 'she does all right as long as I'm with 'er, but as soon as me back's turned ...' Dennis shook his head and walked off, muttering.

One day, Clumsy got back to the little room under the eaves to find his boss stretched out on one of the beds. 'Stable lost its charm, has it?' Clumsy ventured mischievously. He'd spent the afternoon making repairs to the roof of Lord Stomper's east wing and was feeling pleased with himself.

'Don't you be cheeky,' Dennis snapped back. 'Without a decent night's kip, I won't 'old up.'

'Sorry, Boss,' said the little man. 'So how's it going then?'

'I still can't make 'er notice nothin' about what's round 'er,' Dennis complained, banging a fist to his brow in frustration. 'Lost me touch, I 'ave.'

'Not bloomin' likely,' Clumsy protested. 'You have the gift.'

Dennis turned over and pulled the blanket around his shoulders. 'Maybe so,' he muttered. 'But I'm missin' somethin' all the same.' It was a long time before he could manage to fall asleep.

A few days later, Dylan went into the stables with a big bunch of Stomper's finest carrots. Desiree, he knew, was out with Dennis in the paddock, and he dropped the carrots in her manger in the hope that the treat would cheer her when she returned. He was about to leave when the stable door suddenly flew open. There, in the rectangle of light, loomed the silhouette of the horse-whisperer. 'Dylan! Get yourself out 'ere!' he ordered harshly. 'And be quick about it!' Dylan felt himself bridle at the strident command. 'Come on, Dylan!' shouted Dennis. 'Get on with it! It's all up to you now.'

Born to obey! Born to obey! The dreadful words echoed in Dylan's mind and the memory of that terrible encounter in the mud and rain surged over him. With a struggle, he controlled the feelings rising inside him and forced himself to step out into the stable yard. Tiger rose silently from his watching place in the loft and slipped off to fetch Red Tabby and the others.

'I've cracked it!' cried Dylan's old tormentor in a voice shaking with emotion. 'It's bin starin' me in the face all along! Simple, it is. Come on, Dylan – all you 'as to do is dance!'

Dylan gave a bleak whinny and looked away. *My mother's life is in danger,* he thought. *How's dancing going to help?*

'Listen, Dylan,' Dennis persisted, 'You were only a bit of a foal when she saw you last. Now you're all grown up, you look different to her, like. But she'll know you right enough if you'll only tap those hooves! Then p'raps she'll start gettin' well. See?'

Dylan didn't quite, but he nodded his head anyway.

'Stay put,' said Dennis, 'I'll be right back,' and he strode out of the yard towards the paddock.

The rain had stopped and the flagstones of the stable yard glistened in the weak morning sun. Alerted by Tiger that something important was afoot, first one then another of the Happy Days troupe gathered at a discreet distance, all anxious to see what might come of Dennis's sudden inspiration. Clumsy stood shyly to one side, his chubby hands clasping and unclasping in nervous anticipation for his boss. Everyone watched as the horse-whisperer led Desiree up from the paddock. She came along listlessly, her head hanging down, her steps laboured and slow.

Dennis halted when they reached the centre of the yard. 'Stay there my beauty,' he whispered and hurried across to where Dylan, still uncertain of quite what was expected of him, stood waiting. 'Come on now, Dylan! Dance!' he commanded in a voice that hissed with intensity. 'Dance like you've never danced before!'

Dylan took one look at his mother's sad, blank expression and suddenly everything Dennis had said started to make sense to him. He took a deep breath to calm himself, and then he began. 'Tip-tip-tippity tap' went his front hooves. 'Tap-tap-tappity tip' his back hooves replied. Desiree raised her head, confusion on her face. 'Tip-tip-tippity tap' Dylan's hooves went again. 'Tap-tap-tappity, tip'. A distant memory seemed to flicker in the sick mare's eyes, but it vanished as swiftly as it had come.

'I know what's missing,' Red Tabby whispered to Stomper. 'We need music.' Stomper raced off and quickly returned with a guitar. 'Tap-tip-tappity tip' went Dylan once more. Stomper picked up the beat, strumming the opening bars of 'Duelling Hooves.' Dylan gave him a grateful look. 'Tippity-tap. Tap-tappity tip' went the hooves. 'Strum-strum, strummety-strum' went the guitar. 'Tip-tap, tip-tap, tip-tap tum' Dylan's hooves kept on.

Slowly, Desiree began to follow Dylan's movements as he danced across the flagstones. When her eyes at last met his, the blankness had all but gone. Red Tabby held her breath and Dylan felt as if his heart might burst with longing. Feebly, hesitatingly, Desiree began to join in. 'Tip-tip-tippity tap' her front hooves began. 'Tap-tip-tappity tip' her unsteady back hooves replied. Dylan moved alongside his mother, and for a few moments they danced almost as they had done when he was a foal. Then Desiree faltered and stopped.

Madame Lulu looked on with tears coursing down her cheeks. Chia slapped Dennis warmly on the back. 'Well done, man!' he whispered, hardly able to contain his enthusiasm. 'Well done, indeed!' For a moment, Dennis's mouth curved awkwardly into an unfamiliar shape that Clumsy, who was watching his boss intently, could have sworn was the distant cousin of a smile.

Desiree stood quietly, her muzzle pressed against Dylan's neck. Her legs trembled and her flanks were flecked with foam, but a new light shone in her eyes. Stomper put aside his guitar and, with Dylan and Dennis's help, guided her back to her stall. Madame Lulu could hardly believe it, but now there could be no doubt. Dylan's long-lost mother was well and truly found.

From that day on, Desiree began to improve. Dylan, when he wasn't in rehearsals, spent every waking moment at her side. He was able, at last, to start telling her about his adventures: how Red Tabby had rescued him when Emlyn the dairyman sold him to Dangerous Dennis and Clumsy; how they had escaped together and found the Happy Days troupe; how they had become fast friends and part of the circus family; and how, all thanks to his old enemy, he had now found his heart's desire.

For her part, Desiree told Dylan all about her life since the old travelling theatre had failed and they had been so cruelly parted. How she had been passed from one owner to the next until an eccentric old bachelor bought her and took her to his comfortable manor farm.

'What went wrong?' Dylan wanted to know.

'Well, he died, you see,' Desiree explained. 'So then I was sold on to a traveller who penned me in the paddock by that railway line and never returned.'

And all the while, Red Tabby lay stretched out on the rail above the manger, listening intently as mother and son shared their stories, and purring deep purrs of contentment.

42

Countdown

The day of Banjo's TV Spectacular was fast approaching and the pace of rehearsals grew even more hectic. Madame Lulu and Prudence could be seen hurrying here and there with great piles of costumes draped over their arms. Banjo's television director and Ringmaster Chia spent hours huddled together, going over every detail of the show. Then, a week before the broadcast, Banjo's team of technicians arrived to inspect the old hangar and prepare it for the big event.

Amidst all the bustle and excitement, no one heard Banjo's long, white limousine edge up the drive. When at last Red Tabby spotted it, she rushed off to fetch Stomper from the billiard room where the band was practising. Stomper caught up with Banjo in the library. He was standing behind the large rosewood desk peering intently at a framed document hanging on the wall.

'This thing here states that the Happy Days Circus is actually owned by the animals,' said Banjo as Stomper came in. 'By Lion and Tiger and someone called Irma – who's she?'

'Irma the elephant,' answered Stomper, his eyes dancing with amusement at his friend's bewilderment.

Banjo turned back to the framed parchment and ran his finger down the text. 'Yeah, her and Dylan and his mate, Red Tabby. This can't be real, surely?'

Stomper took the framed parchment down to give Banjo a closer look. 'Madame Lulu must have told you. They own it lock, stock and barrel,' he assured his old friend. 'All the animals do, along with Ringmaster Chia and Madame Lulu herself. Everyone's an equal partner.'

'Too much!' said Banjo. 'I thought she was spinning me a line.'

'It's the whole truth, Banjo, I promise you,' Stomper insisted. 'In fact, it's a first. This document set a legal precedent for animal rights.'

Banjo's eyes gleamed with excitement. 'Yeah! That's what she said, too,' he exclaimed. 'What an angle! Our sponsors have got to hear about this.' He delved into his jacket and pulled out his mobile phone.

'Mobiles don't work in Great Park,' Stomper told him as he carefully hung the parchment back on the wall. 'We've no signal here. But there's a phone at the foot of the grand staircase.'

Banjo went off muttering to himself. 'You thickhead, Banjo! Why didn't you listen to the woman? What an angle! Oh, boy!'

Out in the stable yard, Banjo's director and floor manager stood watching intently while Lion and Tiger paced through their act. In one hand, the floor manager held a clipboard, in the other a stopwatch. Chia hovered nearby, an anxious expression playing on his face. 'We'll need to shave some time off that,' the floor manager told Chia as the two great cats finished their performance.

'Perhaps that might be managed,' answered Chia uncertainly, as he cast a glance towards Tiger and Lion. 'I'll have a discreet word.'

'Did you hear that?' Lion asked Tiger tetchily as they padded away. 'Someone tell that TV man that great art can't be rushed.'

'I have a meeting about costumes,' announced the director. 'We'll take a break. When we're back, it's Irma and the Meerkat Clowns.' And off he stalked to find Madame Lulu.

With the floor manager gone to look for coffee, Chia sat down on a bale of hay and wiped the perspiration from his brow. He was finding the pace of events rather hectic and was glad of the chance for a breather. Red Tabby, who'd been watching the goings-on from close by, jumped up on the bale beside him. 'Not quite our style, is it?' she ventured. Chia gave a wry smile. 'Not really, dear Tabby,' he agreed. 'But we'll all have to put up with it, at least until the Spectacular is over.'

'Which is why it's a bit awkward for me to ask this,' Tabby went on. The ringmaster looked at her quizzically. 'You see, Dylan's had an idea!'

Chia clasped his hands together in excitement when he heard what Red Tabby had to say. 'Brilliant! Wonderful! Inspired!' he cried. 'As long as she's really up to it,' he added. 'Of course, it would mean some changes to the programme. I'll see what Banjo has to say.'

Down at the hangar, Banjo's technicians were hard at work transforming the rusty old structure into a magical circus arena. 'Oh!' gasped Prudence in admiration. 'It's almost like our dear old Big Top.'

Everyone except Desiree had come down from the big house for a 'walk through' with the director before the full dress rehearsal began. They gazed about them in awe.

Charlie pointed up towards the hangar roof. 'Look up there!' he exclaimed. Overhead, the crew had rigged all the aerial equipment: the trapezes, the high wire, the rope ladders and safety net.

'All shipshape and Bristol fashion,' Red Tabby enthused. Dylan threw her a questioning look. 'It's an old seafaring expression,' Tabby told him. Dylan nodded, none the wiser. 'It means everything's purrfect,' she explained patiently.

Backstage, the crew had set up dressing rooms with proper mirrors ringed with powerful light bulbs. Rows of colourful costumes hung neatly on racks. Wide ranks of seating for the audience rose on three sides of the hangar, while on the fourth side a lavish purple velvet curtain – emblazoned in gold with the words 'The Happy Days Circus' – hung thick and heavy from ceiling to floor. Dylan was so pleased that he cantered right around the hangar, his hooves throwing up little puffs of saw-dust as he went.

Dennis and Clumsy stood in the doorway watching the preparations. 'Good isn't it, Boss?' asked Clumsy.

'Not bad,' Dennis admitted, then turned abruptly and walked off. 'Goin' to look in on Desiree,' he mumbled.

'See you later, Boss,' Clumsy called after him, then ventured into the hangar to join in the fun.

The day of the great show arrived at last. The phone rang endlessly with calls of congratulation from friends and fans of the Happy Days Circus. A delivery van drove up filled with lavish bouquets addressed to Prudence, Irma, Celia and Madame Lulu. A really huge bunch of roses came for Chia and he hurried away with the bouquet tucked under his arm and a secretive look on his face.

The very air around the old hangar seemed to hum with excitement. Even Stomper's rooks swooped down from the ancient oak and gathered in the nearby trees to watch the proceedings.

'You have never looked more magnificent!' cried Red Tabby as Lion's professional dresser groomed his great mane in preparation for the night's performance. Red Tabby herself was resplendent in her sparkling waistcoat of green velvet and gold lamé.

'Just like the old days,' purred Lion. 'It's good to work with people who have a true appreciation of the artiste.'

'Not a stray pink hair roller to be seen,' Tabby whispered to Tiger.

Tiger concealed a grin behind a big paw. 'Don't get too used to all the pampering, Lion,' he advised, 'After tonight, it's back to fending for ourselves.' Lion's face fell.

'I can do that,' piped a small voice from a corner of the dressing room, and out hopped Roo who'd been following every stroke of the dresser's brush.

Lion peered down at the little kangaroo. 'You've been a dresser?' he asked doubtfully.

'Not yet, mate, but I've been watching,' Roo replied. 'From now on, if you want someone who understands the artiste, just call on me.' Lion's dresser gave Roo a wry look.

'Standby all performers. All performers for the Grand Parade if you please!' The voice on the dressing room intercom commanded everyone's attention. 'Musicians take your places!'

The hubbub of the audience as they settled into their seats could now be distinctly heard from the other side of the purple curtain. All talk of dressers and artistes was forgotten as the performers gave last minute tweaks to their costumes and make-up.

'Looks like this is it,' Tabby muttered to Dylan.

'Tabby, do take care up there on the trapeze,' Dylan begged as they waited backstage.

'I will,' promised Tabby. 'And Dylan,' she added earnestly, 'good luck to you and Desiree.'

'Ladies and Gentlemen. Boys and girls. Listen up.'

Prudence looked up from adjusting her pink tutu. 'That's not Ringmaster Chia!' she blurted.

Chia appeared at her side and put a reassuring hand on her arm. 'That's Banjo,' he whispered. 'He's warming up the audience. It's what they do in television before they switch on their cameras.'

'I hope he doesn't warm them up too much,' muttered Lion. 'With all those lights in there, I don't know how my curl is going to hold.'

The buzz of the crowd faded away into silence. Banjo stood in the ring in the beam of a great spotlight, a microphone in his hand. 'Ladies and Gentlemen, tonight we are in for a treat. The Happy Days Circus, whose show you are about to witness, is unlike any other circus you or I have ever known. It is the first and only one of its kind in the entire world. And why? Because it is owned entirely by the performers themselves. The very artistes whose skill and talent will thrill you tonight.'

'That's us! That's us, isn't it?' cried the meerkats, jumping up and down in excitement.

'And me!' agreed Dancing Dog and he wagged his curly tail happily.

'It's all of us,' added Irma, firmly, '*and* Ringmaster Chia and Madame Lulu, and Lord Stomper too.'

'Going live in ten seconds,' came the steady voice of the floor manager over the intercom. The show was about to begin.

'Enjoy yourselves, folks,' cried Banjo, handing the microphone over to Chia. 'In five seconds!' Sea Lion raised his flipper. 'In four, three, two, one, and you're on!' Sea Lion's flipper swept down and the band, with Lord Stomper on guitar, struck up the Grand Parade March. Banjo's purple curtain parted, lifting slowly to each side. The crowd roared a welcome and the first Happy Days Circus Christmas TV Spectacular began.

High above the hangar, against a background of twinkling stars, an orbiting satellite captured the broadcast signal from Banjo's cameras. Silently, it beamed the signal earthwards again to millions of upturned dishes and antennae and onto the television screens of countless eager families gathered in their homes to watch.

In one particular hilltop cottage, a voice that Dylan would have found familiar called out from the parlour. 'It's starting, my dear. Don't want to miss anything.'

'Just bringing in the tea, Emlyn, love,' came the reply.

Not long after Emlyn had swapped Dylan for an electric delivery van, he had traded the joys of bachelorhood for the bliss of married life with Widow Medlar. With the tea poured, Emlyn and Doris settled down comfortably in front of their television, never dreaming what a surprise lay in store for them.

43

Pas de Deux

The hard work of the past weeks – the long rehearsals, the late-night music sessions, the tired and aching muscles, the fingers sore from endless cutting and sewing – all now seemed worthwhile.

The exuberant crowd cheered one amazing act after another until it seemed the roof of the old hangar would blow clean off with the sheer force of their enthusiasm. Irma and the Meerkat Clowns, Red Tabby, Prudence and Charlie, Lion and Tiger, Sea Lion's family with Roo, Dancing Dog, Ranga and Marmaduke; each in turn brought the live audience and the viewers at home to the edge of their seats.

In the television control booth, Banjo watched spellbound as Charlie and Prudence, swinging in great arcs high on their trapezes, tossed a shining green and gold ball back and forth between them. Suddenly, there came a shocked gasp from the audience. Prudence seemed to have misjudged her throw. The ball sailed high over Charlie's head. Charlie lunged for it and missed. Down plunged the ball, unfolding as it fell until the unmistakable figure of Red Tabby emerged, legs outstretched, ginger fur flying. Just as it seemed nothing would stop her dreadful fall, Charlie swung the third trapeze, timing it to perfection. Effortlessly, Red Tabby caught the crossbar, swung onto it and, an instant later, stood waving to the crowd below in her green velvet and gold lamé costume. The audience quickly realised it had all been a clever trick, and another eruption of shouts and cheers rocked the hangar. Banjo's cameras caught it all.

'You promised me you'd be careful up there!' Dylan exclaimed sternly as Red Tabby, trembling with the excitement of her triumph, came backstage. Charlie and Prudence grinned from ear to ear.

'Oh, you needn't worry, dear Dylan,' said Prudence. 'We'd never let anything happen to our Red Tabby.'

'All the same,' Dylan mumbled.

'And now, good people,' came the rich tones of Chia's voice over the loudspeakers. 'The moment you've all been waiting for.'

'We're on next, I believe,' murmured a soft voice from the backstage shadows. The other performers turned to look as Desiree stepped shyly forward to stand beside her long-lost foal.

'I am honoured to announce,' the ringmaster's voice proclaimed, 'the return to show business of the celebrated artiste, Desiree de Polka, dancing for us tonight in the company of the star of the Happy Days Circus, her illustrious offspring, Dylan de Polka!'

'It's only this once, mind you,' Desiree reminded Dylan gently as the lights dimmed. 'I'm a bit old for the dancing life now.'

A hush fell as Dancing Dog rattled out a stirring roll on his snare drum, and mother and son, chestnut coats gleaming, stepped into the spotlight. From his seat high in the back of the stands, Clumsy watched in eager anticipation. Beside him sat his boss, a peculiar mixture of happiness and anguish playing on his face.

The lilting strains of a waltz floated up from the little band and the two dancers fell into a gentle tap routine that Desiree had first taught Dylan when he was a foal. Its languid pace charmed the crowd while Sea Lion's new arrangement of the well-known tune added a special magic of its own. For a while during the routine, Dylan stood aside, leaving the arena to his mother. Her elegant, fluid movements cast a captivating web of enchantment over the audience.

'Every inch a star,' whispered Madame Lulu to Chia as they stood watching Desiree from backstage.

Chia gave her a warm smile. 'She most certainly is,' he agreed and added to himself: *Like another fine lady I know.*

When the act ended, the crowd sat in awed silence. Then, like huge waves breaking on a rocky shore, a tumult of applause washed over Dylan and Desiree. Shouts of 'Encore! Encore!' echoed through the hangar, but Desiree merely gave a slight shake of her head, bowed deeply and, together with Dylan, trotted from the ring. When Clumsy, still applauding wildly, turned to congratulate his boss, Dennis had gone.

As the crowd continued to applaud Dylan and Desiree's performance, the television floor manager stood at the ringside frantically signalling to Chia to get on with the show.

'Thank you, mums, dads, aunties, uncles and little people everywhere,' boomed Chia once he could make himself heard. 'And now, for our final act, please welcome back the star of the Happy Days Circus Christmas Spectacular in an astounding, never-before-seen extravaganza guaranteed to set your feet tapping. I give you the incredible, the amazing, the one-and-only Dylan de Polka and his new act: "Duelling Hooves".'

With a thrilling riff on his guitar, Stomper led Sea Lion's band into the intro of their new tune. Backstage, Desiree looked on with quiet pride as Dylan, in the glare of the spotlight and at full gallop, made a complete circuit of the hangar then halted in the centre of the ring.

A nod to the band and 'tip-tap-tippity-tip tap' went his rear hooves. 'Tip-tap-tippity-tip tap' his fore hooves echoed. Then 'tap-tip-tappity-tap tip' and the duel was on: rear hooves challenging fore hooves; fore hooves battling rear hooves. Banjo sat in the control booth, heart in mouth, his foot thumping to the exhilarating beat. Rarely had he heard such a fabulous tune. Never had he witnessed such talent and agility. Faster and faster went Dylan, with each step becoming more intricate than the last until it seemed there really were two dancers in the ring, each vying passionately for the champion's crown.

'Again! Again!' the crowd roared almost before the dance was over. Sea Lion caught Dylan's eye. Dylan, puffing hard but flushed with triumph, nodded eagerly and off the band went once more.

'Stand by for the Grand Finale March! All performers for the Grand Finale March!' The voice of the floor manager on the dressing room intercoms could scarcely be heard over the uproar in the hangar as the crowd stamped and whistled their appreciation. At last, they let Dylan go and he rejoined his mother backstage.

Chia strode into the centre of the ring. 'Dear friends of the Happy Days Circus,' he boomed. 'Thank you for watching our show this evening, here in this arena and in your homes. We salute you – we thank you – but now it's time to wish you a Happy Christmas and bid you farewell until we meet again!' The crowd rose in their places and stood clapping in time to the stirring chords of the bandmaster's Grand Finale March.

As Desiree trotted side-by-side with Dylan around the circuit of the hangar, she nuzzled his cheek. 'Your father would have been proud of you tonight,' she told him. 'And I'm prouder of you than you could ever know.' Red Tabby, riding on Dylan's back, purred with happiness.

At the foot of the purple curtain, Chia waited with the enormous bouquet of red roses in his arms. Once the troupe had bowed and bowed again to the cameras and to their cheering audience, Chia moved forward. With a smile and a gracious nod of his head, he held out the roses to Madame Lulu. In the control booth, Banjo nearly jumped out of his stylish leather boots. 'He's doing it!' he exclaimed to his director. 'He said he was going to and he *is*. He really *is* doing it!'

Madame Lulu took the bouquet from the ringmaster's hands and drew out a small gold card that peeped from amongst its red blossoms.

'Camera Three,' the director hissed into his microphone. 'Give me a close-up on Madame Lulu. Camera Two, cover the ringmaster. Camera One, zoom in on that little gold card. I want the world to know what it says.'

As Madame Lulu opened the card, television viewers across the land could read Chia's carefully composed words: 'I love you more than all the stars in the sky. Please will you marry me?'

Madame Lulu paused for a moment then turned to the troupe, her green eyes sparkling. 'Ringmaster Chia wants me to be his wife,' she said quietly. Red Tabby stared in astonishment as a soft blush washed over the renowned impresario's fair skin.

'What should I do? Should I say "Yes"?' Banjo's microphone picked up Madame Lulu's soft voice, amplifying it for the whole world to hear.

The Happy Days troupe began chanting: 'Yes! Yes! Yes!' – 'Say yes!' And the audience took up the cry. 'Say yes! Say yes!' they roared.

Madame Lulu handed the bouquet to Prudence. Still clutching the small gold card, she took Chia's face in her hands and kissed him.

In the parlour at Hilltop Cottage, Emlyn's bride, who loved a good romance, dabbed at her eyes with a tissue. 'Oh, Emlyn, how beautiful!' she sighed, but Emlyn just leant forward in his easy chair, gaping at the television in disbelief as the end credits rolled on the screen.

'It really is him, Doris. Look! That's Dylan. You remember him, don't you? The one who used to spill my milk over your patio. Who would've believed it? My Dylan a television star! That's a surprise and no mistake.'

After the show, everyone gathered backstage to celebrate their success. 'Man! I can't get that "Duelling Hooves" out of my head,' Banjo told Stomper. 'Hey! We're going to have to cut a record together!'

Tired but overjoyed, the performers lingered at the hangar long after the last of the audience had gone, getting under the feet of the television crew who were trying to pack up and go home.

44

Chia in a Pickle

'Where are you off to then, Roo?'

Charlie's voice coming out of the blue made the little kangaroo jump with surprise. Roo looked first this way then that. 'Aah, oh!' she faltered.

Charlie pointed to the little kangaroo's pouch. 'What have you got in there?' he asked.

Roo glanced down at her pouch, which displayed an alarming bulge. 'Well, you see, the thing is, it's – well, it's a banana!' she said awkwardly. She plunged a paw into her furry pocket and produced a fat, yellow crescent. Charlie raised a disbelieving eyebrow.

Roo looked down again at the still prominent bulge below her tummy, and her little shoulders sagged. 'Oh, all right,' she sighed. 'It's not just one banana. It's a whole bunch of bananas.'

'Those seem very familiar,' Charlie observed when she had emptied her pouch.

Roo looked distinctly guilty. 'Sorry, Charlie,' she mumbled. 'I know I shouldn't take circus food without asking, but he's starving.'

'Who's starving?' asked Charlie, mystified.

Roo gathered up the fruit. 'Come with me,' she said and hopped off down the path towards Lord Stomper's woodlands.

Charlie hurried after her. When they reached the edge of a dense thicket, Roo put a finger to her lips. 'He's in there,' she whispered, pointing into the thicket. 'But he's very scared.'

Roo led Charlie through the undergrowth until they reached a small glade beneath a canopy of overhanging branches. On the far side, Charlie could see what looked like a round ball of dark-brown fur. Roo signalled to Charlie to stay put and tiptoed across the glade. 'It's me,' she said quietly. The ball of fur stirred. 'I've brought you some lunch.'

To Charlie's surprise, the ball of fur stretched and unfolded until there, in the corner of the glade, stood a small brown bear with a large pair of spectacles set firmly on his nose. 'This is my friend …' began Roo, but before she could finish, the bear caught sight of Charlie and, with a whimper of fright, rolled himself up in a ball again.

Several of Charlie's bananas and a good while later, three figures emerged from the thicket and made their way towards the big house. Twice, the small bear tried to turn back, but Charlie and Roo persuaded him to carry on.

'It's those rooks again,' Roo told Chia when they'd at last found the ringmaster. 'He's heard all about Great Park from them, same as me.'

Chia looked intently at the little bear, who was peering back at him timidly from behind Charlie's broad back. His 'spectacles' turned out to be lovely white markings that circled his gentle eyes.

'Remarkable,' said Chia. 'Spectacled bears are quite rare. You're a long way from home, aren't you?'

'From South America,' the newcomer admitted gloomily. 'In a crate.'

Charlie, Roo and Chia exchanged concerned glances. 'What's your name?' Chia wanted to know. There was an awkward silence.

'I don't think he's got a name,' Roo whispered.

'Then may we call you Ted?' asked Chia.

The bear nodded happily. 'Ted,' he repeated. 'Ted. Ted. Ted.'

'Can Ted stay then, Mr Chia?' asked Roo,

'He can for now,' Chia agreed, but a worried look crept into his eyes as he watched Roo and Charlie lead the little refugee off to meet the others.

That evening Chia called everyone to an emergency meeting in Stomper's ballroom. 'We're in a bit of a pickle,' he began once Madame Lulu and Red Tabby had joined the circle.

'Where's Lord Stomper?' Prudence asked. 'He's good at pickles.'

'He's on the phone, talking to Banjo,' Madame Lulu told her. 'He won't be long.'

'Dear friends,' Chia went on, 'it seems that Great Park is becoming known as a safe haven.'

'Safe haven?' asked Tiger.

'For homeless animals,' explained Chia.

'Is that a pickle?' asked Red Tabby.

'If it were just Roo and Ted, of course not,' replied the ringmaster.

'You mean more might come along to the park hoping for a home?' asked Tiger.

'Exactly,' said Chia. 'If too many turn up how will we ever manage to care for them?' The others exchanged anxious glances, for nearly everyone present had known what it felt like to be homeless.

'That needn't be a problem,' said Stomper, who had finished his call with Banjo and stood listening at the doorway. 'We've certainly got the space.'

'But can we afford it?' asked Madame Lulu. 'After all, we're still saving up for a Big Top.'

'No problem there, either,' said Stomper, grinning. Everyone looked at him, keen to know what he meant.

'"Duelling Hooves" was released yesterday in America,' he said, 'and Banjo says it shot straight to the top of the charts. We've got a mega-major hit!'

The others stared at him in stunned silence. *Charts?* wondered Prudence. *Hits?* puzzled Charlie.

'And there's more,' Stomper pressed on. 'Banjo wants Sea Lion's Band to record an album. He's sending a contract over tomorrow.'

'Then can we get our Big Top now?' asked Charlie.

'I don't see why not,' said Stomper.

The next day, after Stomper and Sea Lion had signed Banjo's generous recording contract, another important meeting was called. Madame Lulu had gathered some large sheets of paper, coloured pencils, rulers and a pair of compasses. She had just laid everything out on the big table in her room when Prudence and Red Tabby arrived. It was time to design the new Big Top.

'It must have lots of stripes,' Prudence began. 'And flags all around.'

'In every colour of the rainbow!' suggested Madame Lulu.

'And lots of gold trim,' added Red Tabby.

'In fact, exactly the same as our old Big Top!' Madame Lulu joked.

'Only bigger!' Prudence added triumphantly.

Soon, three heads were bent busily over the table, with pencils and rulers flying across the paper sheets. Chia poked his head in at the door in the hope of being offered some hot chocolate.

'Can I be of any use?' he asked.

'There's some washing-up to be done down in the kitchen,' Madame Lulu teased, with a wink at Red Tabby. Chia's face fell.

'I mean can I be of any use here?' he protested.

'Oh, here? No, I think we can manage, don't you?' Madame Lulu looked round at the others with a mischievous grin. Prudence, who had always regarded Ringmaster Chia with awe, stared wide-eyed at the impresario's strange behaviour.

As Chia trundled back down the stairs, he heard Madame Lulu's cheerful voice call after him, 'Hot chocolate in half an hour if you're good.'

Chia grinned broadly. 'Thank you, my dear,' he called back. 'And remember to allow enough space in the Big Top for Lion's extra-large dressing room.'

At the foot of the grand staircase, Chia found Clumsy waiting for him, looking agitated. The little man shifted from one foot to another as the ringmaster descended the last few steps. 'Is there something I can do for you?' Chia asked in a kindly tone.

'It's about Mr Dennis and me and what's to become of us, Mr Chia, sir,' Clumsy said.

Chia led the little man into Stomper's library and, once they were both seated, waited to hear what was on his mind.

Clumsy fidgeted awkwardly under Chia's scrutiny. 'I mean, now that Miss Desiree's better, sir, me and Dennis needs to think to our future and all.'

'Well,' Chia answered, 'Lord Stomper rather hoped you'd stay on here for a while. We could certainly use the extra help.'

'That would suit me, Mr Chia, and I'm obliged to his Lordship,' said Clumsy. 'But it's Mr Dennis, sir. Even now, he's too proud for his own good. He's always liked his independence, see?'

'Oh!' said Chia, his brow puckering into a frown. He chewed his lower lip thoughtfully while Clumsy nervously cracked his knuckles. For a moment the two men sat in silence.

'So you'll be going back to your railway carriage then?' asked Chia at last. He stared across at the little man almost lost in the big leather chair.

'Seems like it, Mr Chia, sir. Unless ...' Clumsy hesitated. 'Well, it's just that I has this here idea,' he hurried on. 'Only Mr Dennis don't know about it yet. If his Lordship and yourself, sir, agrees to it, then I might get him to see things our way.'

Chia clasped his hands together in anticipation. 'Very well, Clumsy,' he said. 'I am most interested to hear what you have in mind.'

45

The Truth About Dennis

Exactly a week after Clumsy and Chia had talked in the library, Stomper skidded into the stable yard on his motorbike, tyres squealing as he braked. 'Anyone seen Clumsy? Or Dennis?' he called.

Red Tabby hurried out of the stable to greet him. 'Clumsy's down in the paddock mending the fence,' she told him as he clambered off the bike. 'What's up?'

'It's on its way!' Stomper replied mysteriously and headed off in the direction of the paddock.

Lion came padding around the corner of the stables. 'What's all the excitement about?' he asked.

'It's on its way,' Tabby repeated as she raced off after Stomper.

Before long, Red Tabby, Dylan, Desiree and all the rest of the Happy Days troupe were gathered in the paddock, their necks craning skywards. 'It's coming! It's coming!' cried Marmaduke, and soon everyone could hear the roar of engines and the unmistakable 'thwop-thwop-thwop' of rotor blades. Then, over the far trees, swooped a huge, twin-engined helicopter. Beneath its dark silhouette, on strong steel cables, dangled Dennis and Clumsy's old railway carriage. Lion and Tiger exchanged cautious glances. 'I know we all agreed to this,' muttered Tiger, 'but let's still keep an eye on the pair of them shall we?' Lion nodded gravely.

Slowly, the helicopter lowered its burden into a corner of the field just beyond the paddock. For a moment after the cables were released, the railway carriage wobbled uncertainly. Everyone held their breath, but at last it settled into its place.

'Home, sweet home! Right, Boss?' murmured Clumsy happily. Dennis made no reply but stood gazing impassively at his old carriage. Clumsy felt his spirits sink. *What's he brooding about now?* he wondered.

'We'll have it licked into shape in no time,' declared Stomper, who had noticed Clumsy's concern. 'You'll see. All shipshape and Bristol fashion, as Red Tabby would say.'

'I'm most grateful to your Lordship, sir,' Clumsy replied. 'I'll be getting on with my housework then.' He was over the fence and well into the field beyond the paddock before Dennis moved to follow him.

When Stomper and Red Tabby returned to the stable yard, a strange sight met their eyes. There on the flagstones stood Stomper's motorbike, jiggling and shaking as if it had suddenly come to life.

'What's going on?' asked Stomper.

Red Tabby circled the motorbike with her usual curiosity. Strange scratching sounds mixed with frantic mewing could be heard coming from under the sidecar's canvas cover.

'I think you've got a stowaway,' she said.

Stomper laughed and unfastened the cover. Out of the sidecar jumped a large grey and white tomcat. He might have looked quite handsome had it not been for his dishevelled condition.

'Who on earth are you?' Stomper exclaimed.

'And who pulled you through a hedge backwards?' added Red Tabby.

The tomcat shook out his coat and smoothed his whiskers. 'No one,' he retorted. 'Cloudwatcher's the name. I've come to meet that famous feline aerial artiste – on a bet.'

'A bet, was it?' replied Red Tabby. 'Why then, Mr Cloudwatcher, you can tell your betting chums you've met her – face-to-face!' And she watched with barely-concealed amusement as confusion overcame the swaggering tomcat. Then, all at once, for reasons she couldn't fathom, she felt herself purring with delight. Stomper, quick to notice the stranger's effect on Tabby, cleared his throat noisily and walked off, whistling a cheery tune. Cloudwatcher and Red Tabby settled on their haunches and eyed each other warily.

Dennis and Clumsy had only just moved into their refurbished railway carriage home when Ringmaster Chia came hammering on the door. 'Big snow storm brewing,' he announced when Clumsy answered his knock. 'Better batten down the hatches.' Clumsy thanked him and hurried off to collect up his chickens.

'Perhaps we'd better make ready, too,' Madame Lulu suggested when Chia returned from delivering the news. Every-one helped. Stomper and Irma piled extra firewood beside the ballroom fire, while the others brought in fresh food supplies and plenty of warm bedding.

For three whole days and nights the blizzard raged. It dumped its downy cargo over Great Park until the grounds had all but disappeared beneath the thick, white blanket of snow. Cheered by a seemingly endless supply of good food, and, for Chia and Lord Stomper, brimming mugs of Madame Lulu's delicious hot chocolate, the troupe, along with Ted, Roo and Cloudwatcher, huddled together before the roaring fire.

Down at the old railway carriage, a thin plume of smoke blew sideways out of the chimney, fleeing before the blizzard. Clumsy stuffed more wood into the firebox of the little woodstove and gave his pot of soup an extra stir.

'Nearly ready,' he said and glanced towards his boss. Dennis sat on the edge of his bunk, silent and unmoving. Ever since the TV Spectacular, he had been unusually quiet. Clumsy shook his head and frowned. 'Come on, Boss,' he offered, trying hard to make his tone sound unconcerned. 'There's nothing like Clumsy Golightly's homemade soup!' He was about to ladle out the soup when Dennis suddenly began to speak.

'It was Desiree de Polka that first got me wantin' to work with 'orses.' The horse-whisperer's voice was husky and he sat stiffly, consumed with grief. 'First saw 'er when she was performin' at a theatre near where I 'ad me lodgin's. She was a bit of a foal at that time, settin' out as a dancer. A proper little cracker she was too.' Clumsy stood very still, hardly daring to breathe for fear of losing the moment.

Unaccustomed tears welled up in Dennis's eyes and his words began tumbling out as if he couldn't stop them. 'Got meself a job as a groom, I did. And that's 'ow I got into the 'orse-whispering game. But they paid so bad in them days. In the end, I fell to tradin' 'orses instead of 'elpin' them. Ever since, it's been all wrong turnin's, Clumsy. All wrong turnin's.' Dennis pulled an old rag of a handkerchief from his pocket and rubbed his damp eyes mournfully.

So that's what it's been about all these years, thought Clumsy. He felt a wave of happiness wash over him. Now everything was bound to come right. His boss had changed back to his old self before his very eyes. Clumsy filled a mug with aromatic soup and held it out. Dennis took it gratefully.

46

The Vow

By the early morning of the fourth day, the storm had blown itself out, and the troupe woke to a snowbound world glistening beneath blue skies.

Red Tabby and Dylan ventured out onto the terrace of the big house to find the sea lion pups already at play, sliding down the huge snowdrifts. As the pups barked their delight, their breath made silvery puffs in the crisp, still air.

The little meerkats, who had never seen such a snowfall before, crowded the tall windows of the ballroom, chirruping and chattering with excitement. In every direction, endless white expanses sparkled in the sunlight.

Red Tabby took one look at the glittering scene and climbed up onto Dylan's back. 'I suppose we're going exploring,' remarked Dylan with an amused whinny.

'Right first time!' declared Tabby.

'Where are you two off to then?' asked Ranga from the doorway of the ballroom. He had a large woolly scarf wrapped round and round his neck, and he hugged himself with both arms against the chill.

'We're going out for a bit of a stroll,' Red Tabby replied as she snuggled up warmly in the long, blond locks of Dylan's mane. 'Don't worry. We promise to be back for tea.'

Desiree appeared beside Ranga. 'You two *will* take care on the ice, won't you?' she asked anxiously.

'We will, Mum,' Dylan replied fondly. 'See you all later,' he added, and off he trotted, along the terrace and down through the stable yard.

Out in the ice-locked park, only the crunch of Dylan's hooves disturbed an otherwise silent world. Before long, the two friends found themselves nearing the ancient oak tree that had first drawn them to Great Park. From amongst the mistletoe entwining its branches came the rustle and croak of Lord Stomper's rooks. Dylan halted.

'Where has the wall gone?' he asked. Between them and the open fields beyond lay nothing but billowing drifts of snow.

'Buried, I should think,' Red Tabby replied and jumped down onto the drift's glistening surface. Her feet slithered and slipped, but with the help of sharp claws, she quickly reached the crest.

'Try it, Dylan,' she called. Dylan stepped gingerly forward. His great hooves broke through the brittle crust, but beneath, the snow was firm, packed tight by the winds that had howled through Great Park during the storm. In moments he stood on top of the drift beside his friend.

'Do you remember when we first got to know Lord Stomper?' he said.

'I do!' exclaimed Tabby. 'It was over in that field by the little river. I can taste those fried fish as if it were only yesterday!'

'Red Tabby,' Dylan said hesitantly. 'There's something I've been meaning to say to you.'

'And what might that be?' she asked fondly.

'It's just that …' Dylan took a deep breath. 'Dear Tabby, I'm truly sorry I went off looking for my mother without telling you. And I'm truly sorry I caused you so much worry. I only meant to fetch her back to Great Park. I never meant to alarm you.'

'I know that, Dylan,' Red Tabby replied warmly. 'I know that perfectly well.'

'And Tabby!' Dylan burst out again. 'You and I are *so* lucky. If only all the animals in the world could have our good fortune!'

'If only!' Tabby agreed. 'Come on, Dylan, we'd better keep moving. My paws are getting terribly cold.'

And so, with Red Tabby back up in her usual place on Dylan's back, and well wrapped up in his mane, the pair continued to pick their way over the frozen ground.

'Here's an idea, Dylan,' Tabby said after a bit. 'What do you think of this? Suppose we vow – come what may – never, ever to be parted again?'

Dylan gave a pleased snort. 'And friends forever?' he asked.

'Friends forever!' Tabby agreed.

By now they had come quite a distance and, ahead of them, they spotted the old hangar. Beyond it, under a blanket of sun-sparkled snow, Stomper's new fields and hillsides stretched into the distance.

'Oh!' gasped Tabby. 'Oh!' and felt her heart yearn for far off, unexplored spaces.

Dylan knew his friend of old and easily guessed her longing. 'Shall we?' he invited.

'Let's. We've lots of time. Prudence won't have tea ready just yet.'

'Then hold on really tight, dear, dear cat,' Dylan warned. 'Hang on for your very life – for we're away to the edge of the world!' And the two set off at full gallop, across the untrodden landscape – rejoicing in their freedom.

About the author

 The written word has always been Katherine's first love, but a talent for film-making steered her into a different career choice. With a friend, she founded a London film company, editing and producing award-winning TV documentaries. Over the years, her projects took her to Italy, Greece, India and then to Canada, where, in the course of her adventures, she met and married a well-known Toronto actor and became a Canadian citizen.

Working between Vancouver, Toronto and Montreal, she created and produced TV series for children; collaborated on scripts for television and film; and wrote extensively for various magazines. She was, for ten years, Contributing Editor of Britannia, a North American magazine celebrating the British way of life. Later, she founded and wrote 'The Street', a monthly newsletter for Coronation Street's many overseas fans.

In 1998, she and her husband, Michael, returned to the UK to live near their film-maker daughter, and their grandchildren. The green and rolling countryside of Somerset soon worked its magic in her imagination and the adventures of Dylan de Polka and Red Tabby were born.

Katherine Reynolds: Member: Society of Authors and SCBWI.

Come and visit Dylan and Red Tabby's website

For more information about the stories, the characters,
the author, book signings, school visits,
and new places to buy the books

www.dylanandredtabby.com

Our illustrator

Charlotte Roffe-Silvester (née Micklem), like several of her relations, inherited a love of drawing from her grandmother, the renowned portrait painter, Hilda Kidman. Charlotte studied textile design at the Central School of Art and Design, and then went on to work in the field of furnishing prints. In 1982 her first child was born. Twenty-five years later, after six children and eight house moves, she is now beginning to re-establish herself in the art world. She is happy to try new artistic challenges while being inspired by the natural world.

Need an extra copy (or two)?

To order extra copies of Born to Dance please visit our website:

www.ideas4writers.co.uk/dylanandredtabby.htm

We accept all major credit and debit cards, PayPal, cheques, postal orders, bank drafts and bank-to-bank electronic transfers

Born to Dance is also available from Amazon.co.uk
or you can ask any UK bookshop to order it for you

For a list of shops that stock the book please see Dylan and Red Tabby's website: www.dylanandredtabby.com

Enquiries, etc

To arrange book signings, talks, school visits, and for any questions or enquiries please use the following email address:
borntodance@dsl.pipex.com

If you would like to contact the publisher please use this address:
mail@ideas4writers.co.uk